Hidden Bones

Murder in Swartz Creek

Crime Thriller

by

Mark R. Beckner

Becknerbooks Publishing

First Edition: June 2025

ISBN: 979-8-9908287-0-4 (Paperback)

Credits

Sally Beckner – Copy review and editing

Writing companion – Roxy

Dedication

This book is dedicated to our precious dog Roxy, who sadly passed away while writing this book. I based the dog character in this story on our dear Roxy. She was my writing companion and my wife's walking buddy. Roxy would often stay up late with me as I wrote. Little did I know that her time was limited when I started this book. She was a Shepherd, Collie, Poodle mix, and a super dog and friend to all who knew her. We miss her dearly. Rest in peace, Roxy. We loved you with all our hearts.

Roxy is pictured on the front cover.

Preface

After retiring from the Boulder Police Department following 36 years in law enforcement, I began my new career as a writer of fictional crime dramas. My stories evolve from my imagination, as well as from my time as a police officer. While each story is fictional, the police and forensic work are based on reality. I rely on the knowledge and experiences gained over my long tenure and from continued interest in following actual crime events.

This book is my sixth crime thriller. The setting is Swartz Creek, Michigan, a small town where I attended high school. Many of the locations will be recognized by those familiar with Michigan.

In this story, when a dog named Roxy uncovers a shallow grave, it prompts a renewed investigation into an eighteen-year-old case of three missing Swartz Creek High School students. Multiple suspects, intrigue, and heart-pounding drama will keep mystery and crime thriller readers happy.

Thank you so much for your support. Independent authors rely on readers willing to take a chance on our work. Finally, please leave me a review; it would be much appreciated. I hope you enjoy the story.

Please visit my website for additional information.

beckner books.com

Other books by Mark R. Beckner:

> **Behind The Lies**
> **Death From Desire**
> **Naked Evidence**
> **Silent Waters**
> **Cactus View Book Club**

These books are available in print, ebook, and audiobook. In addition to Amazon, books may be found on Apple, Smashwords, Barnes & Noble, Hoopla, Kobo, and other sites.

Chapter 1

The male teenager, with light brown hair and small stature, shivered in the cold air of the dark wooden barn. His hands were tightly bound behind him with a rope around a dark wooden post. His arms bore the scratches and slivers from being tied up for so long. A second rope was tied around his neck, preventing him from bending over, and an oily rag wrapped around his mouth to prevent him from screaming. Except for short periods when he was given water and minimal food, his mouth was gagged. The boy's legs were bound to the post as they ached from hours of standing. A crack in the barn door was the only thing that told him it was night.

Any effort to call out for help was muffled by the gag in his mouth. While he didn't know where he was, he knew it was somewhere in the countryside. The cold only added to his discomfort and feeling of helplessness. He feared the next time the doors opened, his captor would step in to continue the abuse.

Only two days prior, he had been in class at his high school. How could he have been so gullible to fall for the charisma and promises of his captor? Maybe the fact that he had few high school friends made him vulnerable to the faked friendship. Why did he agree to meet up with this monster? Of course, he didn't know him to be a monster at the time. The promise of a job with potential college credit sounded too good to be true. As it turned out, that was the case. And now, he only longed for his life and freedom. He worried about what his mother must be thinking. Was she trying to find him? Would the police rescue him? Finally, exhaustion overtook his pain, his eyes grew heavy, and he slowly fell asleep.

The boy was awakened when the barn door opened. He could see it was early dawn as the sun brightened the eastern sky.

The man walked up to him and stared. Finally, he said, "I'm sorry, but today is your last day."

The boy's eyes widened with fear. He tried to speak, but the gag and dryness of his mouth prevented him from doing anything but making grunting noises.

"I can't keep you here, and I can't let you go. You'd go to the police, and that would be the end of me. And I'm not going to jail."

The boy shook his head back and forth, trying to communicate he would not tell anyone. He pulled his arms, hoping to break free of his bondage.

"It's unfortunate because I like you. But we all have our burdens to bear. Yours was to be my friend for a short time. Mine is that I must now kill you. Mind you, I don't want to kill you. I'm not the type of person that kills for no reason. I just can't trust you to keep quiet."

The boy's eyes were wide with fear as he continued shaking his head back and forth, still trying to convince his captor he wouldn't talk. He shivered from the cold air and increased fear of what was about to happen.

"I know," said the man as he looked into the scared eyes of the sixteen-year-old boy. "This is the hardest part."

The man reached up with both hands, cupping the boy's face with one hand on each cheek. He looked directly into the boy's frightened eyes and smiled. He then gently slid his hands down to the boy's neck, one hand on each side. The boy shook his head back and forth while letting out a squeal.

The man looked him in the eye and said again, "I'm sorry. I really did like you." He then slowly tightened his grip around the boy's thin neck.

Unable to use his hands or feet to defend against the attack, the boy gagged, then soon succumbed to the iron grip strangling his throat. Once he stopped breathing and his body went limp, the man released his grip. He then cut the ropes holding the boy captive. He picked the boy up, slung him over his shoulder, and carried him out of the barn.

Chapter 2

Eighteen Years Later

It was mid-morning on a warm September Saturday in Swartz Creek, Michigan. The leaves on the oak, red maple, and sugar maple trees were morphing into the rainbow colors of yellow, orange and red. The changing colors and dark green pines created a mosaic of fall beauty. The creek, for which the town was named, rippled through town at a slower pace than in the spring and early summer when melting snow and spring showers filled the creeks and rivers. It was as close to a perfect fall day as possible in the little town of Swartz Creek, which was precisely why Dylan Hudson and his best friend, Jason Chapman, wanted to head to the nearby ponds to fish.

Dylan Hudson was fourteen years old and had just started his freshman year at Swartz Creek High School with his neighbor and best friend, fourteen-year-old Jason Chapman. Dylan was slender with blond hair and blue eyes, which he inherited from his mother. His friend, Jason, had darker skin, brown eyes, and curly black hair, the result of being a mixed race. His mother was African American, and his father was Caucasian. Jason's athletic physique was like his father's.

Both boys had planned to play in the woods along the creek and small ponds behind the property where Dylan lived. They often liked to look for turtles, frogs or fish, mainly for catfish and small sunfish. However, Dylan's mother, Karen, was hesitant to allow Dylan to go.

"You know I have to work today, right?" asked Karen Hudson, a physician assistant at the local Swartz Creek Clinic.

"Sure, Mom," said Dylan. "But we can't just sit home all day. It's beautiful outside. I promise we will be careful and back in time for dinner."

"Jason, have you talked to your mother about this?" asked Karen.

"Yes, she's okay with it," answered Jason.

Karen thought momentarily as she brushed her blond hair back behind her right ear. "All right, you can go if you stick together and take your sister and Roxy."

"Oh, come on, Mom, do we have to take Abby?"

"Yes. She is only twelve, and I don't want her to be alone all day. And you need to exercise Roxy. Plus, I'm more comfortable when Roxy is with you out in the woods," said Karen.

Roxy was a six-year-old mixed-breed dog the Hudson family rescued as a puppy. She looked similar to a Golden Retriever but was actually a mix of German Shephard, Collie, and Poodle. Her color was a golden-reddish brown. She had a long snout and ears that flopped over, much like a Collie. Roxy was energetic and friendly, but Karen knew Roxy was also protective of the family. She still had vivid memories of the time three male teenagers went missing in Swartz Creek approximately eighteen years ago. She always believed the heartache and trauma caused in the community during that time influenced her sometimes overly protective mothering.

"And take your phone with you," said Karen.

Dylan wasn't happy about having his little sister tag along, but he knew Mom wouldn't let him go otherwise. "All right, we'll take Abby with us," agreed Dylan.

"Good," said Karen. "Your dad will be home around five o'clock. Be sure to be here by then."

"Okay," responded Dylan.

"And stay out of the water!"

"Okay, Mom."

Having overheard the conversation, Abigail (Abby for short) was happy to be going. She liked going to the creek and ponds but knew Dylan would not be thrilled with her tagging along.

After Karen had left for work, Dylan told Abby she would have to watch over Roxy.

"For the whole time?" asked Abby.

"Yes. We don't even want you to come. You're only going because Mom won't allow us to go without you."

Abby stuck her tongue out at Dylan, then turned and walked away.

Jason returned after going home to get his fishing pole and small tackle box. "Are we ready to go?" he asked.

"Yep," said Dylan. "Abby, are you ready?"

"I'm ready," replied Abby as she descended the stairs from her upstairs bedroom. She had a small white nylon net in her right hand and Roxy on the end of a leash in her left hand.

"Where's your fishing pole?" asked Jason.

"I decided to work on my insect project for school. You don't want me around anyway, so I'll look for bugs while you fish."

"Fine with me," barked Dylan. "Let's go."

The Hudson's lived in a more rural area on the south side of town in a small cul-de-sac off Seymour Road. Their home sat on a one-and-a-half-acre lot that bordered a wooded area. The creek ran southwest along the backside of the wooded area. Between their home and the creek was a mix of woods, farmland, and several small ponds. About a half mile to the northwest was an old Indian burial ground, named the Chippewa Burial Grounds.

Dylan, Jason, and Abby hiked about a quarter mile to a small pond. Given the cooler night temperatures, most of the summer algae had died. This was good, as Dylan knew less algae was better for fishing. While Dylan and Jason readied their fishing poles, Abby unleashed Roxy, allowing her to jump into the pond and splash around, as she so loved to do.

"You're scaring the fish!" shouted Dylan. "And I don't think mom will like Roxy smelling like pond water."

"She loves the water," replied Abby.

"Well, take her somewhere else," grumbled Dylan. "We'll never catch fish with her splashing around."

"Come on, Roxy, let's go find somewhere else to play," commanded Abby. Abby had to summon Roxy several times before she hopped out of the water, shook herself off, and saddled up next to Abby. "Let's go look for some critters," said Abby.

Abby headed north on a weed-covered path leading through a stand of fall-colored trees. After she left, Dylan and Jason baited their fishing lines with worms from a plastic whipped cream bowl, now serving as their worm container.

The boys fished the pond for catfish for the next hour or so. Jason caught two small catfish, while Dylan caught one. Neither boy kept the fish; they just enjoyed the process of catching them.

"Where did Abby go?" asked Jason.

"She went off looking for bugs or something," replied Dylan.

"Yeah, but we haven't seen her since she left," said Jason.

Dylan cocked his head and thought for a moment. He then lifted his head, cupped his hands around his mouth and shouted, "Abby, where are you?" He got no response. He yelled a couple more times and still got no response.

"Maybe she went home," said Jason.

"Yeah, maybe," agreed Dylan. "But I don't think so. She would have told me she was going."

"Roxy!" shouted Dylan, "Come here!" Roxy did not come.

"What do you think?" asked Jason.

"I'm getting a bit worried. Abby shouldn't have gone so far away that she can't hear me," replied Dylan. "We need to go look for her. Come on."

Dylan led the way as they headed north into the woods. They followed an overgrown path for about 200 feet. Dylan stopped and again called out for Abby. Still, no response.

"I hope she's okay," said Jason. "Where could she have gone?"

"I don't know," grumbled Dylan, "but it pisses me off for her to take off like this. She should have stayed home."

"What if something happened to her?" asked Jason.

"Like what? She's probably just lost and can't find her way back."

"I think Roxy could have found her way back," replied Jason.

Dylan paused. "Yeah, I suppose you're right. Now you're making me worried. Let's keep walking. If we don't find her, I'm in big trouble."

The boys continued walking down the path, occasionally pushing aside hanging branches. Dylan and Jason called out to Abby and Roxy as they walked.

"Maybe you should call your mom," suggested Jason.

"No, we just need to find her. My mom would be real pissed if she knew we lost Abby."

The boys continued for about fifteen minutes until they came upon an open field surrounded by wire fencing. Across the field, they observed an old, white, two-story farmhouse. An old green Ford F-150 pickup was parked near the house.

"Who lives there?" asked Jason.

"I think it's some old man."

"Do you think Abby might be up there somewhere?"

"No. Why would Abby go up to some old farmhouse? She knows better than that."

"Where do we look from here?" asked Jason.

"Let's go back. Maybe Abby's returned and looking for us."

The boys started the march back to the fishing pond, occasionally calling for Abby. As they drew closer to the pond, Dylan heard Abby calling out, "Dylan! Where are you?"

Dylan sighed and immediately felt a sensation of relief. He bent over with his hands on his knees, took a deep breath, and shook his head. He then stood up straight.

"Abby! We're over here. Just stay where you are."

After five more minutes, the boys reached the pond where the woods opened. Abby stood near the pond next to a wet and muddy Roxy, who had something significant in her mouth. Dylan could not make out what it was.

"Where have you been!" shouted Abby as Dylan and Jason approached. "I've been looking all over for you!"

"Me?" asked Dylan. "Where have YOU been? You were supposed to stay in this area!"

"I would have, but I couldn't find Roxy."

"What do you mean you couldn't find Roxy? And look at her. She's all muddy. What is that in her mouth?"

"I think it's a bone," replied Abby.

"A bone? Just explain what happened, Abby."

"I was looking for bugs like I told you. I thought Roxy was close to me, but she was gone when I looked for her. It took me a while to find her. She finally came running to me with this bone in her mouth."

"Where did she get this bone?" asked Dylan.

"I don't know."

"Maybe Roxy found the old Indian burial grounds," offered Jason.

Dylan looked at Jason. "You think this is from an Indian grave?"

"I don't know. It's just an idea."

"Give me the bone, Roxy," said Dylan as he took the bone from Roxy's mouth. "This is a large bone. It could be from a cow or something."

"Yeah, maybe," said Jason.

"You didn't see where Roxy got this?" asked Dylan.

"No. She came running to me with the bone in her mouth."

"Maybe Roxy can lead us back to where she got it," suggested Jason.

"Maybe," agreed Dylan. "But we need to get home now. We will have to shower Roxy off before letting her back in the house and before Mom gets home. We can always come back tomorrow and search for where she got it. She obviously had to dig for it. Look how muddy she is."

"I can go after church tomorrow," said Jason.

"Yeah, that's a good idea," agreed Dylan. "We'll pretend to go fishing again. Now, Abby, you can't say anything about this to Mom, or we will all be in trouble. You got that?"

"Don't worry, I won't say anything."

"Okay. Let's stash this bone under a bush for now."

"Why can't I take it home?" asked Abby.

"Maybe tomorrow. I want to try to find out where Roxy got it first. There could be a whole cow or pig skeleton out there somewhere."

"Or a dug-up Indian grave," replied Jason.

"If that's the case, we won't be showing this bone to anyone," said Dylan.

Back home, Dylan directed Abby to use the outside hose to clean the mud off Roxy. Meanwhile, Dylan and Jason discussed the bone.

"Roxy must have found some animal remains somewhere," suggested Jason.

"Well, yeah," agreed Dylan. "It will be interesting to find out what she dug up. I don't think it was big enough to come from a cow, and I don't know of any nearby pig farms. Most likely another dog or coyote. Maybe even a wolf."

Dylan opened his iPad and searched for dog and coyote skeletons. Both boys studied the drawings and photos that popped up.

"It looks like it could be the large upper bone of a dog's back leg," said Jason. "At least that looks the closest."

"Yeah, I can see the rounded ends like the bone Roxy found," agreed Dylan. "That's probably it. Maybe a coyote or wolf."

"It could also be a human bone," said Jason.

"Why do you say that?"

"Well, in our biology class last year, we studied the human skeleton. It also looks kind of like a human bone. Your mom could tell us."

"I'm not showing her that bone until we are sure Roxy didn't dig up an Indian grave. We need to go back tomorrow to find out."

The sliding back door opened, and Roxy hopped into the room with her tail wagging. She stopped in the kitchen and shook herself off, sending tiny water droplets everywhere.

"Abby!" yelled Dylan. "Why did you let her in all wet?"

Abby came through the door. "She shook off outside. I thought she was done."

"Go get a towel and clean this up. Mom will be home soon."

"Why do I have to clean everything up?"

"Because it was you who allowed Roxy to go dig up some bones."

As she walked away, Abby stuck her tongue out at Dylan.

"Do you know where the burial site is?" asked Jason.

"Yes, I've been there before. It's on a dirt road just off Seymour Road. Woods and farmland surround it. We probably passed it looking for Abby."

"What time should we go?"

"We have church and then Sunday dinner at one o'clock. Be here at two, and I'll be ready," said Dylan.

"Okay, see you tomorrow," replied Jason as he walked out the door.

Thirty minutes after Jason had left, Karen Hudson arrived home from work. "How did your fishing go?"

"We caught a couple of catfish," said Dylan.

"What about you, Abby?" asked Karen.

"I just looked for insects and turtles."

"Hmmm," sighed Karen. "It looks like Roxy had a bath. Did you let her in the water?"

Dylan looked at Abby, hoping she wouldn't say more than she should.

"No," said Abby. "But she did get dirty digging in the dirt. I had to clean her off when we got back."

"Thank you, Abby. I appreciate that."

"We're going to go again tomorrow if that's okay," said Dylan. "It was a lot of fun catching those catfish."

"Not until after Sunday dinner."

"Oh, we know. Jason's coming over at two o'clock."

Karen smiled, "Okay."

Chapter 3

During the Hudson Sunday dinner, Dylan's father, Jack Hudson, forty-one years old, stocky, with the same military-style haircut he had in the army, asked Dylan about the catfish he had caught.

"I only caught one, but Jason caught two. They were small ones. We're going after the bigger ones today."

Jack then turned to Abby. "And you were looking for bugs and turtles?"

"Yes. I caught a few bugs, but I let them go."

Jack smiled. "Maybe I'll come along today, and we can go after some bigger ones."

Dylan and Abby looked at each other.

Jack smiled. "I can see you don't want me tagging along. But if you catch a big one, I want a picture."

"Yes, we'll take a picture for you," replied Dylan.

"Same as yesterday, I want you to take Roxy. I feel more comfortable knowing Roxy is with you," said Karen.

"Yeah, I like taking Roxy," agreed Abby. "She finds all sorts of critters and things."

Dylan gave Abby a sideways glance.

"What type of critters?" asked her father.

"Ummm, you know, like chipmunks and stuff."

"Well, I hope she doesn't bring any of them home."

Right on time, Jason Chapman arrived at the Hudson house at two o'clock with his fishing rod and small tackle box. Dylan and Abby were ready as well. As they left the house, Dylan grabbed his father's spade from the garage.

"What are you going to do with that?" asked Jason.

"If we find where Roxy was digging, we may need a shovel."

"Ah, yes. Good thinking."

The foursome of Dylan, Jason, Abby, and Roxy hiked to the same pond from the day before. Once they arrived, Dylan grabbed the bone from under the current berry bush. He allowed Roxy to smell the bone.

"Come on, Roxy," said Dylan. "Take us to where you found this. Go on!"

Roxy danced around and barked a few times while looking at Dylan holding the bone.

"No, go find the other bones, Roxy," said Dylan as he pointed.

Abby started walking along the path leading north of the pond. "Let's go, Roxy!"

After several more commands, Roxy finally started after Abby. She caught up with Abby and trotted past her along the path, her tail flopping back and forth. Jason placed the bone back under the bush, and the boys followed.

After about a quarter mile, Jason said, "Is this the way to the Indian burial grounds?"

"No," replied Dylan. "Abby, is this the way you went yesterday?"

"I'm not sure. I kind of got lost."

"Follow me," said Dylan. "I know how to get there."

Dylan went off the path in a northeast direction. Walking through trees and thick underbrush was more difficult without a path to walk. He used his shovel to push small branches out of his way. Roxy followed and eventually passed everyone. She kept her nose to the ground, taking in all the wonderful smells of the forest.

"Ouch!" yelled Abby. "Some of these bushes have stickers."

"They're called thorns, Abby," chuckled Dylan.

"Where's Roxy?" asked Abby.

"She's up ahead. I can still see her."

The fallen leaves crunched under their feet as they navigated their way through maple, oak and pine trees. After about one hundred yards, a clearing appeared with old flat headstones sticking out of the forest ground. The grass and weeds around the headstones had not been mowed in some time. A sign near the entrance said Chippewa Burial Ground. Roxy was sniffing around some of the headstones.

"Look at this," said Jason. "I've heard of these old graves but never been here. This one has a date of 1853."

"Some of these don't even have dates on them," said Abby.

"Mom told us this burial site was here before Swartz Creek even existed," said Dylan. "Let's try to find where Roxy was digging."

"Come on, Roxy," said Abby. "Show us where you found the bone."

Abby followed Roxy around while the boys checked every gravesite. Nothing appeared to be disturbed or out of place.

"I guess that eliminates it being a human bone," said Dylan.

"But where did Roxy find that bone?" asked Jason. "There has to be a carcass of something out here somewhere."

"Where is Roxy now?" asked Dylan to no one in particular.

"She went through those trees," said Abby as she pointed west.

"Let's go," said Jason as he thrashed his way through more bushes and tall grasses.

"Roxy! Wait up!" shouted Dylan as he ran after Jason. Abby tried to keep up as best she could.

After another fifty yards, Jason caught up to Roxy near a barbed wire fence on the edge of a dead cornfield. He found her digging a hole in the forest dirt about ten feet outside the fence. He grabbed Roxy by her neck collar while pulling her back.

"That's enough, Roxy."

Jason looked into the hole and could not believe what he saw. More bones. Roxy had led them to her digging site.

"We found it!" shouted Jason.

Dylan soon reached Jason's location and could see several bones mixed among the dirt and leaves dug up by Roxy, who now had another bone in her mouth. This bone was much smaller than the one she found the day before. Abby soon joined them. A musty smell rose from the disturbed soil.

"What do you think was buried here?" asked Jason.

"I can't tell," answered Dylan. "There are a lot of bone fragments here."

Jason reminded Dylan, "You have your shovel. We could dig it up."

"That's creepy," moaned Abby."

"How else will we find out?" said Jason.

Dylan looked at Jason before sticking the blade of his shovel into the dirt. He turned over a couple spades of black earth when another bone appeared. Jason bent over, looked at it, then picked it up.

"This bone is small. Maybe a finger?"

"Creepy," mumbled Abby.

"What are you kids up to!" came a loud, gruff voice.

All three teens were startled. Roxy stared intently at the older gentleman standing on the other side of the barbed wire fence.

"Well, what are you doing here?" the man asked.

"Uh, our dog found some bones here, and we were just checking it out," said Dylan.

"Bones!" shouted the man. "Are you digging up an Indian grave?"

"No, no. The graveyard is back that way," insisted Dylan while pointing easterly.

"That's the official graveyard," said the man. "There are burial sites all over this area. No one knows for sure how many were buried here. Some of them are well over two hundred years old. It's illegal to dig up old graves."

"We didn't mean any harm," said Jason. "We thought this was an animal."

"What are you doing out here?" asked Abby.

Both Dylan and Jason gave Abby a look that said shut up.

"I live here," said the man. "See that old farmhouse across the way there?"

Dylan and Jason looked over the bushes and through the fence. They both saw the old white farmhouse and green Ford pickup they had seen the day before, although from a different location.

"We're sorry. Our dog dug up this grave, and we thought it was just an animal," explained Dylan.

The old man looked at each of the kids. "You all look like good kids. Where do you live?"

"We live on Blossom Lane, just off Seymour Road," explained Dylan.

"You're about a mile from home," said the man.

Sensing the man was not an immediate danger, Roxy started digging at the dirt again.

"Roxy! No!" shouted Dylan.

"Here, let me help you," said the man as he bent over and stepped through the gap between two strands of barbed wire. He looked to be about sixty years old with a slight pot belly and gray hair under a dirty U-Haul baseball-type hat. It was apparent he hadn't shaved in several days. He wore baggy jeans and a red long-sleeved flannel shirt. The sleeves were rolled up to his elbows.

Dylan didn't know if they should run or stay to help. He looked at Jason, who shrugged his shoulders. Abby just stood in silence.

The old man nodded his head toward Jason. "What are you? Hispanic?"

Jason was surprised by the question. "No. My mom is African American, and my dad is white."

"Well, nothing wrong with that, but we don't see many mixed-race kids in Swartz Creek."

"What's your name?" asked Abby.

"My name is Charles Kotter, but I go by Chuck."

Dylan looked at Abby, shrugged his shoulders, and turned his hands upward, making a "what are you doing?" gesture. Abby ignored him.

"What's your name?" asked the man.

"I'm Abby."

The man then nodded toward Jason. "And what's your name?"

"Um, I'm Jason."

The man then looked at Dylan. Before he could even ask, Dylan said, "I'm Dylan."

"Give me that shovel," Kotter said as he reached over and grabbed it from Dylan's hand. He then started to backfill the hole.

"Where did you come from?" Abby continued.

"I'm originally from Pennsylvania," said Kotter.

"That's where you live?"

Kotter chuckled. "No, I live in that old farmhouse over there."

Abby looked through the fence and saw the farmhouse across a large field. Dylan and Jason also looked.

"You walked all the way over here?"

"I was walking the field when I heard a dog bark. I then saw the three of you digging up this dirt."

"We're sorry," said Dylan. "We didn't mean any harm."

After patting down the top of the grave, Kotter looked at Dylan. "I believe you, but you can never tell anyone about this. Some people steal from old graves, especially Indian graves. They like to steal any valuables that may have been buried with the bodies. Old artifacts can be sold for good money. You didn't take anything from this grave, did you?"

"No," said Dylan.

"Good. You don't want the Indian spirits to haunt you at night."

"Indian spirits?" asked Abby.

"Well, sure. Anytime you disrupt an old Indian grave, you disturb and anger the spirit. Taking something out of the grave only makes it worse."

Abby thought about the bone Roxy had dug up but decided not to say anything.

"Now help me gather some leaves, and let's cover up this dirt," directed Kotter.

Dylan, Jason, and Abby quickly gathered leaves and piled them on the disturbed dirt. Kotter helped spread them out.

"That should do," said Kotter. "I don't believe you have to worry about any spirits now unless, of course, you tell someone about this grave."

"Why does that matter?" asked Dylan.

"Spirits don't like to be disturbed. If you start talking about what you found here, it won't go over well. Do not tell anyone about this Indian grave."

"We won't say anything," replied Dylan.

"I know you won't. You seem like smart kids."

The way he said it sounded like a warning to Dylan.

Jason had been looking across the field of dead cornstalks at Kotter's worn-looking white farmhouse with a covered porch. A large reddish-brown barn sat west of the house. Kotter noticed Jason's seeming interest in the house.

"What are you thinking?" asked Kotter.

"Huh?" said Jason.

"You're eyeing my house. Would you like to see it? It's one of the oldest farmhouses left in Swartz Creek. I'm trying to get it registered as a historical site to protect it from ever being torn down."

"Oh, no, I was just looking at it."

"I've got an airplane in the barn if you want to see it."

"You have an airplane?"

"Yep. You can't see it from here, but there's an asphalt runway across the field."

"Do you fly it?"

"Not as much as I used to, but yeah, I still fly it. The sights from up high are incredible. I've given lots of people, even other kids like you, rides in that plane."

Dylan interrupted, "It's getting late, and we need to get home."

"I understand," said Kotter. "I've lived here a long time, and I can tell you kids are curious. I can give you more history on Swartz Creek and the Chippewa Indians. I'll even show you my airplane. Come back tomorrow if you're interested."

"We have school tomorrow," said Dylan.

"What time do you get out?"

"Three o'clock."

"I'll be here if you want to come by. There's a gate along the south fence line. That would be the easiest way to get to my place. You'll find a dirt tractor trail runs across the field from the gate to my house."

"We'll see," said Dylan. "We have to get home now."

"Of course. Don't get lost on the way home."

"We have Roxy," said Abby. "She knows the way."

Kotter smiled as he watched the three teenagers trudge through the brush and trees as they headed home. When Dylan arrived back at the current bush, he reached under and retrieved the bone.

"What are you going to do with that?" asked Jason.

"I'm taking it home. I don't want anyone else to find it."

"You heard what the old man said," Jason reminded him.

"He's just a crazy old man," said Dylan. "We don't even know for sure where this bone came from or whether it's a human bone."

"How are you going to find out?"

"We could ask my mom. As a physician's assistant, she would be able to tell us. But first, I think we need to talk some more to the old farmer."

"You want to go back?"

"Why not? I have more questions about this Indian burial stuff, and I'd like to see this airplane he talked about. You're not afraid of Indian spirits, are you?"

"Of course not," smirked Jason.

"I am!" exclaimed Abby.

"He was just trying to scare us, Abby," said Dylan. "Indian spirits aren't going to come after you or anybody else. You don't have to come."

"I found the bones," replied Abby.

"No, you didn't. Roxy found the bones. But if you promise to keep your mouth shut, you can come along."

"I won't say anything."

Dylan turned to Jason. "Can you go after school tomorrow?"

"Sure. I'll just tell my mom we're going fishing again."

"Yeah, same here."

When he returned home, Dylan wrapped the bone in an old towel from the garage and hid it behind a bag of fertilizer. *That should be good for now.*

Chapter 4

The hours of the school day seemed to pass ever so slowly. Dylan was anxious to return to the woods and visit the old farmer, Chuck Kotter. There was something about the old man that aroused Dylan's curiosity. Was he just some crazy old man, or did he really know what he was talking about? Dylan also wanted to see the old man's airplane, as Dylan had always liked airplanes. In fact, he had gotten a battery-powered model airplane last Christmas. After the final bell rang, Dylan met Jason at the school bus in the high school parking lot.

"I'm anxious to see that airplane Kotter talked about," said Dylan.

"I've been thinking about it too," replied Jason. "But are you sure we should go? We don't really know who he is."

"If Abby goes, there will be three of us," replied Dylan. "He can't kill us all."

Jason flashed a frown at Dylan. "Let's hope he doesn't kill any of us!"

Dylan laughed, which made Jason smile as well.

"Besides, you're strong enough to take the old man on yourself," insisted Dylan.

"If nothing else, we can all run faster than him," replied Jason.

After the bus dropped the boys off at the corner of Blossom Lane and Seymour Road, the boys agreed to meet back at Dylan's house in thirty minutes. This would allow time for Abby to get home from middle school.

Karen Hudson was home when Dylan entered the house. He explained that the three of them were going back to the pond and would be home in time for dinner.

"Why such sudden interest in going to the woods?" asked Karen.

"We've just found the fishing to be fun, and the weather has been perfect for it," answered Dylan.

"Well, dinner will be at six. Be home on time."

"We will."

Soon after Abby had arrived home from school, Jason arrived. Once Abby had changed her clothing, the three of them headed out the door.

"Hey," shouted Karen. "I want you to take Roxy. She needs exercise, and I feel more comfortable knowing she is with you."

"Of course," said Dylan. "Come here, Roxy."

Roxy ran to Dylan with her tail wagging, anxious for another adventure into the woods. Once Roxy was on her leash, the three explorers crossed the large backyard and entered the woods. Neither Dylan nor Jason remembered to take their fishing poles. They were more focused on getting to see Kotter's airplane. After entering the woods, Dylan allowed Roxy to go off-leash. She dutifully led the way to the pond, then onto the path heading toward the burial ground and old man Kotter. The three kids struggled to keep up.

As they got closer to the south property line of Kotter's farm, Roxy veered off in a northeast direction at a faster trot.

"Roxy!" called out Dylan. "Where are you going?"

All three started running after Roxy, calling her as they ran. Jason tripped and fell, bumping his knee on a rock. "Ouch!" he shouted.

"Are you okay, Jason?" shouted Dylan.

"Yeah," answered Jason as he brushed himself off.

Abby continued to run after Roxy.

"Come on, let's go," urged Dylan as the two boys followed Abby and Roxy.

Once they caught up to Abby and Roxy, they found themselves back by the east side of the barbed wire fence. Roxy was again pawing at the leaf-covered burial site from the previous day. Dylan reached over and grabbed Roxy by the collar. "No!" he shouted as he pulled her back.

"Damn," said Jason. "Your dog is determined to dig those bones up."

"Why does she only come to this one?" asked Dylan.

"Maybe because it's fresh," replied Jason.

"It's only fresh because Roxy dug it up the first time," said Dylan.

"Do we know that?" asked Jason.

"What do you mean?"

"Well, maybe it was dug up before Roxy found it."

"Who would have dug it up?"

"I don't know, it's just a thought."

The boys smoothed the dirt again, then stomped it to pat it down. Abby pushed the leaves back on top.

"Now we need to find that gate Mr. Kotter was talking about," said Jason.

"Let's just spread the wires and go through right here, just like he did," suggested Dylan.

Jason shrugged his shoulders. "Let's go."

Dylan held the strands of barbed wire apart as Abby bent over and stepped through. Roxy followed her, quickly jumping between the two wires. Jason was next but snagged the back of his sweatshirt on one of the barbs. Dylan unhooked the sweatshirt, allowing Jason to continue through. Jason then held the wire open as Dylan stepped between the wires, careful not to snag himself. The three of them then walked along the dried-out, brown cornstalks toward the two-story white farmhouse. After clearing the cornfield, they came across a long strip of asphalt running east to west parallel to the cornfield. A faded white stripe ran down the middle.

"This is the runway Kotter talked about," said Dylan. "He must have told the truth about having an airplane."

As they approached the house, they could see the once bright white paint had faded over time. The south-facing side had sections of peeling paint, revealing weathered wood underneath. A red brick chimney ran up the south side, extending above the gray shingled roof. A large, covered porch extended across the west side of the house over the main entrance. On the porch sat a small metal table with brown wooden rocking chairs on each side. A wicker couch with red cushions sat to the right of the table and chairs. As the kids approached, they saw a folded newspaper and a coffee cup on the small table. When they arrived at the steps to the porch, they stopped. Looking through the wooden screen door, they could see the primary door was standing open.

While Roxy sniffed around the frame of the porch, Abby asked, "What do we do now?"

"You go up and knock on the door," replied Dylan.

"I'm not doing that!" exclaimed Abby.

Dylan laughed. "Come on, let's all go up. There's nothing to be afraid of."

Jason and Abby followed Dylan up the stairs to the screen door. Roxy bounded up the steps behind them. Dylan knocked on the door and waited. Several seconds later, Chuck Kotter came to the door.

"Well, I'm surprised to see you here," said Kotter as he opened the screen door. "Come on in."

Dylan hesitated.

"You came all this way. Don't stop now," said Kotter.

"We have our dog with us," replied Dylan.

"She's welcome. I love dogs."

With that, Dylan walked through the door with Jason, Abby, and Roxy following. When they entered, they could see the kitchen was to the right, and the living room was to the left. The furniture looked old but in good condition. The kitchen had a large square oak table with six wooden chairs surrounding it. The sun shone through the southern window into the kitchen. There was a slight musty smell to the home. It reminded Dylan of his grandmother's house.

"Come in and sit down," said Kotter. "You're probably thirsty from your walk over here. Would anyone like a soda? I have coke and root beer."

After a pause, Abby spoke up. "I'd like a root beer!"

Dylan added, "Sure, I'll take a root beer as well."

"Me too," said Jason.

Kotter opened the white refrigerator and grabbed four cold root beers, then handed them out, keeping one for himself. Kotter was dressed similarly to the day before but now wore a blue denim shirt. Dylan also noticed Kotter was now clean-shaven.

Kotter then took a bowl out of his sink, rinsed it out and filled it with water. He placed it on the floor for Roxy, who quickly began lapping up the water.

"She seems like a great dog," said Kotter.

"She is," agreed Dylan.

"I guess you decided to come see the place and my airplane. Is that right?"

"Yes, we'd like to see it," agreed Dylan.

"After you've finished your drinks, I'll take you to the barn. You haven't been digging up any more graves, have you?"

"No, sir. And we didn't dig up the last one. That was Roxy."

"Ahh, but I found you with a shovel digging into the grave. I'd call that digging up a grave, no matter who started it."

Jason glanced at Dylan. "I suppose you're right," said Dylan. "But we thought it was an animal Roxy found. We would never dig up the grave of a human."

"Just checking," responded Kotter with a smile. "I sure don't want those Indian spirits coming after you."

"No, sir," said Dylan.

"How long have you lived here?" asked Jason.

"Oh, it's been about thirty years now. I took this farm over from my parents after they got too old to handle it. It's been in the Kotter family for probably fifty years."

"How old are you now?" asked Jason.

"I'm fifty-eight. How old are you?"

"Um, I'm fourteen, but I'll be fifteen in January."

"I see. And how old are you, Dylan?"

"The same. I'll be fifteen in November."

"What about you, Abby?"

"I'm twelve. I'll be thirteen in March."

"So, you've been in Swartz Creek for thirty years?" asked Dylan.

"More than that. I was raised here and went to Swartz Creek High School, just like you. I then left for a while to, you know, see the world. Even went to California for a couple of years. That's a crazy place. After about ten years, I came back to Michigan. Worked at General Motors for a bit, then moved to the farm to help my parents."

"You must know a lot about Swartz Creek," said Abby.

"Oh, you bet I do. Did you know Swartz Creek was founded in 1836 by a German pioneer named Adam Miller?"

"I didn't," said Dylan.

"You've all heard of Miller Road, right?"

"Of course," replied Jason. "It's the main road in town."

"It's named after Adam Miller," continued Kotter. "In fact, Swartz Creek was first known as the Miller Settlement. It wasn't until 1877 that the village was named after the creek on the other side of those trees. It wasn't established as a city until 1959."

"So, you've been here a long time," said Dylan. "That's why you know so much about the burial grounds."

"Yes. The Chippewa Indians, originally known as the Ojibway Indians, were the first inhabitants of this territory. And Ojibway translates to puckered moccasin people."

"Oh, come on," laughed Dylan. "You're just making this stuff up."

"No, you can look it up. They were called that because their moccasins had a puckered seam across the top."

Dylan and Jason looked at each other, not knowing whether to believe the old man or not.

"So why did they put an Indian burial ground in the town?" asked Jason.

"They didn't!" exclaimed Kotter. "The burial grounds were here long before the white men came. Much of the burial grounds were destroyed by early settlers. It was a real bone of contention between the town folks and Indians. It wasn't until the owner of this land established a treaty with Chief White Bird that the plot of land over there became protected."

"Was the owner your parents?" asked Jason.

"No. The fight over the burial grounds occurred before my parents lived here. Even after the treaty, vandals often came to vandalize the stones or dig out buried treasures. That's what I thought you three were doing."

"No, it really was Roxy who dug out the dirt," said Abby.

"You seem like good kids. I believe you, Abby."

"The burial ground with the fencing looks pretty good now," said Dylan.

"Yes. The Swartz Creek Historical Society restored the burial site in 2009. The headstones were either repaired or replaced. The wrought iron fence along the front and the sign were put in at that time. We don't have the problems there we used to. The site now officially belongs to the Chippewa Indian Tribe based in Mount Pleasant."

"We still have Indians in Michigan?" asked Abby.

"Most people refer to them as Native Americans now, but yes, there are plenty of Indians throughout the United States. Many of them live on reservations."

"This is all interesting," stated Dylan, "but what is all the crap you were telling us about spirits coming after us?"

Kotter turned and stared into Dylan's eyes for several seconds, sending a chill down Dylan's back.

"You don't believe it?" asked Kotter.

"Well, uh," stuttered Dylan. "I don't believe in ghosts."

"Let me just say that you're fortunate I stopped you when I did. I've heard the stories since I was younger than you. And it wasn't all that long ago that three boys disappeared in Swartz Creek, never to be found again."

"What!" said Abby. "I never heard of that!"

"It was before you were born, Abby. But it happened. Rumor is that they had all been digging for treasures in the burial ground."

"What happened to them?" asked Jason.

"Nobody knows. They just disappeared. Poof! They were gone."

"Even if that is true, we weren't in the burial grounds," insisted Dylan.

"Like I told you, the official burial grounds are a small area. The original burial grounds were much larger. My corn probably grows on top of some of them."

There was silence for several seconds.

"We probably should head back," said Dylan.

"But you haven't seen my airplane yet."

"We need to be back for dinner, and it's getting late."

"You can't leave after coming all the way out here and not see the plane. Come on, I'll show it to you right now."

Kotter stood up and walked to the screen door. He pushed it open and called out to Roxy. "Come on, pup, let's go see an airplane."

Roxy gleefully ran out the door as the three teens got up and followed.

"It's in my old red barn," said Kotter as he walked toward the barn's double doors. He then pulled them open for the kids to see. Just inside the doors was a white with red trim Cessna 172 Skyhawk single-engine airplane.

"Wow, look at that," said Abby.

"Does it still fly?" asked Dylan.

"Does it fly? Of course it flies," replied Kotter.

"How many people can it hold?" asked Jason.

"It's a four-seater. Go ahead and get inside for a look-see."

Jason was the first to open the passenger side door and climb in. Dylan and Abby followed him. Jason sat in the pilot's seat while Dylan sat in the front passenger seat. Abby climbed into one of the back seats. Roxy hunched down with her front legs extended and barked as though she wanted to jump in.

Dylan, who always had a fondness for planes, was mesmerized by all the controls. "Where do you fly this thing?"

"Wherever I want. I can take off and land right here on my own runway. Would you like to take a ride in it?"

"Do you mean right now?"

"Yeah, I got nothing better to do," replied Kotter.

Dylan looked at his phone and saw the time was 5:45 pm.

"We can't. It's close to six o'clock. We have to get home."

Dylan helped Abby out of the back seat as Jason exited out the pilot's side door.

"We would like to take a ride, but we have to get home," explained Dylan. "We're already going to be late."

"All right," responded Kotter. "Tomorrow is supposed to be a great day weatherwise if you want to take a ride."

"We'd like that," said Jason.

"Come on, Jason," urged Dylan. "We need to try to get home by six."

Kotter stood and watched as the three teens and Roxy ran across the cornfield toward the southern gate. Dylan looked at his cell phone. A message from his mom said *where are you?* Dylan stopped to text her back, *on our way.*

Chapter 5

Dylan, Abby, and Roxy walked through the back door at six-fifteen. Their parents, Jack and Karen Hudson, were already seated and eating dinner at the dining room table. Roxy ran to her food dish and immediately started to gulp down her food.

"There you are," barked Jack in his military command voice. "What time did your mother say to be home?"

"We're sorry," replied Dylan. "We were having so much fun we lost track of time."

"Hmmm. Go wash up, then come sit down to eat."

After several minutes, Dylan and Abby joined their parents at the dinner table. A meatloaf, mashed potatoes, gravy, and broccoli were still on the table. Karen passed the dishes first to Abby and then to Dylan. They both took large helpings of each. The food was no longer hot, but neither Dylan nor Abby was about to complain.

No one at the table said much until Jack asked Dylan how the fishing was.

"Um, it was fine. But we didn't catch any big ones."

"I'm surprised you caught anything at all," replied Jack

Dylan looked at his father in a quizzical manner. "Why do you say that?"

"Well, I'd like to know how you caught them without your fishing rod."

Damn, thought Dylan. He knows I didn't take my rod or tackle box. He didn't know how to respond.

"Would you like to tell us where you were?" asked Jack.

Dylan hesitated before speaking. "Okay. Saturday, when we went fishing, Roxy dug up an animal bone in the woods. On Sunday, we went back to find where she had been digging. We found it and covered everything up. We went back today to make sure no other animals got into it. We then played in the woods and lost track of time."

"Where did Roxy dig up this bone?"

"North of the big pond in the woods," replied Dylan.

Karen interrupted, "Is that why you had to shower her off on Saturday?"

"Yes. The dirt was damp, and she got it all over herself."

"What kind of bone was it?" asked Karen.

"Some animal bone, I guess."

Abby just sat and listened to the questioning. She was relieved not to be hammered with questions. Being the youngest sometimes had its privileges.

"You put the bone back on Sunday?" asked Karen.

Abby looked at Dylan, wondering what he was going to say next.

Dylan didn't know whether his father had seen the bone, so he figured it was best to tell the truth to this question.

"I have it wrapped in a towel in the garage."

"In the garage!" exclaimed Jack. "I thought you covered it back up?"

"We were going to, but didn't know for sure if that's where Roxy found the bone. It's a big bone."

"I'd like to see it," said Karen. "Maybe I can tell what type of animal bone it is."

Dylan started to get up from his chair.

"Finish your dinner, then we can look at this bone Roxy found," said Karen.

Dylan quickly finished his dinner and carried his dirty dishes to the sink. Abby did the same. He then went to the garage to retrieve the bone. When he returned, both parents were again sitting at the dining room table. Dylan placed the towel-wrapped bone on the table and pulled back the towel.

"That's a good-sized bone," said Jack.

Karen leaned over to look at the bone. She then picked it up with both hands and looked at both ends.

"This is not an animal bone," said Karen. "This is a human bone. It looks like a humerus bone, the big bone of the upper arm. This end is the proximal or ball end that attaches to the shoulder. The distal end connects to the elbow."

"You're not joking, are you?" asked Jack.

"Not at all," responded Karen. She then looked at Dylan, then Abby. "You're telling us Roxy dug up a human grave?"

Dylan didn't know how to respond.

"Were you in the Chippewa Burial Grounds?" asked Jack.

"No!" exclaimed Dillon. "This came from just a spot in the woods near the farm with the big white house."

Jack looked at Abby. "Abby, were you in the burial grounds with Roxy?"

"No, I promise," pleaded Abby. "She ran off, and I found her with this bone in her mouth. Roxy led us back to the hole in the ground. That's where we think the bone came from."

"We probably should call the police," suggested Jack.

"This bone has obviously been in the ground for some time. Let me take it to work tomorrow and show it to Doctor Phillips. If he agrees with me, we'll call the police," suggested Karen.

"Yeah, I suppose it's not an emergency," agreed Jack. He then turned to Dylan and Abby. "You've told us everything you know about this, right?"

"Yes," said Dylan. Abby just nodded her head.

"And you're sure you weren't on the cemetery grounds, right?"

"Yes. This was not in the cemetery," replied Dylan. He knew he wasn't telling the complete truth, but Dylan didn't think it would matter that they had visited the cemetery or had been confronted by Chuck Kotter. And he definitely didn't want to get into the narrative of visiting the Kotter farm. Besides, Kotter had nothing to do with Roxy digging up a bone.

Later that evening, Dylan called Jason to let him know what had transpired. Jason appreciated that Dylan did not reveal the trip to the Kotter farm.

"I'm not sure my mom would be very happy if she knew about that," said Jason.

"How much have you told your mom?" asked Dylan.

"Not much. Just that we were going fishing, and Roxy dug up some old bones. I didn't say anything about Mr. Kotter and the airplane."

"Would you still like to take a flight?"

"I'd like to. He seemed nice enough. I really want to get a ride in that airplane."

"I know, that would be so cool," agreed Dylan. "My mom is taking the bone to work tomorrow to confirm it is a human arm bone. She called it a humerus bone. My dad's also working tomorrow. We could always go get a ride in that plane, then never go back again."

"Will you bring Abby?"

"We have to. If not, I'm afraid she'd tell Mom everything."

"You're not going to tell your mom?" asked Jason.

"She'd never let us go."

"Yeah, probably not. I won't say anything to my mom either."

The following morning, Karen Hudson arrived at the Swartz Creek Clinic a few minutes before ten o'clock. She carried the towel-wrapped bone in a paper bag. With patients already waiting, Karen had no time to show Dr. Phillips the bone until his scheduled office hour at three-thirty. It was three-thirty-five when Karen saw him in his office. She knocked on the open door.

"Karen, come on in," said Dr. Phillips. "What can I do for you?"

"I want to show you something," answered Karen as she sat the bag on a chair, reached in, and pulled out the towel-wrapped bone. She set the bone on the edge of the doctor's desk and unwrapped it. "What type of bone do you believe this is?" asked Karen.

Dr. Phillips grabbed the bone and looked it over. "Looks like a humerus bone. Where did you get this?"

"My son and daughter found it in the woods behind our house."

"What?"

"Yes, they were fishing over the weekend, and our dog dug it up somewhere in the woods."

A puzzled look crossed Dr. Phillips's face. "Where exactly was this?"

"We live on Blossom Lane. It was somewhere behind our house in the woods or near one of the ponds. Our kids could show us."

Dr. Phillips sat in silence for a moment as he examined the bone. "Isn't that near the Chippewa Burial Grounds?"

"I don't know how close they were to the burial grounds, but Dylan said where Roxy dug it up was not in the cemetery."

"This is definitely a human bone," said Dr. Phillips. "And if it was in the ground, it has been there for some time. There is no flesh on this bone."

Karen nodded her head in agreement.

"Call the police," advised Dr. Phillips. "They need to look into this."

"I'll do it right now," replied Karen.

"It was four o'clock by the time Dylan, Abby, and Jason had assembled at the Hudson house in preparation for their trip back to Kotter's farm.

"No one but us knows about Kotter and his airplane. If we do this, we can't tell anyone," Dylan warned.

"I'm not saying anything," agreed Jason. "My mom thinks I'm playing basketball at the park. What did you tell your mom?"

Dylan looked at Abby, then back at Jason. "We didn't say anything. Our parents don't know we're going anywhere. Neither of them will be home before six. But if we need to, we can say we were playing basketball with you."

"Does Abby play basketball?"

"I'll say I was watching," said Abby.

"Okay," agreed Jason. "Let's go then."

With that, the three of them started their trek back to Kotter's farmhouse, with Roxy happily running along. As they got closer to the farm, Dylan hooked Roxy up to a leash to keep her from running back to the buried bones. This time, they traveled west along the southern fence line to the gate. Opening the gate was much easier than squeezing between barbed wire fencing. Once through the gate, they followed the weed-covered dirt road that split the cornfield to Kotter's house. They arrived shortly after four-thirty. It was cooler than the previous day, with a slight breeze. They found both the screen door and the primary door to the house closed.

"I hope he's home," said Jason.

They slowly climbed the steps and walked to the door. Dylan opened the screen door and knocked hard on the solid wood door. It wasn't but a few seconds before the door swung open. There stood Chuck Kotter. Instead of a long-sleeved shirt, Kotter was wearing a cotton Detroit Lions t-shirt. Kotter flashed a big grin.

"Did you come back for a soaring plane ride?"

"We did," answered Dylan.

"And your parents are okay with this?"

Dylan hesitated, then said, "Yeah, but we need to be home by six o'clock."

"That should be no problem," said Kotter. "Let me get my jacket, and I'll join you in the barn. You can open the doors."

"What about Roxy?" asked Abby.

"We can put her in the barn. She wouldn't like it in the airplane," said Kotter.

Dylan and Jason each took one barn door and pulled them apart. The plane they saw the day before was still there, looking as impressive as the day before. Seconds later, Kotter joined them in the barn.

"Go on, get inside," shouted Kotter.

Abby climbed in first, going to one of the back seats. Jason followed and sat next to Abby. Dylan sat in the front co-pilot's seat. Kotter walked around the plane, checking the tires and ailerons on each wing. He then opened the front left hood to check the oil.

"Everything looks good," said Kotter as he climbed into the pilot's seat. "Everyone fasten your seatbelts and make sure they are snug. I'm going to give you the ride of your life."

Abby thought, *what does that mean?*

On his second attempt, the engine roared to life. Kotter revved the engine for a minute to get it warmed up. He then released the brake, and the plane began to taxi out the barn doors. Roxy barked as the plane moved forward.

"Hold on, I need to put Roxy in the barn," said Dylan.

Kotter stopped the plane long enough to allow Dylan to hop out, put Roxy in the barn, and close the doors. He could still hear her barking as he walked away. Once Dylan was back in the plane, Kotter maneuvered the plane onto the worn blacktop runway, turned left and taxied to the east end. He would take off into the west. Once he got the plane aligned with the center line, Kotter applied the brakes and revved the engine once more. With the engine roaring, he released the brakes, and the plane lurched forward and started down the runway.

"I'm scared," said Abby as the plane picked up speed.

Dylan comforted her. "It's okay, Abby."

The engine roared as the Cessna 172 Skyhawk sped down the runway. Dylan could feel the vibrations as the prop reached full speed. At fifty-five knots per hour, Kotter told them to hang on. At sixty knots, Kotter pulled back the yoke, lifting the nose of the plane gently off the blacktop surface. The plane gently lifted off the runway, leaving a trail of dust behind.

Dylan, Jason, and Abby were all looking out the windows in awe at seeing the ground drift away. The engine's noise softened as the wings sliced through the late afternoon air and climbed toward the clouds. The landscape below stretched out the higher they flew. Objects on the ground grew smaller.

"This is so cool!" exclaimed Dylan.

"I can see the creek," said Jason.

Abby was too enthralled with the view to say anything. She was also still a bit frightened. At 2,000 feet above the ground, Kotter banked the plane to the left, the side Abby was sitting on.

"AHHH!" screamed Abby as she found herself looking down out her window.

"It's okay, Abby," assured Jason. "He's just turning the plane."

Kotter continued the turn until he was headed east, back toward the woods and the city of Swartz Creek.

"Look, there's our house," said Dylan.

"I can see mine too," said Jason.

Abby was too mesmerized and still too scared to say much. As they flew overhead, Kotter pointed out the burial grounds.

Within seconds, they were flying over Swartz Creek High School. "I've never seen it like this," raved Jason. "Look at the football field."

Abby finally spoke up. "And there's my middle school."

Kotter then turned the plane back to the west, making a deep angled turn.

"Whoa!" shouted Jason.

Abby tightly gripped the armrest on her side of the plane.

Once the plane was level again, Kotter told them the land below them once belonged to the Chippewa Indians. He repeated some of the history he had talked about earlier. When he was safely over the rural and wooded countryside, he told the three kids he would show them some fun.

"What do you mean?" asked Dylan.

Kotter didn't respond. He pulled back the yoke, causing the plane to climb higher. He then said, "The higher you get, the more you can see,"

Abby gripped her armrests as the plane climbed at a steep angle. She could only see the sky out her window, and her stomach felt a bit queasy. After what seemed like a long time, Kotter leveled the plane back out.

"Look at the view now," directed Kotter.

Everyone looked out the windows and could now see so much more of the landscape and horizon.

"Whoa, look at all the lakes," muttered Jason.

"What's that city over there?" asked Dylan.

"That would be Lansing," said Kotter.

"Lansing? That's almost an hour away."

"Yep, but we are high enough to see it. You get to see a lot up here. We are far enough out now. Would you like to feel some G forces?

"G forces?"

"Yes. The effect of speed and gravity."

"Is it dangerous?"

Kotter grinned. "Are you afraid?"

"Um, no."

"How about you, Jason?" asked Kotter. "Are you afraid?"

"No."

"I'm kind of afraid," said Abby.

"It will be all right, Abby," Dylan assured her.

"Okay," said Kotter, "Hang on." As he said this, he pushed the yoke down hard. The plane immediately dipped forward until Dylan and Jason believed they were headed straight into the ground. Abby had her eyes closed. It felt as though they were free-falling straight to earth.

"Ready?" shouted Kotter.

"Ready for what!" screamed Dylan.

"Hang on!" yelled Kotter as he sharply pulled back the yoke, bringing the nose of the plane rapidly upward. The path of the plane made a sharp U shape.

"OH MY GOD!" screamed Jason from the back of the plane.

Dylan's head felt cemented to the back of his seat as the G forces pulled on every muscle in his body. Abby let out a loud, long scream. Once the plane had leveled off, Kotter laughed.

"Well, was that fun, or what?"

"I thought you were going to kill us!" exclaimed Jason.

"That's nothing; watch this!" said Kotter as he banked the plane sharply to the right and held the yolk steady, putting the plane into a downward spiral. Dylan, Jason, and Abby could hardly move in their seats. Their heads were tilted in the direction of the intense G forces as their hands tightly gripped the armrests. Abby continued to scream from the back. Kotter flew three tight right turns before pulling out. Just as they were catching their breath, Kotter put the plane into a left-turning spiral. Heads snapped in the opposite direction. Dylan could see the ground getting closer. He willed himself to scream out the words, "We're going to crash!"

"No, we're not!" yelled Kotter. "Just hang on!"

After what seemed like a long time, Kotter pulled the plane out of the spiral and back to level flight.

"You're crazy!" yelled Jason. "My neck hurts."

Jason looked at Abby. Her face was pale. "Are you okay, Abby?"

"I don't feel so good. I think I'm going to throw up."

"Don't do that!" yelled Kotter. "Here. If you're going to throw up, do it in this bag."

Abby held the white plastic bag near her mouth as she tried to settle her stomach.

Kotter looked at Dylan. "This plane is awesome, isn't it?"

"It is," agreed Dylan, "but I didn't expect that kind of ride."

Abby leaned over and placed the bag up to her mouth. She gagged as vomit erupted from her throat and mouth, leaving behind a sour and acid taste in her mouth and throat. Fortunately, the vomit made it into the bag. The smell of vomit filled the cabin of the airplane, which made Dylan and Jason queasy as well.

"We probably should go home now," said Dylan.

"Yep, that's enough for today," agreed Kotter as he turned the plane back in the direction of his farm. Kotter then handed Abby a bottle of water. "Here, this should help."

Abby took the water, rinsed her mouth, then spit the contents into the bag. She then took a drink to wash the acid from her throat.

Kotter flew the plane back to the farm and safely landed it on the runway, then taxied back to the barn. He then helped Abby out of the plane while the boys got themselves out.

"How are you feeling, Abby?" asked Kotter.

"Better now."

"Sorry you got sick. Sometimes that happens."

"What did you think, boys?"

"It was scary but kind of awesome as well," replied Dylan.

"I thought you were going to kill us," said Jason. "But, yeah, now that it's over, it was a blast."

Dylan looked at his phone. "We need to get home."

As Kotter pulled the barn door open, Roxy ran to Dylan, wagging her tail. Dylan rubbed her head. "Good girl."

"You did tell your parents you were going for a ride, correct?" asked Kotter.

Dylan lied. "Yes, but we didn't know it would be a ride like this."

"You might want to leave that part out," laughed Kotter.

"Don't worry. We will."

"Let me know if you want to go up again."

"Okay, thank you, Mr. Kotter."

Chapter 6

Detective Sergeant Greg Thompson, the only detective in the Swartz Creek Police Department, arrived at Dr. Phillips's office at four-thirty in the afternoon. Thompson had been with the Swartz Creek Police Department for twenty-three years. Although his brown hair was partially gray now, at fifty-three years old, he still had a full head of hair, which he combed to the side. He also sported a full mustache, and he stood at six-foot-two with a husky build. He was dressed in black pants and a gray sports coat. Karen Hudson was also present.

Karen told the detective the story of her children finding the bone after their dog had dug it up while playing in the woods. As best she could, Karen described the approximate location. Dr. Phillips confirmed that the bone was a human upper arm bone called a humerus.

"You're sure that's a human bone?" asked Thompson.

"Positive. I've seen plenty of them to know," responded Dr. Phillips.

"This is most likely associated with the Chippewa Burial Grounds," said Thompson. "But I'll treat it as evidence until we can be sure. Do you have a large plastic bag I can put this bone into?"

Karen found a bag and handed it to Thompson.

"And could I use one of your plastic gloves?" asked Thompson.

Karen retrieved a glove from the dispenser in an adjacent examining room. Thompson put the glove on his left hand. He gently picked up the bone with his gloved hand and placed it into the plastic bag. He then tied a knot at the open end of the bag.

"Many people have already handled that bone," said Karen.

"I'm sure," replied Thompson. "I don't need to be one more. I'll take this back to the police department and submit it for forensic testing. A simple DNA test can tell us if this is a Native American bone."

Both Karen and Dr. Phillips thanked Detective Thompson before he left. Back at the police department, located downtown on Miller Road, Thompson showed Police Chief Paula Ward the bone and explained how it was discovered.

Ward had only been the police chief for three years. She previously worked at the Lansing Police Department for twenty years, rising to the level of Lieutenant. When the opportunity opened to become the Police Chief in Swartz Creek, Ward applied and was hired. She was forty-six years old with dark red hair and a slim build. After getting passed over for a captain's position in Lansing, the decision to come to Swartz Creek was an easy one. Having grown up in Grand Blanc, Michigan, Ward was familiar with the area. Since the police department consisted of her and only five other officers, including Detective Thompson, Ward had to be a hands-on Police Chief. No sitting behind a desk or attending meetings all day. The Chief even had to help with patrolling the city from time to time.

"You think a dog dug up a burial site?" asked Ward.

"That would be my guess," answered Thompson.

"Having heard the stories and reviewed the files of the three high school boys who disappeared sixteen to eighteen years ago makes me want to be sure. I'd like you to pack up this bone as evidence and then send it to the state lab in Lansing for examination. I want to know everything about it. How old is it, how long has it been buried, age of the deceased, DNA, everything."

"Will do, Chief."

"And tomorrow, You and I are going to have those kids show us where that bone was dug up,"

"What time do you want to do it, Chief?"

"We'll talk to the parents tonight and explain what's happening. Hopefully, we can set it up for tomorrow after they get out of school."

"Got it, Chief."

Once Thompson had left her office, Chief Ward sat back in her chair, concerned over the finding of a human bone. There were several possibilities. If the grave of a Native American had been disturbed, members of the Chippewa tribe would be upset. If the bone turned out to belong to one of the missing victims from sixteen to eighteen years earlier, another set of problems would arise, including renewed attention to the case. Chief Ward wasn't in Swartz Creek when the young men went missing, but she remembers the news at the time. Since becoming Chief, she's been told about it many times by community members, family members, and retired police officers. The only current member of the police department who was in the department at the time was Detective Sergeant

Thompson. At the time the boys went missing, Thompson was a patrol officer.

Karen arrived home from the clinic around six-thirty in the evening. She found Dylan and Abby together in Dylan's bedroom. Karen thought it a bit strange as when they were home, they didn't usually hang out in each other's bedroom.

"What's going on?" asked Karen.

"What do you mean?" replied Dylan.

"You're usually either doing something or talking to your friends on your phone. You don't typically hang out in each other's bedroom."

"We were just talking about the bone Roxy found. Did you find out anything about the bone?" asked Dylan.

"Well, Dr. Phillips confirmed it was a human bone. As I believed, it's a humerus bone. The police have it now."

"The police? Why?" asked Dylan.

"They must investigate whether it's an old bone from a Native American burial site or something else."

"You mean like an animal bone?"

"No, it's definitely human. Remember when we talked about the three boys that went missing over an eighteen-month time period?"

"Yeah," said Dylan.

"Well, it's possible that bone belonged to one of the victims."

"From that long ago?" asked Abby.

"Sure. Bones can last a long time."

"Now you're scaring me," said Abby.

"That was a long time ago, Abby. But if the bones are those of one of the missing boys, it would be nice for the parents to know. And maybe the police could solve the crime."

Abby gave a half smile.

"Are you feeling okay, Abby?" asked Karen. "You look a bit pale."

"Yeah, Mom, I'm fine. Just tired."

"Have you two eaten anything yet?"

"No," answered Dylan.

"I'll make you a sandwich. I'll call you when it's ready."

Karen had just spread mayonnaise on four slices of bread when her phone rang. It was a call from Jack.

"Hey, what's up?" answered Karen.

"Are the kids home?"

"Yeah. I'm fixing them sandwiches now. What's up?"

"I got a call from the police chief. She and a detective want to come talk to us and the kids tonight."

"I talked to the detective this afternoon. He picked up the bone to be examined."

"Yes, and now they want to talk to our kids about how they found the bone and then go out to the site tomorrow after school. I can get off work if you can't be there."

"I'm supposed to be at the clinic again tomorrow."

"That's fine. I'll arrange my schedule to be home when the kids get out of school tomorrow," said Jack. "I'll be home tonight by seven-thirty. That's when the police will be there."

"Oh, okay. I'll let the kids know."

When Karen told Dylan and Abby that the Police Chief was coming by that evening, they both looked at each other.

"Why is the Chief coming here?" asked Dylan.

"She wants to know more about where and how you found the bone. Are you hiding something?"

"No. I was just wondering."

Chief Ward and Detective Sergeant Thompson arrived at 7:20 pm. Jack Hudson had not yet arrived home. Karen offered the officers something to drink, but both politely declined. She then called Dylan and Abby downstairs and introduced them to the officers.

"My husband will be home any minute now," said Karen. "Do you mind waiting until he gets home to start?"

"Not at all, Mrs. Hudson. We appreciate you allowing us to come this evening."

"Go on and have a seat."

While they waited, Roxy greeted Ward and Thompson with wide eyes and a wagging tail. Ward reached down and scratched the top of Roxy's head. Roxy then curled up between Ward's feet.

"You have a sweet dog here," Ward said.

"She was rescued from a shelter and has turned out to be a great dog."

"I can see that," smiled Ward.

Two minutes later, Jack Hudson arrived home and introduced himself to the officers. Chief Ward then began to question the children.

"Dylan, please tell us how you found the bone," said Ward.

"I didn't find it. Abby found it."

"You found the bone, Abby?" asked the Chief.

"No, Roxy found it."

"All right, tell me how Roxy found the bone."

"I don't know. We were playing in the woods, and I couldn't find Roxy. I kept calling her until I found her with a bone in her mouth."

"You didn't see where she got the bone?" continued the Chief.

"Eventually, we did," interrupted Dylan. "We didn't have time to find out where Roxy was digging. So we went back the next day and followed her back to the hole."

"Where was this hole?"

"I would describe it as north of the big pond, west of the cemetery, and close to the fence of Mr. Kotter's farm."

"Are you talking about Chuck Kotter?" asked Detective Thompson.

"Yeah."

"Is it a white farmhouse with a red barn?"

"Yeah, that's the one," replied Dylan.

The Chief continued. "When you returned the second day, what did you do when you found the hole?"

"We were going to put the bone back and cover it up. We didn't know what it was. We thought it was an animal bone."

"But you didn't put it back, correct?"

Dylan looked down. "No."

"Why not?" asked Chief Ward.

"We weren't sure what we had. We thought it could be a human bone. I was going to show it to Mom, but I was afraid."

"Why were you afraid?"

Dylan hesitated.

"It's okay, Dylan," said Karen. "You won't be in trouble. We just need the truth."

"We were kind of afraid of what Mr. Kotter told us."

"Mr. Kotter?" asked the Chief. "What did he tell you?"

"He said if it were an Indian burial ground, we would be haunted by Indian spirits, and bad things would happen to us. I didn't believe that stuff, but it still scared me a bit. I didn't want to dig up the grave again."

The Chief paused, then continued. "When did you talk to Mr. Kotter?"

"It was when we returned to find where Roxy found the bones. He saw us digging and came out to talk to us. That's when he warned us about disturbing Indian grave sites. He helped us cover it up."

"He helped you?"

"Yes. He warned us not to tell anyone, as it could upset the Chippewa Indians if they found out we disturbed a grave."

"Did he say anything about the three teenagers who disappeared sixteen years ago?" asked Detective Thompson.

"No."

"Did he threaten you in any way?"

"No. He just said if we disturbed a burial site, it would upset the spirits or something."

"He scared me," said Abby.

"Oh, yeah?" asked Thompson. "How did he scare you?"

"The way he talked about the spirits and warned us not to say anything about the bones."

"Have you had any other interactions or conversations with Chuck Kotter?" asked the Chief.

Dylan and Abby looked at each other but said nothing.

"Well, I can tell from your body language that you aren't telling us everything," said Chief Ward. "This is important. You need to tell us everything you know."

Jack spoke up. "Tell these officers everything you know. You won't be in trouble. They're trying to find out where these human bones came from and who they belong to."

"But, I think we will be in trouble," pleaded Dylan.

Jack frowned. "Have you done something against the law?"

"No, nothing like that."

"Then tell the officers what else you know."

"It has nothing to do with the bones," pleaded Dylan.

"Dylan, any information you provide may help us solve three murder cases," said the Chief. "Did you have more conversations with Mr. Kotter?"

Abby blurted out, "We went to his house and flew in his airplane."

"WHAT!?" screamed Karen.

"When did you do that?" asked Jack.

The Chief held her hands up. "Hold on, hold on. Let's hear what they have to say."

Karen couldn't stop. "What do you mean you flew in an airplane?! When!" she screamed.

Karen and Jack stared at Dylan. He finally broke the silence.

"Earlier today."

"TODAY!" screamed Karen. "You mean, while I was at work, you were with some old man flying in an airplane!

"Let's calm down," pleaded Chief Ward. "Everyone is safe right now. Screaming won't help. Let's hear what the kids have to say. It could be very important. We can deal with what Mr. Kotter did later, but for now, we need to know what happened today."

Karen sat with her head in her hands, breathing heavily.

Ward looked at Jack. He nodded yes to continue. Detective Thompson knew Chuck Kotter had been a suspect in the disappearance of the three boys seventeen years earlier, but he didn't want to bring it up at such an emotional time.

"If I understand this correctly," said the Chief, "you, Abby, and Jason went for a ride in Mr. Kotter's airplane today. Is that right?"

"Yes," muttered Dylan.

"Speak up!" demanded Jack Hudson.

"And Jason Chapman was with you, correct?"

"Yes."

"How did you get a ride in Mr. Kotter's airplane?"

"He showed us the plane yesterday and invited us to come for a ride."

"Wait," interrupted Karen. "Are you saying you went to his house yesterday as well?"

"Please, Mrs. Hudson," pleaded the Chief. "I know this is hard, but let me ask my questions, and then you can have all night to question your son."

Karen looked away, shaking her head.

"Why were you at Mr. Kotter's house yesterday?" continued the Chief.

"He invited us over to see his plane. We talked about a lot of stuff and he invited us to come back for a plane ride."

"What type of stuff?"

"He told us mostly about the history of the burial grounds and the history of Swartz Creek. He even gave us each a soda to drink."

"Did Mr. Kotter ever talk about three missing teenagers from sixteen to eighteen years ago?"

"Yeah. He mentioned it while talking about the burial grounds. It was kind of like a warning."

"A warning?"

"He asked if we had heard about the three missing teenagers. It sounded like they may have been stealing from the burial site or something like that."

"Did Mr. Kotter indicate where these boys might be?"

"No."

"Did he threaten you in any way?" continued the Chief.

"No. He just warned us not to mess with the Indian graves."

"Why did you go flying with him today?"

"Both Jason and I wanted to see what it was like."

"Did he entice you to go with any promises, gifts, money, that sort of thing?"

"No. He just invited us to go. He didn't pressure us at all."

"Did he tell you not to say anything to your parents?"

"No. He asked if we had told our parents."

"And what did you say?"

"I said yes."

"YOU LIED ABOUT TELLING US?" screamed Karen.

Chief Ward held up her hand, then turned to Abby. "Abby, you've heard my questions. Do you have anything else to say?"

"It was scary," said Abby.

"What was scary about it?"

"He made the plane do dives and loops and stuff. I thought we were going to crash. It made me sick, and I threw up."

"OH MY GOD!" screamed Karen. "I'm sorry, but that's child abuse!"

"I have to agree," said Jack. "I have a mind to go beat the crap out of that guy right now."

"We understand," assured the Chief. "Let us conduct an investigation. As you know, if we don't do this right, we could be left with nothing. Mr. Kotter may have knowledge about the missing boys from years ago."

"The Chief is right," said Thompson. "Your dog and children may have broken this case open. We can always charge Kotter for his actions with your kids, but now isn't the time."

"Did Mr. Kotter use the plane ride to scare you into not talking?" asked Chief Ward.

"I don't think so," said Dylan. "He was just showing us how the plane could dive and turn. Stuff like that."

"Okay, we need to go talk to Jason Chapman now," advised the Chief. "Are we going to be okay here?"

"It will be fine," said Jack. "Thank you."

After the police left, Karen glared at Dylan. "How could you?"

"Mom, we didn't mean to do anything wrong. It was all in fun."

"Fun? You could have all been killed."

"We need you both to go to your rooms for the night," said Jack. "Your mother and I need to talk about consequences."

"You said we wouldn't be in trouble," protested Dylan.

"Yeah, well, that was before we knew all the crap you did with this Kotter fellow. Now get up to your rooms."

When Dylan got to his room, he quickly texted Jason. *The police are coming. They know everything. Tell the truth.*

When the police arrived at Jason's house, both of his parents were waiting. The Chief went through a similar series of questions with Jason. As with the Hudson's, the Chapman's were disturbed by what had occurred. The Chief was relieved that both stories were similar. This led her to believe she was hearing the truth about what happened over the last few days. Detective Sergeant Thompson agreed.

The following morning, Dylan and Jason, as usual, sat together on the bus to school. "Are you grounded for life?" asked Jason.

"No, but they took my iPad away for two weeks, and we can't go to the woods or pond anymore. Mom really laid into me. She rarely swears, but she did last night."

"I think our parents must have talked," said Jason. "I had my iPad taken away as well. At least we still have our phones."

"Yeah, that's so they can track us now," replied Dylan. "They installed an app on my phone. My dad and I have to meet with the police tonight so that I can show them where the gravesite is."

"That should be fun," replied Jason.

Later that day, and after school had let out, Chief Ward and Detective Thompson met with Dylan and his father, Jack, at the edge of the woods. The weather had turned overnight when a cold front moved in. A ceiling of gray clouds covered the sky. Everyone wore a light jacket to keep warm. Chief Ward was in uniform, while Detective Thompson wore dark slacks and a lightweight beige jacket.

"Take us to the burial site," said Ward. Everyone followed as Dylan worked his way through the woods. Upon arrival, he pointed out the leaf-covered dirt grave.

"This is where your dog found the bone?" asked Thompson.

"We believe so. This is where Roxy came back and started digging."

Thompson bent over and brushed leaves off a small area, exposing loose black dirt. "This looks like it."

"Okay," said the Chief. "Greg, stake this out and wrap it with crime scene tape, then stay here. I'm going to call the State Police to see if they will lend us a couple of crime scene investigators to process this grave. It may be a while."

"Just bring me a sandwich and some coffee, and I'll be fine,"

Ward then looked over at the Kotter farm. "Is that the house and barn you were talking about?"

"Yeah, that's it," answered Dylan.

The Chief turned to Jack Hudson. "You and Dylan can leave now. If we have any other questions, we will be in touch."

Hudson nodded, "Okay, thank you. Let's go, Dylan."

After several more words with Detective Thompson, Ward walked back through the woods towards the Chippewa Burial Grounds. She walked through the cemetery looking for any signs of disturbed gravesites. Finding none, she worked her way back to her car and then drove to the police station. From there, she called the commander of the local state police post to ask for assistance. After listening to the Chief's story, the commander agreed to have forensic experts at the scene the following morning. Chief Ward then stopped at the local

Subway to pick up an Italian sub sandwich and coffee. She knew Detective Thompson liked the Italian sandwiches the best. Ward then returned and trudged through the woods to Thompson's location. She was slightly out of breath when she arrived.

"Here, I got you an Italian sub and coffee."

"Oh, thank you," replied Thompson.

"The state police agreed to send us a team in the morning," advised Ward. "I suspect they won't arrive until at least nine or ten. Will you be okay until I get our night officer here to relieve you?"

"That will be fine."

The Chief paused momentarily, then said, "I've read the police reports on the missing teenage boys, but you were here. What was the sense back then?"

"It was rough," replied Thompson. "We lost three teenage boys in a manner of two years. Like now, we didn't have the manpower to handle the case, so we sought out the help of the Sheriff's Department, the State Police, Gaines Township, and anyone else who was able to help. We even had a couple of FBI guys in town for a while."

"Did anyone have a theory of what happened to them?"

"There were a couple of theories. One is that they may have simply run away. Each kid seemed to have some problem of some kind. But the primary theory was that it was too coincidental to have three male teenagers go missing in such a short span. Most around here believed they were kidnapped and probably killed."

"What do you think?"

"I think they're all dead. And we may have found one of them right here. If this turns out to be one of our missing boys, it's all going to come back."

Ward nodded. "What do you know about Chuck Kotter?"

"He was a person of interest, that's for sure. I didn't interview him, but I know he was interviewed by us and the Sheriff's Department. I think he even allowed them to search his house."

"Why was he investigated?"

"He's always been a bit quirky. He was also known for his friendliness toward teenage kids. As I recall, he allowed the kids to use his property for parties."

"I read where there were other suspects as well," said Ward.

"A lot of people were interviewed. There were a couple more looked at as suspects, but I can't remember who they were. I'm sure they're in the reports."

The Chief groaned. "If these bones belong to one of those teenagers, it's all going to blow back up."

Thompson nodded in agreement. "I'll see you in the morning."

Chapter 7

It was approximately 9:30 am when two members of the state's forensic team arrived at the burial site. The Chief and Detective Thompson were waiting. The team introduced themselves as Boyd Tremont and Cindy Sayer. They were both wearing what appeared to be blue scrubs under navy blue jackets with fur collars. State Police shoulder patches adorned the upper sleeves. Both were wearing plastic shoe protectors and latex gloves. The Chief recited the events that led to the discovery of the dug-up bones.

"Other than what you've told us, has anyone disturbed the site?" asked Sayer.

"Not to our knowledge," answered Ward. "It was left unguarded for about twenty-four hours until Dylan Hudson, a fourteen-year-old boy, could bring us here. He said it looked the same as when he last saw it."

"We'll take it from here," advised Sayer. "The medical examiner should be here in an hour or so. We'll package everything up for him to take to his lab for analysis."

"We appreciate it," Ward replied. "Detective Thompson will remain here until you're done. He can answer any further questions you have. I have to go meet with the mayor now."

After the chief left, Sayer asked Thompson whether the finding of the gravesite had been made public.

"No. We weren't sure what we had. We still don't know if this is the remains of a crime victim or an old burial site."

Sayer and Tremont carefully began to dig through the topsoil with hand shovels. They took small amounts of dirt each time so as not to miss anything of evidentiary value. Soon, they were both finding bones of a human skeleton.

"Here is an arm with a missing humerus bone," said Tremont. "I also see some broken finger bones."

"This isn't a real shallow grave, but it's not a deep one, either," offered Sayer. "I doubt this is an Indian burial site."

"I would agree. I just found a rotting belt with a rusted buckle," replied Tremont. "And some cloth fragments such as from clothing. I haven't found any Indian artifacts."

Tremont continued to carefully dig and brush the rich soil from around each bone he found. "I believe we've got a full skeleton here."

Detective Thompson telephoned Chief Ward to fill her in on their findings. "They don't believe this is an Indian burial site. This is probably one of the three missing boys."

"I'm not surprised," sighed Ward. "We'll have to send out a press release once they are done collecting everything."

"We won't know who it is until DNA testing is done," replied Thompson.

"True, but it's still a dead body found in the woods. We have to say something before those kids tell everyone."

"You're right."

The medical examiner arrived on the scene as Tremont and Sayer packed the final items in plastic bags. They continued to dig until they could find no more bones or items of clothing. Included in the items found was a silver ring with a black onyx stone. The items were placed in a large black body bag and carried out of the woods to the medical examiner's van. Sayer notified Chief Ward when they were done.

When Detective Thompson arrived back at the police department, Chief Ward was writing her press release. The release was generic and did not refer to the three missing boys from eighteen years earlier. The Chief added that while the cause of death was unknown, it would be investigated as a homicide until proven differently. The press release was sent just after 4:00 pm. The Chief then called the City Manager, Gary Engles, to inform him of the news.

By 4:30 pm, Chief Ward was fielding phone calls from local news agencies wanting additional information. Most of the questions resulted in the Chief saying, "We don't know yet."

During a break, Thompson asked, "Why don't you let your Public Information Officer answer these calls?"

Ward frowned, "Very funny. Maybe I'll assign you as the Public Information Officer, smartass."

"I don't think I'd be very good at it. I'd get angry at the stupid questions they ask."

"I know it's getting late, but I think we should go interview Chuck Kotter," Ward suggested.

"I'm sorry to say I think you're right," responded Thompson.

By five o'clock, the story was being aired on local news channels. Karen Hudson called Dylan and Abby downstairs to watch the news. "You need to see this."

Dylan and Abby listened as the news of a found skeleton was being discussed. The reporter mentioned the cases of the three missing Swartz Creek teenagers sixteen to eighteen years ago and speculated that the discovery of the unknown body could be related.

"Now, do you know why I was so angry?" asked Karen. "You probably spent the day with a deranged child killer!"

Neither Dylan nor Abby responded. They were already in enough trouble. Once they returned to their rooms, Dylan turned to Abby. "He was a bit scary at first, but he didn't seem dangerous once we got to know him."

"He sure scared me in that airplane. I thought he was trying to kill us," replied Abby.

"Yeah, it was a bit scary, like a roller coaster. But it was sure fun. Besides, he was also in the plane. I don't think he wanted to kill himself."

On the drive to Kotter's farm, Chief Ward asked Thompson more about Kotter.

"I was a patrol officer back then," responded Thompson, "so I didn't have the same level of involvement as our Chief. We also had a lot of outside assistance with the investigation. But I do remember that many folks around here thought Kotter might be involved."

"What made them think that?" asked Ward.

"He's always been a bit odd. As I recall, he was involved in some of the high school activities when he was younger. He seemed to like hanging out with the students. As I mentioned earlier, I remember he used to host high school parties at his property around the years the boys went missing. For some people, that was a red flag. They felt like he was grooming students or something. Oh, one other thing. One of the boy's jackets was found on the roadside not far from Kotter's home. I remember a large search party was formed to comb the area, but nothing else was found."

"Interesting," nodded Ward. "And now we've found a body just outside his fence."

Thompson looked at Chief Ward. "It does make him look like a suspect, doesn't it?"

Ward nodded. "What about a wife or children?"

"As far as I know, he's never been married or had children. He moved back to help his parents, then took over the farm after they passed."

They soon arrived at Kotter's farm. Thompson drove the white Ford Explorer down the long gravel driveway and past the barn to the front of Kotter's home. The sun was still in the western sky, casting shadows across the landscape. They could see a light on through the kitchen window. Thompson parked the car in front of the covered wood porch. Both officers approached the door. Thompson loudly knocked four times. Chief Ward saw Kotter look out the kitchen window. Several seconds later, the door opened.

"Good evening, Mr. Kotter," began Ward. "I'm Police Chief Paula Ward, and this is Detective Sergeant Greg Thompson with the Swartz Creek Police Department."

"I know who you are," responded Kotter in his gruff voice. "What do you want?"

"We would like to talk to you about the grave site found by the kids you helped."

"Yeah, we covered it back up after their dog messed with it. And then I saw you had people desecrate the grave by digging up the body or what's left of it."

"That's what we need to talk to you about. May we come in?"

Kotter tilted his head and stared like he was thinking about it. He then stepped back while opening the door. "Sure, come on in."

Kotter walked them to the kitchen table, where the three of them sat down. Ward and Thompson sat across from Kotter.

"Why aren't you wearing uniforms?" asked Kotter.

"We normally wear uniforms when patrolling," explained Ward. "Right now, we're investigating the circumstances of the skeleton found buried in the woods."

"That's probably a Chippewa Indian you just dug up," grunted Kotter.

"We don't believe so," said Thompson. "No Indian artifacts or clothing was found. We only found evidence of modern-day clothing."

"Many Native Americans wear regular clothing these days," responded Kotter.

"There have been no Native Americans buried outside the Chippewa Burial Grounds for many years," explained Thompson. "This site is not that old."

"So, what do you want from me?"

"This grave was found just ten feet outside your property line. It took some time to bury the body there. Do you recall seeing activity in that area sixteen to eighteen years ago?"

Kotter chuckled. "If I did, I certainly don't remember it now. It's not that easy to see from here."

"No, but you saw the three kids and a dog there on Sunday."

"That's because I was out checking my property. I could tell they were trying to dig something up."

Thompson continued. "Do you remember the period of time between sixteen and eighteen years ago when three high school boys went missing?"

"Of course. Anyone living here remembers that."

"Did you know any of the boys?"

Kotter shook his head without responding.

"Let me give you the names," said Thompson. "Mike Taggert, sixteen years old; Richard Cranski, also known as Peaky, seventeen; and Stanley Pollock, fifteen."

"I remember the name Peaky. That's a hard one to forget."

"How did you know him?" asked Thompson.

"I didn't know him. Your officers investigated me as a suspect. They told me his name, and that is one you don't forget," Kotter said in an irritated voice.

"There's no need to get upset, Mr. Kotter," said Ward. "We suspect the body in that grave is going to be one of the boys. That's why we're asking these questions. I've reviewed some of the reports and found that you were involved in several school functions. You even had some parties at your farm for the high schoolers. Are you sure you don't remember any of these boys?"

"You know, I put up with this crap sixteen years ago. I never had kids, okay? But I liked kids. I let them use my property as a place to have some fun. For that, I got accused of being a suspect."

"Speaking of fun," continued Ward, "I heard you took Dylan, Jason, and Abby up in your airplane on Tuesday."

Kotter stared emotionless at Chief Ward.

"Is that true?" asked Ward.

"Yes, the kids wanted a plane ride. They told me it was okay with their parents, so I took them up."

"You did more than give them a ride, didn't you?"

"What do you mean?" grumbled Kotter.

"You scared the hell out of Abby."

"She was having fun until she got sick."

"Was it a good idea to put them at risk with a wild flight?"

"There was no risk," argued Kotter. "I had full control of the plane at all times."

Ward looked intently into Kotter's eyes. "I don't think the parents care how much you think you had control. Doing the stunts they described put them at risk. That could be considered endangering a child."

"Is that what this is about? Are you just trying to charge me with something?"

"Mr. Kotter," interjected Thompson. "Were you trying to scare the kids from digging in that grave because you knew it was one of the three missing teens?"

"Okay, that's enough," shouted Kotter. "I would like you to leave now."

"One more question," said Thompson. "Is there any reason your DNA might be found on the clothing or items recovered from the grave?"

"I asked you to leave."

"Will you first answer my question?" asked Thompson.

"The only way my DNA would be there is if you planted it there," snarled Kotter.

Thompson and Kotter locked eyes until Ward spoke.

"Thank you, Mr. Kotter," said Ward. "We'll see our way out."

On the way back to the station, Thompson asked Chief Ward what her thoughts were.

"He's tough to read," said Ward. "I would certainly keep him on our suspect list, especially if that body ends up being one of the boys. I find it very coincidental that it was found just outside his property. Second, he was known for catering to high school kids. And third, he just seems a bit off."

"He's always been somewhat difficult," replied Thompson. "But he's also never caused any real problems."

"Maybe," replied Ward. "Let's see what our evidence tells us."

It was getting dark by the time they returned to the police station. Chief Ward wanted to know who the other two prime suspects had been. Thompson lifted the large case file boxes onto his desk. He searched through the boxes until he found the three files - one on Chuck Kotter, one on Miguel Morales, and one on Kent Franklin.

"Tell me about Morales," said Ward.

"Let's see, he's a Hispanic male in his mid-twenties at the time who worked at the library. Scanning this, it looks like he hosted the children's reading hour on Saturdays. He was also gay."

"That's it?"

"From what I remember, some parents were concerned about him. They thought he was grooming children for sex."

"What about the third suspect?"

"That would be Kent Franklin. He was seventeen and still in high school. He was described as an odd kid, kind of a loner type. Apparently, he was seen with one of the victims the day before he disappeared. At the time, he lived in Gaines Township."

"How extensively were each of them investigated?"

"I was in patrol, so I wasn't directly involved, but in reviewing the files, each one was looked at closely. There just wasn't enough evidence. We weren't sure whether our victims were dead, kidnapped and still alive, or had just run away."

"Yeah, that would be a problem," agreed the Chief. "But after this long, I think we can assume they are dead. What are the odds of three high schoolers going missing within eighteen months and never being heard from again?"

"I'd say the odds are very, very low."

"Do you believe our bones belong to one of those missing boys?" asked Ward.

"I do. Who else would be buried in a relatively shallow grave out in the woods?"

"A stranger from another city?"

Thompson smiled. "At least we could then turn it over to another department."

"I doubt we will be that lucky. Do we have the DNA charts on our three victims?"

"I remember seeing them. I believe we got samples from each family."

"Then we should know soon enough whether our buried body belongs to one of our victims," said Ward. "Are you tired?"

Thompson smiled. "Extremely."

"Me too. Put down the files and call it a night. Tomorrow, we'll track down our other two potential suspects."

"Thank you, Chief."

Karen Hudson spent the evening scouring the internet for any information she could find. Local sites were already full of comments on Facebook and X, still commonly called

Twitter. Karen was unhappy to see references being made to Dylan, Abby, and Jason and their affiliation with Chuck Kotter. Some posters speculated that the children had probably been sexually assaulted.

Karen turned to her husband, Jack. "This is awful, Jack. Have you seen some of the things people are posting?"

"No, I stay away from that nonsense."

"But other people will read this and believe it to be true!"

"Karen, just ignore it. Social media is full of lies and nonsense."

Karen called Dylan into the room. "Did you talk to anyone about what happened?"

"Um, we told some friends at school," admitted Dylan.

"Why would you do that, Dylan?"

"We didn't see any harm in telling our friends."

"Well, now you're being talked about on the internet. This could put you in danger."

"How could we be in danger?"

"If Mr. Kotter reads all this, he could come after you, Abby, and Jack. Who knows what he's capable of?"

Dylan stood silently.

"Don't you have anything to say?"

"I don't believe Mr. Kotter would hurt us."

"Dylan, that's what men like Mr. Kotter do. They play nice until their victims trust them. He used to hold parties for high school kids at his farm."

"Mom, we're not going back. Stop worrying."

Karen sighed. "I appreciate that."

"Can I have my iPad back now?"

"Nice try, but no."

Dylan turned and left the room. He went upstairs to speak with Abby.

"Mom thinks we're in danger now."

"From Mr. Kotter?" asked Abby.

"Yeah. I think mom's still upset over the airplane flight."

"It scared me to death."

"Lots of people do things like that in airplanes. I think he just wanted to give us an exciting ride. Kind of like a roller coaster."

"Well, I didn't like it."

"I understand. Good night, Abby."

Chapter 8

When Detective Thompson arrived at work at 8:30 am, Chief Ward was already in the office.

"What time did you get in?" asked Thompson.

"I woke up at four-thirty and couldn't get back to sleep, so I came in to read more reports. I'm going over the suspect list they had sixteen years ago. Kotter would have been forty-two back then. There are quite a few people who described him as a bit strange but also friendly to the high schoolers. The parties at his farm were well-known and not favored by some parents. Others thought it was a safe venue for the kids to party without getting into trouble. At the time, his farm was not in the city limits, so our department didn't have jurisdiction over the party complaints."

"Yeah, I remember that," agreed Thompson.

"Do you know if he gave kids airplane rides back then?"

Thompson thought for a moment. "Yes, he did."

Ward raised her eyebrows. "Could he have been using the rides as an enticement for the kids?"

"Possibly," answered Thompson.

"According to these reports, Kotter never agreed to a DNA sample. Apparently, we didn't have enough probable cause to get a court order."

"If those bones are one of our victims, do you think we'll be able to get a warrant this time?" asked Thompson.

"Oh, no doubt. With the body being buried just off his property and his insistence on covering it back up, it will be easy to get a judge to sign a warrant."

"I agree," said Thompson. "What about the other two suspects?"

"Kent Franklin is an interesting one because he was a fellow student and was seen with one of the victims the day before he went missing. Let me see, the victim was sixteen-year-old Mike Taggert. Taggert was a sixteen-year-old white male described as an awkward kid without many friends. And Franklin is described as an odd kid who didn't talk much. It says here that he had very few friends. He lived with his mother. This could be what attracted Franklin to befriend Taggert."

"This is bringing back some memories," replied Thompson. "I think there were some similarities in all three victims. I remember Chief Braxton was focused on Kent Franklin as a prime suspect because of his personality."

"We'll have to contact Braxton to pick his brain," said Ward.

"You won't be able to do that," replied Thompson.

"Why not?"

"He retired ten years ago and passed away six years ago."

"Damn," grumbled Ward. "We need to talk to someone who was involved in the investigation."

"There are two people I know of who might have more information."

"Who would that be?"

"Our City Clerk and Administrative Assistant, Marilyn Branch, knows everything that goes on, and I know Chief Braxton had her assist with reading and organizing all the reports. She knew as much about the case as anyone."

"I hadn't thought of Marilyn, but you're right. She seems to know everything about this town."

"She's been around for about thirty years," said Thompson. "She's sixty-three now and plans to retire in two years. The other person who may be valuable is our past mayor, Marty Strawski. He was here during that time and seemed to be closely involved. I know he talked to the press a lot."

"Where is Marty now?" asked Ward.

"I'm not sure. I heard he moved up north somewhere to hunt and fish."

"When did he leave Swartz Creek?"

"It was probably three years after the last victim went missing. As I recall, he resigned shortly before the next election. He and Chief Braxton were under considerable pressure."

"Look him up. I'll want to talk to him as well."

"I've added it to my to-do list."

"Okay," said Ward. "The third prime suspect was Miguel Morales. At the time, he was twenty-five, with a slim build and black hair. He's the one who worked at the library. He was described as well-dressed, and people believed him to be gay."

"He had a boyfriend at the time, so I'd say he was gay."

"Right," replied Ward. "Is he still around?"

"No. After all the rumors of him grooming boys for sex, he chose to leave town. I don't know where he is now."

"Was it proven he groomed boys for sex?" asked Ward.

"No. I think some parents were uncomfortable with Morales running the reading program at the library. He didn't hide his homosexuality, and that disturbed a few people. Personally, I don't believe he was involved."

"Maybe not, but we can't eliminate anyone at this point," replied Ward.

"I agree, Chief."

"Where are we on DNA samples?" asked Ward.

"We have samples on everyone except Kotter."

"Do we have comparison samples from each victim?"

"Of course," replied Thompson. "We took DNA from the parents and collected the toothbrushes from the homes of each missing child. We have DNA charts on all three."

"Excellent!" exclaimed Ward.

"Do you think the state lab will be able to pull some foreign DNA from the rotted clothing pulled from the grave?" asked Thompson.

"Highly unlikely. Any DNA was likely lost as the clothing rotted away. But who knows, maybe we get lucky."

"I figured," replied Thompson.

Ward continued, "You've probably done this, but did anyone send missing person bulletins to all departments in the country?"

"Yes. Every year for six years after the last teen went missing."

"I'm sure you also did national database searches for each victim?"

"Yes. Multiple times."

"Great, thank you, Greg. Let's pull Marilyn in to see what she remembers."

Fifteen minutes later, city Clerk and Administrative Assistant Marilyn Branch sat in Chief Ward's office facing Chief Ward and Detective Thompson. Marilyn Branch was sixty-three years old and had worked for the city for the past twenty-six years. She worked closely with the city administration, including the police department. Employees often consulted with Branch about her knowledge of city history. Her white hair was styled to curl just over her ears, highlighting her dark brown eyes. Branch had already been told what the meeting was about.

"Thank you for helping us out," said Chief Ward.

"That's what I'm here for," smiled Branch.

"I understand you've read the entire case file. Is that correct?"

"Over time, yes. As reports were filed, I was tasked with reviewing them for accuracy and errors. Chief Braxton had his hands full."

"I can imagine. Do you remember if any suspects were specifically focused on back then?"

"Chuck Kotter was probably suspect number one. He was the least cooperative of those interviewed. He was also known for befriending teenagers in town and even allowed them to use his property for parties. I remember a time the police were called out to his farm during one of the parties. Some students had gotten into a fight or something."

"Was Chuck charged with anything?" asked Thompson.

"I don't believe so. At that time, the farm was still in the county, so Swartz Creek Police had no enforcement jurisdiction, but they were always there to help the county."

"Were you present for the interviews of Kotter?"

"One of them. He was brought into the police department for an interview with an expert from the State Police."

"Did you watch the interview?"

"No, I wasn't allowed to. But Ron allowed me to later listen to the recording."

"Are you talking about Chief Ron Braxton?" asked Ward.

"Yes."

"Okay, go on."

"Well, I thought Kotter came across as arrogant. He was argumentative during the interview, claiming he was simply targeted because he allowed parties on his property. When he was asked for a voluntary DNA sample, he refused. He asked if the police had a warrant."

"They didn't have enough to get a warrant?" asked Ward.

"That's what Chief Braxton told me. He said the only reason they had to question Kotter was because he was friendly to teenagers. They never found a body, so technically, the case was only about missing persons, not a homicide."

"It's still not a homicide," said Ward. "We suspect the teens must be dead, but no one knows for sure."

"He did let them look around his property."

"Kotter let the police search his property?"

"He said they could look around so long as they didn't disrupt or damage anything. I think he did it to get the police off his back."

"Interesting," pondered Ward. "He would allow them to search his property but not provide a DNA sample."

"I knew Chuck Kotter outside the investigation. He has always thought the government was too much into everyone's lives. Providing his DNA was too intrusive for him. I had a conversation with him once about the parties he allowed. He told me it wasn't that he enjoyed teenage parties; it was more about giving the kids a safe place to have a good time without being watched or hassled. He knew his property was outside town limits, and with no neighbors around, there were no complaints of noise or anything. The only complaints we got were from parents who were pissed he allowed the parties. We all knew the kids drank and smoked pot up there."

"Do you believe Kotter was involved in the disappearances?" Ward asked.

Branch hesitated. "I don't. He was an easy target because of his gruff attitude and the parties. But I never saw him show any type of unusual interest in kids. I believe he has a fondness for teenagers, in a good way."

"What about the body just found at his property line? Does that change your mind?" asked Ward.

"If it ends up being one of the missing teens, then maybe. On the other hand, because he was suspected by many, I could see someone trying to set him up by burying the body near his property."

Ward paused before saying, "Huh, I hadn't thought of that. What do you know about the other two suspects?"

"Chief Braxton focused more on Kotter, but my number one suspect would be Miguel Morales. He seemed to like children almost too much. He is also gay. And I know that shouldn't matter, but given that all the missing kids were young teens and male, you have to think he might have had something to do with it."

"Did he cooperate with the investigation?" asked Thompson.

"As far as I remember."

"Did you ever see anything inappropriate when he was with kids?"

"The only time I saw him with kids was during some of the library programs he ran. He gave a lot of hugs. Maybe I'm old-fashioned, but that didn't seem appropriate to me."

"Did he only hug the male kids?"

Branch paused. "No, he hugged both boys and girls."

"What age group are we talking about?" asked Ward.

"Probably kindergarten to second grade."

"Ever see him interact that way with teenagers?"

"No, not that I recall."

"Thank you, Marilyn," said Ward. "What about Kent Franklin?"

"Well, he was about the same age as the victims. He was attending Swartz Creek High School at the time. As I re-member, he was an odd kid. Quiet and didn't seem to have many friends. Very introverted. I recall Chief Braxton refer-ring to Kent as a loner. What arose suspicion on him was that he was seen with one of the victims the day before he went missing."

"The victim she is referring to is sixteen-year-old Mike Taggert from Gaines," said Thompson. "Taggert was de-scribed as a small-statured, awkward kid who lived with his mother. According to several witnesses, it would have been unusual to see Franklin hanging out with Taggert. They were last seen walking from the high school parking lot."

"The day he went missing?" asked Ward.

"No, the day before," answered Thompson.

"That's not very strong evidence,"

"No, it's not. I think more of it centered around Franklin being a loner with few friends."

"Do we have his DNA?"

"Yes."

"Marilyn, is there anything else you can think of that may be important to our investigation?" asked Ward.

"Not right now."

"Well, thank you for answering our questions and giving us more background information. It's very helpful."

"You're welcome."

After Branch had left, Ward looked at Thompson. "That was helpful. It was a good idea to talk with Marilyn, but I don't think we're much closer to having a solid suspect."

"No, but it was good to get the background. Out of the three, who would you suspect the most?"

"I don't think it's Morales," replied Ward.

"Why not?"

"He doesn't fit the profile, at least in my mind. He obviously liked working with younger children and had done so for several years with no complaints. It was only when a teenager went missing that people started pointing a finger at him simply because he was gay. He also had a partner, so sex would not have been a motivation."

"Who then?" asked Thompson.

"Kent Franklin presents an interesting question. What was he doing with Mike Taggert the day before he went missing? That's the only report we have of someone being seen with one of our victims just prior to his disappearance. He was also a loner. That's a typical trait of many serial killers."

"Yeah, I see your logic," agreed Thompson. "What about Kotter?"

"He's like a jigsaw puzzle to me. In some ways, I can see him doing it. But sometimes it seems too obvious. He's bold to refuse a DNA swab, as he has to know that refusing a DNA test raises further suspicion. So, either he's confident because he's not the killer, or he refused the DNA swab because he is."

"Do we have enough now to get a court order for a DNA swab?" asked Thompson.

"Probably not. While we believe the victims were probably murdered, we don't have proof of that other than they haven't been heard from in many years. They are still listed in our files as missing persons."

Thompson nodded. "If the bones turn out to be from one of the victims, will we have enough to get the court order?"

"Yes," replied Ward. "At that point, a judge would certainly issue a search warrant for DNA. The bodies were buried just outside his property line. That alone is reasonable suspicion. We won't hear anything from the state lab until next week. There isn't much else to do for now. Go home and enjoy the weekend. It could be the last one you get off for a while."

"I could use the rest. Thank you, Chief."

Chapter 9

It was ten o'clock on Saturday morning. Dylan and Abby Hudson had been left home alone. Karen Hudson worked every other Saturday at the clinic, and this was one of her days to work. Jack Hudson was working at the General Motors Truck Plant, as he did on most Saturdays. It was Dylan's job to look after Abby. Karen would be home sometime around 3:00 pm. Jason Chapman had come over to hang out with Dylan.

"It's been kind of boring not having our iPads to play on," said Jason. "And my mom somehow locked my phone from the internet."

"Yeah, same here," said Dylan. "I wish we could at least go to the pond to fish."

"I can't go there or to the woods," replied Jason.

After a silent pause, Dylan asked, "Did Johnny Baker tease you at school?"

"No, why?"

"He kept asking me what Kotter did to us."

"What do you mean?"

"I mean, like sexual stuff."

"Huh? Where did he get an idea like that?"

"I don't know, Jason, but he claimed Kotter was a pervert who liked to fondle teenage boys."

"What did you say?"

"I told him nothing happened. He said his mother told him Kotter murdered those three missing students from years ago."

"Do you think he did?"

"No, but I'll bet we can find out."

"How?" asked Jason.

"Let's go visit him again."

"I can't do that," protested Jason. "I'm already in trouble."

"Yeah, me too, but there would be two of us, and if he confessed, we would have solved the murders of three students."

"I can't go back there. I'd be in huge trouble," said Jason.

"When do you have to be home?"

"Two o'clock."

"We've got plenty of time to talk to Mr. Kotter."

"What if Johnny is right? We could be his next victims."

"That's why we need to go together. He won't kill two of us. And we can tell him our moms know where we are. Think how famous we would be if we solved this?"

"What about Abby?"

"I'll tell her she has to stay here in case we don't return. She can then tell Mom to call the police. He's an old man, Jason. He can't take both of us. You're strong."

"Well, I am curious to know more."

"Yes! Me too." Dylan then walked to the foot of the stairs and called up to Abby. "Abby, come down here a minute."

"I'm busy," she shouted back.

"It's important. It's about old man Kotter."

Abby appeared at the top of the stairs. "What is it?"

"Just come down here."

Abby walked down the stairs with Roxy and joined Dylan and Jason in the dining room.

"Jason and I are going back to Kotter's farm to find out if he killed those boys."

"You can't go there or to the woods. Remember?"

"We're not going to tell Mom. You need to stay here in case we don't return."

"What do you mean?"

"If we don't return by two o'clock, you need to tell Mom and the police where we are."

"Are you going on the airplane again?"

"No, we're trying to find out if he really did kill those boys."

"You're going to be in so much trouble."

"Mom won't find out unless you tell her. We'll be back before she gets home. You need to cover for us if she calls."

"I don't think you should go."

"It will be fine, Abby. Please do this for us. I'll buy you a candy bar the next time we go to the store."

"A Butterfinger?"

"Whatever you want."

Abby hesitated. "Okay, but you better not forget."

"I won't. Come on, Jason. We need to hurry to have plenty of time to get back."

With that, Dylan and Jason set out on foot to hike back to Kotter's farm. They followed the same route as before until they came upon the gravesite. They didn't go to the gate as they wanted to see what the police had done. It was apparent the site had been excavated. Leaves no longer covered the area, and black dirt was loosely piled into the hole. Dylan and Jason stared for several seconds before Dylan spoke.

"It smells bad here."

"Yeah, let's get out of here," agreed Jason.

The boys helped each other through the barbed wire fencing and then trudged toward Kotter's farmhouse. They were within fifty yards of the house when Dylan's phone rang.

"Oh, oh," said Dylan. "It's my mom."

"Hi, Mom. What's up?"

"Nothing. I'm just calling to check-in. Is everything okay there?"

"Uh, yep. Jason and I are kicking the soccer ball around in the backyard, and Abby is up in her room."

"Okay. I should be home around two-thirty. I'll stop and get a pizza on the way home."

"That sounds great, Mom. Thank you."

After hanging up, Dylan turned to Jason. "Close call."

The boys continued toward the house. As they got to the dirt driveway, Kotter emerged onto the covered porch and yelled, "What the hell are you two doing here?"

"Uh, we just came to see how you were doing?"

Kotter stared at them for a couple of seconds. "Do your parents know you're here?" he hollered in a gruff voice.

"No."

"Then why are you here?"

"We wanted to see you."

"See me? Aren't you afraid I'm going to kill you?"

"No."

Several seconds of silence ensued. Jason swallowed, wondering what would happen next.

"Well, if you want to see me, get up here!"

Dylan and Jason continued to the porch.

"Have a seat on that bench," instructed Kotter.

Both boys sat on the bench. Kotter pulled over one of the chairs from the small table and plopped it before the boys. He then sat facing them.

"Why did you want to see me?"

Neither boy said anything.

"If you're just going to sit there, I'm going back into the house. I have things to do."

"Some people are saying bad things about you," said Dylan.

"Like what!" barked Kotter.

"They think you killed those kids from years ago."

"What do you think?"

"I don't think you did. Did you?" asked Dylan.

Kotter smirked. "If I said no, would you believe me?"

"We wouldn't be here if we thought you were a killer."

"No, I suppose not."

"Do you know what happened to those boys?" asked Jason.

Kotter looked down at the wooden floor of the porch. "No, I don't. If I did, the person who took them wouldn't be alive today."

Dylan and Jason looked at each other.

"What do you mean?" asked Dylan.

"They've been missing for many years, so my assumption is that they are all dead. That means somebody took those boys and murdered them. I can be a gruff old man, but

I've never hurt a child. But I would have no problem hurting whoever took those boys."

"My sister thought you were trying to kill us in the airplane," said Dylan.

For the first time, Dylan saw Kotter smile. "That was one hell of a ride, wasn't it?"

Both Dylan and Jason smiled back.

"It was awesome," said Jason.

"You kids got me into some trouble. You told me your parents knew about the ride. The police questioned me about it. Why did you lie?"

After a pause, Dylan spoke up. "We wanted to go for an airplane ride, Mr. Kotter, but we knew our parents would say no. We're sorry about that."

"You know, I kind of understand that. Parents tend to be overly restrictive these days. Kids need to be kids and experience life adventures."

Dylan felt more relaxed and dared to ask a question he had been thinking about.

"Why did you lie to us about the grave?"

"What do you mean?"

"You said it was an Indian grave. You talked about how we shouldn't disturb it and how we would be haunted if we did."

"That's not a lie," barked Kotter. "How would anyone know it was anything but an Indian gravesite? And I do believe in Indian spirits. I've heard many stories of people who have experienced visits from spirits."

"Oh," said Dylan.

"If that body turns out to be one of the missing teens, I'm probably going to be arrested. It doesn't mean I'm guilty."

"Why would they arrest you?" asked Jason.

"The police and I don't exactly get along. They already see me as a suspect, and if one of the kidnapped boys is found ten feet from my property, I'll be their number one suspect."

"My mom said you used to have big parties with kids on your farm," said Jason.

"That's true."

"Why did you do that?"

"Back in my day, kids had many more freedoms than you do today. We had mini-bikes, motorcycles, and go-karts to drive around on the back roads, through the forests, and to the parks. We could shoot our BB guns in the woods. We could play all day in the woods without parents worrying about us. We played ball in the streets. We could even have parties where parents would allow kids to drink beer so long as they weren't driving. Kids could be kids. These days, kids are restricted from doing so many things. You can be ticketed for almost anything. So, having this farm in the middle of nowhere, I opened it up for high schoolers to have parties. My rule was no drugs, and everyone had to have designated drivers."

"That sounds like fun!" said Dylan.

"It was fun, Dylan. Now, everyone worries about everything. I understand some of it. But we've gone too far."

"If you get arrested, what will you do?" asked Jason.

Kotter smiled. "Don't worry about me, Jason. I'm smarter than those dumb ass cops think I am."

"Hey," said Dylan. "We need to get back before my parents get home. Thank you for talking to us, Mr. Kotter."

"I like you boys. Come back anytime you want to chat, ride a tractor, or take a plane ride," said Kotter as he smiled.

Dylan and Jason returned home in plenty of time. Jason returned to his own home. When Dylan walked into his house, Abby was there to greet him.

"Well, what happened?"

"I think everyone has Mr. Kotter wrong," answered Dylan. "He's actually a pretty cool guy."

"You don't think he killed those boys?"

"No, I don't."

Just before three o'clock, Karen Hudson walked through the door with a large pizza. "I'm home, and I've got pizza," she yelled.

Dylan and Abby came downstairs to join their mother. Roxy, of course, came right along with them.

"Here, I even got you each a root beer."

After they had all sat down, Karen asked them what they had done all day.

"I mostly worked on my drawing in my room. I also watched some TV," answered Abby.

"And what did you and Jason do?"

"We hung out. Played some soccer and then watched some TV in the family room," answered Dylan.

"Well, thank you for staying here and watching Abby."

"Anytime, Mom."

Chapter 10

On Monday, Detective Thompson arrived at work at 8:30 am. Chief Ward was already at her desk in her dark blue police uniform.

"How was your weekend?" asked Thompson.

"I didn't do much other than reading old investigative reports. How about you?"

"I didn't read reports, but I thought about this case all weekend. Are you planning to go out on patrol today?"

"No, I just felt like wearing the uniform today. At times like this, I believe the uniform presents more of a command presence.

"Would you like me to dress in my blues?" asked Thompson.

"That won't be necessary. People don't expect detectives to be in uniform. Only if I need you for patrol."

When do you suspect we will hear from the state lab?"

"It will be sometime later this week," answered Ward. "I also did a database search on Kent Franklin. You can't believe how many Franklins are out there. But I did find a Kent Franklin with the right date of birth. He lives in Jackson, Michigan, on North Waterloo Avenue and works as a hospital janitor."

"Are you going to call him in?"

"Nope. I want you to find him and interview him. I need to stay here. We only have one other officer on duty." Ward then handed Thompson a yellow post-it note. "Here's his home address and the address for the hospital."

"Should I call first?"

"I know it could be a long drive for nothing, but I think it's best to catch people off guard."

"All right, I'll get myself a cup of coffee and be on my way to Jackson. Wasn't there a country song like that? I'm on my way to Jackson...."

Chief Ward laughed. "I believe the words were, I'm goin' to Jackson, by Johnny Cash."

"Yeah, that sounds right," smiled Thompson.

Thompson stuffed some reports into his black leather portfolio, poured himself a cup of coffee, then left for Jackson. Thompson took Interstate Highway 69 west to Lansing, then traveled south on Highway 127 to Jackson. The drive took him an hour and seventeen minutes. He didn't know whether Franklin would be at home or work but decided to try his house first. The neighborhood was a mix of single and two-story homes. Most were wood-sided, which is what many would call bungalow-type homes. Kent Franklin's house was a small, off-white one-story home with a covered front porch. A driveway ran along the north side of the home. Grass and weeds were growing through the driveway's many cracks, and a large oak tree shaded the front yard. Parked in the driveway was a white Kia Sorento. Thompson parked on the street.

Thompson walked up the two wooden steps to the covered porch, then rang the doorbell. In only seconds, the door opened. Thompson observed a thin white male with long brown hair parted in the middle and wearing a white t-shirt.

His dark blue cotton pants reminded Thompson of those a repairman might wear. The man looked a bit startled to see Thompson.

"What do you want?" asked the man.

"Hello, I'm Detective Greg Thompson with the Swartz Creek Police Department. I'm investigating the disappearance of three teenage boys about sixteen to eighteen years ago. Are you Kent Franklin?

After a short pause, Franklin responded, "Yes."

"We have reopened the case after recently finding one of the boys."

Franklin's eyes widened. "You found one of the dead boys?"

Thompson made a mental note that Franklin immediately assumed one of the boys was dead. Thompson decided not to reveal information on the recovered body just yet. "May I come in to ask you a few questions?"

"I talked to the police years ago. I don't know anything about it."

"I understand. However, we are re-interviewing people to see if maybe they can remember something from back then that would help us finally solve the cases. Please allow me to come in for a few minutes."

Franklin stepped back from the door, allowing Thompson to enter the small home. The living room was dimly lit by a shaded lamp sitting on a small table between two cushioned chairs. The living room and kitchen were all one big room. The kitchen table was full of books and some dirty dishes.

"I don't know anything," offered Franklin.

"Why don't we sit down," said Thompson.

Franklin sat in the chair furthest from the front door. Thompson sat in the opposite chair. Only the small table with the lamp separated them.

"I need to go to work in an hour," said Franklin.

"What do you do?" asked Thompson.

"I'm a maintenance janitor at the hospital."

"You do both?"

"Yeah, it's a combination job. I do a little bit of everything."

"Are you married or have children?"

"No. I've never been married."

"Is there a reason for that?"

"Yeah. I've never met a woman worth marrying. Why are you asking me these questions?"

"I'm just trying to get background information on you. We know nothing about you since you graduated. What have you done the last sixteen years?"

"I got on with my life. I left Swartz Creek after graduation. I've lived in several different places and settled down here. I have a good job that pays the bills, and I try to live a quiet life."

"Why did you leave Swartz Creek so soon?"

Franklin didn't answer.

"Kent, why did you leave Swartz Creek?"

"You know why. Some people in town thought I killed Mike Taggert and those other two boys."

"You were seen leaving high school with Taggert the day before he disappeared."

"That doesn't mean I killed him."

"No, but that is why some people believe you were involved in his disappearance."

"I've already talked to the police about all this. Mike and I were just friends. Neither of us had many friends. We were quiet and, I don't know."

"What do you mean you don't know?"

"We didn't click with other students. We were considered oddballs. I finally found someone I could connect with, and then someone killed him. I hated Swartz Creek."

"How do you know someone killed Mike?"

"Huh?"

"I said, how do you know someone killed Mike?"

"Isn't that why you're here?"

"All I said is that we found one of the boys. I didn't say who it was or whether he was alive or dead. Tell me what you did to Mike."

Franklin had a stunned look on his face. Thompson saw his face turn a reddish hue.

"I didn't do anything to Mike. He was my friend."

"Kent, it's time to tell the truth. We now have foreign DNA to compare to yours," lied Thompson. "It will come back as a match to the DNA we took from you over sixteen years ago."

"I didn't hurt Mike!"

"What did you do with Mike the day before he disappeared?"

Franklin was slumped over with his head in his hands. "I told you guys all this already. I don't want to relive this."

"Just tell me what happened, Kent."

"You're trying to trick me."

"I'm not trying to trick you. Tell me what you did to Mike, and the pain will disappear, Kent. Give his family some closure."

Thompson could see that Franklin was crying.

"Kent, what did you do to Mike?"

"I told the police all this before," cried Franklin. "Why are you doing this to me again?"

"How did you know Mike was dead!" screamed Thompson.

Franklin's eyes widened. "You told me."

"I never said he was dead. But you knew he was dead. The only way to know that is if you killed him!"

Franklin looked up at Thompson. "I didn't know he was dead. I just assumed it. He's been missing since high school. And you told me you found one of the boys. You're here because it was Mike. That's true, isn't it?"

"How did you kill him, Kent? Did you get into a fight?"

"I didn't kill him."

"Where did you go the last time you were with Mike?"

"We went to Mike's house and played video games on his Nintendo."

"When was the last time you saw him?"

Franklin stared at the floor. "It was the day we went to his house and played video games."

"After playing games, what happened?"

"Nothing. Mike said he was meeting someone else and had to leave."

Thompson leaned in closer. "Who was he meeting?"

"I don't know. Mike wouldn't tell me. He said it was about a job."

"What type of job?"

"I don't know. He said he couldn't say anything until he got the job."

"Now you're just making things up, Kent. Where did you and Mike go?"

Franklin looked up at the detective. "I told you I didn't know who he was meeting. This is why I left Swartz Creek. The police and kids at school all thought I had something to do with Mike's disappearance."

"You know, Mike. If that DNA comes back to you, you're going to be charged with his murder. It would be much better if you could tell me what happened. His family needs to know."

Franklin wiped away tears.

"Kent, did you bury Mike in the woods by Kotter's farm?"

Franklin looked up at Thompson. "Is that where you found Mike?"

Thompson didn't know whose body it was but wanted Franklin to believe it was Mike. "Yes," answered Thompson.

Franklin leaned over and covered his face with his hands. "Oh, my god."

"What is it, Kent?"

"We had been to Kotter's farm earlier that year."

"You and Mike?"

"Yeah. Kotter would sometimes invite kids to the farm for hayrides and stuff. I even heard some kids got airplane rides from him. Mike and I went one time to ride his tractor. I never once believed the rumors of Mr. Kotter killing those boys."

"You think Kotter killed Mike?"

"Not until just now."

"I don't believe Kotter did it, Kent."

Franklin looked at Thompson. "No, you think I did, right?"

"I do. I can see how much Mike's death has affected you. The game is over, Kent. Let me take you back to Swartz Creek where we can get your statement and relieve the pain these families have suffered with for so long."

Thompson could see a change in Franklin's look and demeanor.

"You have come here and accused me of killing one of the true friends I had in high school. You find his body on Kotter's farm, and you think I buried Mike there. I'm telling you one more time. I didn't kill Mike, and I never would have killed Mike. Now, are you arresting me? Because if not, I need to get ready for work."

Thompson knew he didn't have the probable cause necessary to make an arrest.

"No, I'm not going to arrest you. But if your DNA matches, I will be back."

"Find out who Mike was meeting that night," said Franklin loudly. "That's who killed Mike. Please leave now."

Detective Thompson rose from his chair and handed Franklin a card. "Please call me if you want to talk."

After Thompson left, Franklin sat trying to calm his emotions. He hadn't thought of Mike Taggert in a long time. Detective Thompson's grilling brought it all back. *What would happen if I got arrested for Mike's murder? I was with Mike the day before he disappeared. Maybe my DNA will be found on Mike.* The thought of trying to cope with prison frightened him.

During the drive back to Swartz Creek, Detective Thompson kept replaying the interview in his mind. He was torn between believing Franklin was involved or telling the truth. When he walked into the police station, Chief Ward was on the phone. Thompson could tell she was talking to someone from the state police, but he couldn't tell if she was receiving good or bad news.

When Ward got off the phone, she turned to Thompson. "That was the coroner. While examining the bones, he found the hyoid bone was broken in two. He said there was a slight possibility the hyoid bone was broken when the grave was disturbed, but he's ninety-nine percent sure it was broken from strangulation."

"I've never worked a strangulation," said Thompson. "The hyoid is in the neck, correct?"

"Yes, in the front of the neck."

"What about DNA?"

"Nothing yet," answered Ward. "I was told it would be difficult to get DNA after so many years in the ground and the flesh decayed. They hope to recover some from the victim's leather belt or metal belt buckle. Were you able to talk with Kent Franklin?"

"Uh, yeah. I found him at home, and he agreed to talk to me. He admitted to being a friend of Mike Taggert and admitted to being with him the day before he disappeared."

"That follows what the reports say," nodded Ward.

"Yeah, and he claimed Taggert left to meet someone that evening but wouldn't say with whom."

"Do you believe him?"

"I pushed him hard, but he stuck to his story. He seemed genuine in his friendship with Taggert. He also talked about Kotter inviting kids over to his farm. Not just for parties but for doing things like riding tractors. He even mentioned that some kids received rides in Kotter's airplane."

"Now that's interesting," replied Ward.

"When I told Franklin the body was recovered next to Kotter's farm, he reacted. He assumed Kotter had killed those three boys, and it upset him."

"Was he faking it?"

"I don't believe so. His emotion seemed sincere. I lied and told him we had DNA to compare with his, but he stuck to his story."

"Okay, we still need to find Miguel Morales," said Ward. "He's the third suspect investigated the first time around."

"He's the gay guy, right?"

"Yeah, the one who ran the children's programs at the library. I've been checking each state database for driver's licenses. The only name and date of birth match I've found shows an address in San Francisco."

"Great. I've always wanted to see the Golden Gate Bridge and Alcatraz."

"Uh, I'm not sending you to California. You can talk to him by phone."

"Chief, you know a proper interview can't be conducted over the phone," protested Thompson. "Being present creates tension. And I need to see his body language."

"I agree, and if we develop evidence that incriminates him, I will go with you to California. For now, find a phone number and call him. We already have his DNA so a phone interview will suffice for now."

Thompson just smiled. "Do you want to go get some lunch?"

"I am getting hungry. What time is it?" asked Ward.

"It's one-thirty."

"Sure, let's go.

"Have you ever been to the Ninth Hole?"

"The Ninth Hole?"

"Yeah, it's the café next to the golf course. You've been here three years and haven't eaten there?"

"I don't play golf."

"You don't have to play golf to eat," smiled Thompson. "Come on, I'll drive."

At the café, Chief Ward ordered a chicken salad. Thompson ordered a Philly cheesesteak sandwich with fries.

"Working in Lansing most of your career, you have more experience with murder and violent crime. Do you believe we can solve this case?" asked Thompson.

"Every case can be solved. Now, that doesn't mean every case gets solved, but if you find enough evidence, you can solve any case."

"So, give me your assessment on this one."

"Without DNA, we will need a witness or a confession. Cold cases can be the hardest to solve. But, with new technology, many old cases have been solved. I haven't given up on the DNA yet. The science has greatly improved. What we call touch DNA today didn't even exist when you and I started in policing."

"That's true," agreed Thompson.

The waiter returned with their food. "Can I get you anything else?"

"No, we're good," replied Thompson. "Thank you."

Chapter 11

After Ward and Thompson had returned to the police department, Thompson opened his computer and began a national search for a phone number linked to forty-three-year-old Miguel Morales of San Francisco, California. It didn't take long for Thompson to find a California vehicle registration in Morales' name. Attached to the registration was a phone number. Thompson called the number.

"Hello?"

"Hi, is this Miguel Morales?"

"Uh, yeah. Who is this?"

"Hi, Miguel. I'm Detective Greg Thompson with the Swartz Creek Police Department. I believe you lived in Swartz Creek about sixteen years ago. Is that correct?"

"Uh, yeah."

"Do you recall the disappearance of three teenage boys between sixteen and eighteen years ago?"

"Of course I do."

"Well, we are reopening the investigation into their disappearance. We've recently recovered one of the bodies."

There was silence on the phone.

"Did you hear me?" asked Thompson.

"I heard you. Where did you find the body?"

"The remains were found in a shallow grave near Chuck Kotter's farm."

There was a pause. "That's sad but not surprising," said Morales.

"Why do you say that?"

"After eighteen years, it's not surprising that the boys were kidnapped and murdered. No one believed three teenagers just disappeared over a two-year period."

"Did you know the boys?"

"You're calling because I was a suspect. A gay man who works with kids is always a suspect, right? I worked with kids because I liked them and wanted to help them learn. I didn't kill kids."

"We're simply following up on all leads, Miguel. Did you have any ideas on who may have wanted to harm the boys?"

"No."

"Would there be any reason your DNA would be found on the recovered body?"

"None. I didn't know any of the missing boys. It was a time that was difficult for the whole town. For some more than others."

"What do you mean by that?"

"For anyone suspected of being involved, like myself, it was a difficult time. What was your name again?"

"Detective Sergeant Greg Thompson."

"Detective, I left Swartz Creek because of the rumors in town. I haven't worked with kids since my experience in Swartz Creek, and it was something I loved to do. I wasn't kidnapped and murdered, but I was just as much a victim. I hope you catch whoever kidnapped those boys."

Thompson could hear the sincerity in Miguel's voice. He even felt sorry for Miguel. "Miguel, what do you do now?"

"I now work at a senior center helping older people live a healthier, happier life. I've grown to enjoy it almost as much as working with children."

"I believe you, Miguel. Is there anything you can think of that may help our investigation?"

"You know more about it than I do, Detective. But if it were me, I'd be looking for someone who seemed overly friendly to teenagers, especially the awkward or less popular kids. In my experience, those types of kids are most vulnerable."

"That's very insightful, Miguel. Thank you for talking with me today."

"You're welcome," said Morales. "I hope you catch the monster who did this."

"We're going to do our best. I'll be sure to let you know if we do."

After the call, Thompson walked into Chief Ward's office. "I don't think it's Miguel."

Ward looked up from her paperwork. "I told you."

"Yeah, but you weren't sure," smiled Thompson.

"I've been studying our victim profiles," said Ward. "All three victims share some similarities. For instance, all had either blond or light-colored hair. None of the victims were outgoing or popular. Richard Cranski, also known as Peaky, seemed to be quiet. He was the oldest at seventeen, was slim, and had long blond hair."

"Yeah, I remember that," agreed Thompson.

Ward continued. "Stanley Pollock was the youngest at fifteen years old. He also had blond hair and a skinny build. People described him as quiet and shy. The third victim, sixteen-year-old Mike Taggert, also had light-colored hair. He was described as a skinny, shy, awkward kid."

"In what order did they go missing?" asked Thompson.

"Mike Taggert was first in September. The second was Richard "Peaky" Cranski in the following July. Stanley Pollock disappeared the following April. All disappeared over a period of eighteen months. After that, it stopped."

"Brings back bad memories," said Thompson.

"It's also a pattern that suddenly stopped," said Ward. "What happened back then to make the perpetrator stop kidnapping high school kids?"

"I can't recall anything," answered Thompson.

"Somewhere in these files there has to be an answer," said Ward.

"Maybe the heat got too hot, or maybe the killer simply moved on."

"Yeah, maybe," murmured Ward as she stared at the ceiling.

"What's our next move?" asked Thompson.

"We need to talk to the parents. I've read what they told the police back then, but you never know what bits of information we might get with another interview. We must focus on commonalities with who they knew or hung out with."

"Where do you want me to start?" asked Thompson.

"The father of Peaky is still alive and in the area. He lives just down the road in Durand. His name is Dan Cranski. I'd like you to start with him."

"I'll drive out there right now."

"As much as I'd like that, it will have to wait. We had a burglary last night at the tavern here in town."

"We have more than one, Chief. Which one?"

"Duke's Tavern. An outside cooler was broken into, and lots of beer was taken. I'm waiting for a call from the state, so you'll have to go take the report."

"Teenagers," smirked Thompson.

"That's why I like you, Greg. Smart as a whip. Didn't we have a beer burglary last year?"

Thompson laughed. "It's become kind of a high school senior prank. Happens almost every year in the fall."

"Do we ever find out who did it?"

"Usually. After a while, word leaks out about who was involved."

"What usually happens?"

"Oh, not much. They agree to pay for the new lock and stolen beer, get expelled from school for a week or so, and the county judge gives them probation."

Ward laughed. "Sounds appropriate."

"Do you care if I head home after taking the report?"

"No. There's nothing else pressing for today."

"Okay, see you tomorrow then," said Thompson as he walked out the door.

Shortly after Thompson left, Chief Ward received a call from the state forensics lab.

"Chief Ward, it's Boyd Tremont calling from the state lab."

"Hello, Boyd. Got any good news for us?"

"Yes and no. I'm sorry to say we couldn't retrieve any usable DNA samples from the remains. However, our director has agreed to send you a forensic anthropologist and a decomposition dog team on Wednesday. It's our belief that where your suspect buried one body, he probably buried the other two. The dogs will help us search the woods and property near Kotter's farm. We'll also bring ground-penetrating radar."

"That's fantastic news!" exclaimed Ward. "Will you be able to search the farm property as well?"

"Without more probable cause, we can't get a warrant to search the Kotter farm. The good news is that our behavioral consultant doubts he would have buried any bodies on his property."

"Thank you so much, Boyd. What time can we expect you?"

"We should be there by nine o'clock Wednesday morning."

"I look forward to seeing you. Thanks again."

Once she hung up the phone, Ward let out a yelp. Marilyn Branch heard the yelp and walked into Ward's office.

"Is everything okay in here?"

Ward smiled. "Yes, Marilyn, everything is fine. I just got word the state is sending us some cadaver dogs, a forensic anthropologist, and ground penetrating radar on Wednesday."

Once Branch had left, Ward called Thompson on his cell phone to give him the good news.

Chapter 12

On Tuesday morning, Detective Thompson arrived at the police department a few minutes past eight o'clock. The Chief had not yet arrived. After pouring himself a cup of coffee, Thompson pulled the information on Dan Cranski, the father of Richard "Peaky" Cranski, the 17-year-old teenager who was the second victim. Using the phone number in his file, Thompson called Dan Cranski. After several rings, Cranski answered the phone.

"Mr. Cranski, this is Detective Sergeant Greg Thompson with the Swartz Creek Police Department. How are you doing today?"

"I know who you are, Detective. I've been following the news. I'm doing okay."

"Good, then you're up to date with where we are in the investigation. I know it's probably hard to talk about, but I'd like you to tell me what you remember about Richard's disappearance."

"We called him Peaky."

"Yes, Peaky. What can you remember?"

"Do you know how he got that name?" asked Cranski.

"I do not."

"It's silly really. When he was young, Peaky loved to play peek-and-boo. He played it so much his sister started calling him Peaky. I didn't like it of course, but it caught on and soon everyone called him Peaky. After a while, I came to like it myself. It was his signature, so to speak."

"Interesting. I wondered how he came upon that nickname. Thank you for sharing that. Can you tell me what you remember about his disappearance?"

"He was a good kid. Never gave us much trouble, but he was somewhat shy, which made it hard for him to have a lot of friends. But he had a few."

"Did you suspect any of his friends had a role in Peaky's disappearance?"

"Not immediately, but as the investigation dragged on, you start to suspect everyone."

"Did you suspect anyone in particular?"

"No. Are you going to tell me the body you found is Peaky?"

"We don't know who it is yet, Mr. Cranski. Once we know, I will let you know."

"Then why did you call?"

"As I said earlier, Mr. Cranski, We're following up to see if you remember anything about your son's disappearance."

"I remember the pain and all the waiting. All we did was wait for someone to call to tell us they found Peaky, or at least tell us what happened to him. Not knowing is a hell you never want to go through."

Thompson felt empathy for Mr. Cranski. "I wish I could tell you more. Once we know whose body we recovered, I will call you."

"I would appreciate that, Detective."

Thompson allowed Cranski to talk more about Peaky's life until Chief Ward entered the office.

"Well, I've got some work to do, Mr. Cranski. I'll call you once I know something."

"Okay. Thank you, Detective."

"Who was that?" asked Ward.

"That was Dan Cranski."

"Did he have anything to add?"

"No. He basically talked a lot about his son."

"I don't think we'll get any additional information from the parents," said Ward. "In reading the case file, I found that they were all interviewed multiple times."

"All we need is a little help from our friends," said Thompson.

"What?" asked Ward. "Are you quoting the Beatles now?"

Thompson smiled. "I heard it on the radio this morning, and it made me think. Someone has information that could help us but might not even know it. We need to find that person."

"We need to talk to Marty Strawski," said Ward. "From reading these reports, he was very involved in overseeing the investigation. He held most of the press conferences."

"You're right," agreed Thompson. "Marty was a hands-on mayor. He was very disturbed by these cases. Sometimes, the lines between Marty and Chief Braxton seemed blurred. However, Marty did stand behind the Chief when pressure mounted to have him fired."

"And you said Strawski resigned before his next election, correct?"

"Yes. He was here for almost three years after the last teenager disappeared. However, the case and constant questioning of the police department, and even the mayor himself, took a toll on him, as it did everyone. Prior to the fall election, he chose to retire. Many didn't think he could win another election."

"Were you able to find out where he lives now?"

"Sorry, Chief. I haven't gotten to that yet."

"I understand. Where did Marty live in Swartz Creek?"

"Marty had a place in the county off of Van Fleet Road."

"How did he become the mayor and not live in Swartz Creek?" questioned Ward.

"He rented a small apartment in town. He called his home his weekend getaway."

"I didn't know the mayor of Swartz Creek earned that much money," said a surprised Ward.

"He came from money. The money he was paid as mayor was probably beer money."

"Was the mayor known to be a drinker?"

"Let me put it this way. He could drink his fair share of beer. He was well known at Duke's Tavern."

Ward nodded. "Find out where he lives now, and let's pay him a visit."

"It will be next on my list, Chief."

"I'm also curious. What did Chief Braxton die from?"

"He died about six years ago after a long battle with colon cancer."

"Thanks, Greg. Let me know when you've located Mayor Strawski."

"Will do."

It didn't take Thompson long to find out where former Mayor Marty Strawski lived. He went online to find a Michigan driver's license and property records indicating that

Martin Strawski lived in a small town called Baldwin in the northwest area of the Lower Peninsula. The town lies approximately halfway between Big Rapids and Cadillac.

Baldwin has a population of approximately 1000 residents and is known for its charming, rural atmosphere. Several small businesses and cafes serve the local population and hunters and fishermen who come for the abundant wildlife. The Baldwin River runs along the eastern edge of town, and the surrounding area is covered in forests with numerous small lakes that make up the Manistee National Forest. It is known for its extensive outdoor recreational opportunities.

Baldwin was too small to have its own police department, so Thompson called the Lake County Sheriff's Office to inquire about Marty Strawski. He talked directly with the Sheriff, Mike Johnson.

"Yeah, we know Marty," said Johnson. "He has a place about three miles north of Baldwin. He can sure tell a story."

"Do you see him often?" asked Thompson.

"I wouldn't say often, but he stops by the Sheriff's Office every now and then. He seems to be very interested in police work."

"Yeah, he was in Swartz Creek as well. My Chief and I hoped to interview Marty about the missing teenagers here. He was involved in the original investigation."

"He's talked to me about it," said Johnson.

Thompson gave Sheriff Johnson the address information he had found online. "Is this where Marty lives now?"

"Yes. He has a nice cabin in the woods north of here. He does a lot of hunting and fishing."

"Sounds like a great retirement," said Thompson.

"The hunting is good here," replied Johnson.

"Do you know if Marty is home today?"

"Hang on, I've got his phone number."

After about twenty seconds, Johnson gave Thompson the phone number.

"Thank you, Sheriff.

"No problem. I hope he can help you with your case."

Once the call ended, Thompson called the number provided by Sheriff Johnson.

"Hello," said a gravelly voice.

"Is this Marty Strawski?"

"It is. Who is this?"

"Marty, it's Greg Thompson."

"Well, hello, Greg. It's been a long time. How are things in Swartz Creek?"

"We're doing well, Marty. Still working on the missing teenager cases."

"I thought that case was inactive."

"It was until we uncovered a buried skeleton."

"You found one of the boys?"

"We believe so. We're waiting on DNA analysis to confirm. I'm surprised you hadn't seen it on the news."

"I don't follow the news very closely anymore, Greg. I'm just trying to live a quiet life. It's easy to do when you like to hunt and fish."

"The reason I called is that Chief Ward and I would like to come up to pick your brain on the investigation eighteen years ago."

"I'm not sure how I can help, but if you want to drive that far, I'm happy to do it."

"Honestly, I think my Chief wants to drive through Big Rapids to relive her college days. She graduated from the criminal justice program there. We should arrive around mid-afternoon."

After the call, Thompson walked into Chief Ward's office. She was on her phone but held up her index finger, indicating she needed a minute. Thompson stepped back out and waited. After a couple of minutes, Ward summoned him back in.

"I confirmed that Marty lives in Baldwin and will be there this afternoon if you still want to go," said Thompson.

"I do. I believe face-to-face interviews are always preferable when possible. And it will give me a chance to see my old college campus. I graduated from Ferris State University."

"Yeah, I know."

"They have a great football program now. Did you know that?"

"Yes. They've won several national championships, right?"

"Three of them. NCAA Division Two."

Thompson nodded and smiled. "When are we going?"

"Let me grab my blazer, and we can go. I'll even buy lunch on the way up. I know a good place in Big Rapids."

"I'm sure you do," Thompson said, smiling.

"I'll drive," said Ward.

Ward drove them west to Grand Rapids. From there, they took Highway 131 north through the changing fall colors of the forested countryside, which took them to Big Rapids. The drive took just under two hours and thirty minutes.

"I know this burger bar we used to frequent when I was attending school here," said an excited Ward. "It's been about ten years since I last visited here. It's one of those places where they have peanuts, and you just chuck the shells onto the floor."

"I can hardly wait," deadpanned Thompson.

"Oh, come on. You'll like it."

Ward marveled at how much the college campus had changed as they drove through town. "Some of these buildings have been remodeled or newly constructed."

"I'm sure it was much different thirty years ago," remarked Thompson.

"Thirty years!? I'm not THAT old."

Thompson just laughed.

Just past the campus, Ward turned the car into the parking lot of a standalone, brown-wood-sided restaurant with large windows facing the road. A large red neon sign on the roof faced the road and read, "Burger Bar." Next to the Burger Bar sign was a large, painted picture of a triple-deck burger with cheese, pickles, onions, ketchup, and mustard oozing from the bun.

"This place is literally named the Burger Bar?" asked Thompson sarcastically.

"Yes, I told you that."

"No, you said we were going to a burger bar, not that the name was Burger Bar."

Ward glanced at Thompson with a frown. "What's the difference?"

"One is a description, and one is the actual name of the place."

Ward shook her head as she pulled into a parking space. "You like burgers, right?"

"Sure."

"Then you're going to love this place."

When they walked through the front door, the restaurant was full of young and old alike. Loud chatter filled the air, and the smells and sounds of grilling meat emanated from a rectangular opening behind the bar. Thompson could see cooks grilling through the opening. Multiple posters were plastered on the walls throughout the restaurant, many of which were sports posters. There were several large photos of rock bands and singers who had performed at Ferris State back in the 1970s and 1980s. Thompson noticed three football national championship pennants on one of the side walls, as well as a photograph of the current Ferris State football coach. As they were led to a table, Thompson could feel the crunch of peanut shells under his shoes.

"Isn't this place great?" asked Ward.

"It looks like a sports bar."

"It is a sports bar! And they have great burgers."

Thompson smiled. "What do you recommend?"

"I always get the double cheeseburger with spicy Thousand Island dressing. And I get the onion rings instead of fries."

"I'll go with your recommendation then," said Thompson.

When the waiter arrived, Ward ordered the double cheeseburger with onion rings for both of them. She ordered herself an iced tea. Thompson ordered a Diet Pepsi.

"When did you go to school here?" asked Thompson.

"Twenty-four years ago."

"So, I guess that makes you about fifty years old."

"Where did you learn math? I'm only forty-six! Do I look like I'm fifty years old to you?"

Thompson laughed. "No, not at all, Chief."

"Let's get serious," said Ward. "You've talked a bit about Mayor Strawski. Do you think he can provide anything we don't already know?"

"Hard to say. He spoke to Chief Braxton frequently. Between Strawski and Marilyn Branch, they probably know more than anyone else. I was only an officer at the time, so I wasn't heavily involved in the investigation."

When the meals arrived, Thompson noted the size and fresh grilled smell. "That's a big burger."

"Yes," agreed Ward.

As Thompson raised his double cheeseburger, he opened his mouth as large as possible. He bit into the soft bun, then felt the crunch of onion, tomato, and pickles against his palate. His teeth sank into the gooey, warm cheese and the crispy, slightly charred burger. Thousand Island dressing and juicy grease squeezed out the sides as Thompson bit down. A burst of flavor hit his tongue. It took him several seconds to chew and swallow. He then took a swig of his diet Pepsi.

Ward could tell he enjoyed the moment. "Well, what do you think?"

"Damn, Chief, you were right. This is one good burger."

"Don't ever doubt me again, Greg. Just think how good it would be to drink a beer with it."

"We may have to come back sometime when we're off duty," smiled Thompson.

"Be sure to wipe that sauce off your mustache before we pay Strawski a visit," advised Ward.

Once they had finished with lunch, Ward paid the bill, and they were off on the final leg of their trip. It only took them thirty-five minutes to find Marty Strawski's cabin in the forest outside Baldwin. Ward drove down the dusty 40-yard dirt driveway to the front of the home.

The cabin was a large home built of lightly stained logs with two large picture windows looking out. A large stained wooden deck ran across the front, and a black Ford 250 pickup was parked in front of a two-car garage. Ward parked next to the pick-up.

As they walked up onto the front porch, Marty Strawski swung open the door.

"Hello, Greg. Hello, Chief Ward. So nice to meet you."

"Nice to meet you as well," said Ward as they shook hands.

Strawski walked them into the dining room area, where they all took a seat at the table. The inside of the cabin was decorated with paintings of wildlife, forested lakes, and pine-covered mountains. The heads of a deer and a moose hung in the living room.

"Please sit down," said Strawski. "Is there anything I can get you to drink?"

"We just ate at the Burger Bar, but thank you," replied Ward.

"Ah, yes, the Burger Bar. Great place for a burger and beer," replied Strawski. "Now, what questions do you have?"

"As close as you were to the investigation, I'm curious to know whether you and Chief Braxton ever developed a suspect, or at least someone you thought might be involved," Ward asked.

"I know the police department ran down many leads. We could never get enough information to arrest anyone."

"According to the reports, the primary suspects were Kent Franklin, Miguel Morales, and Chuck Kotter. Were there any more?" asked Ward.

"Certainly there were others the police looked into. And, of course, they had help from the state police. But the three you mentioned were the primary suspects."

"Was anyone considered the most likely suspect by either you or the Chief?"

"Sure. We both believed Chuck Kotter was the most likely suspect. He could have hidden those kids anywhere on his property or in the surrounding woods. I wanted the police to dig up his farm, but the Chief could never get enough probable cause for a search warrant."

Thompson and Ward exchanged glances.

Strawski then looked at Thompson. "You said you found one of the bodies, correct?"

"I did."

"Where did you find it?"

"We found it in the woods just outside Kotter's property line."

"Damn, we must have been right about Kotter. I knew that son of a bitch was involved."

"We don't know anything for sure yet, Marty."

"You know he liked to invite high school kids to parties at his farm. He was probably looking for victims."

"We have already interviewed him once," said Ward. "Once we receive the forensic results, we may have more information."

"Whoever it is, I'll bet Chuck strangled him."

"Why would you say that?" asked Ward.

"Just a hunch. Chuck had arms like cannons. He was very strong. Shooting someone would make too much noise."

"Have you ever been married?" asked Ward.

"Why does that matter?"

"It doesn't. I just like to get a good profile on all our witnesses or anyone associated with a case."

"Yes, I was married for five years in my twenties. It didn't work out. I haven't been married since."

"Any children?"

"No."

"Well, we appreciate your concern and past efforts to solve this case. The disappearance of those kids must have been hard on you."

"Thank you, Chief. I appreciate that. It was hard on everyone. I just tried to do my part to help. When you find out, will you let me know whose body you found?"

"Yes, of course," agreed Ward.

"I'm not trying to tell you how to do your job, but if it were me, I'd search those woods for the other two bodies. I'll bet all three were buried near Kotter's farm."

"We have a search team coming out tomorrow."

"Excellent. I wish you luck, Chief Ward."

"Did you ever suspect any of the parents?" asked Thompson.

"The Cranski kid's dad seemed a bit off to me. It could account for his son's disappearance. If he was whacko enough, I suppose he could have also killed the other two. All three boys were kind of shy or awkward in some way. I'd check into him as well."

Ward looked to Thompson. "Do you have any other questions?"

"Not right now."

"Well, thank you, Marty," said Ward. "We appreciate your time."

"No problem. Call me if you have any other questions."

On the drive back, Thompson questioned Chief Ward. "It seems like most people lean toward Kotter being our number one suspect."

"Seems that way, doesn't it," answered Ward.

"You don't think so, do you?"

"He's clearly a suspect based on circumstances and his fondness for high school students. However, as I mentioned earlier, he acts too boldly for someone hiding something. My judgment of him is that he is honest and doesn't care what others think. But I may also be misjudging him. Some offenders are very skilled at hiding their true nature."

"Maybe this case is just unsolvable," admitted Thompson. "Without DNA or an outright confession, I don't know."

"We need to find the other bodies," said Ward. "Somewhere, there has to be a piece of evidence to lead us in the right direction."

Chapter 13

After dinner on Tuesday, Dylan and Jason were in the driveway at Dylan's house shooting baskets.

"Did you listen to the five o'clock news?" asked Dylan.

"No," answered Jason.

"There's going to be some sort of special team here tomorrow to search for more buried bodies.".

"How?"

"They're bringing in special dogs that can smell dead bodies."

"That's kind of creepy."

"Yes, but wouldn't it be cool to see them uncover more bodies?"

"I don't know about that."

"Think about it. We might be the first ones to know the truth."

"What truth?"

"Whether these are the three missing boys and whether Kotter is involved. We can hide in the bushes and watch. Maybe even hear them talking."

"I don't need to get into any more trouble," protested Jason.

"As long as we remain hidden, we'll be fine. We can be there early to find a good hiding spot."

"The school will know we aren't there," said Jason.

"So what? We're in high school now. They don't call parents because someone skips school."

"I guess you're right."

"Okay then. We'll leave for the bus as usual, then instead of getting on the bus, we'll hike back to the woods to find a good hiding location. We can even be back in school after lunch."

"Well, okay. It would be interesting to see how they work."

"Yes! Let's plan on everything as normal tomorrow, but we'll skip the bus and walk to the burial grounds."

Jason nodded.

Wednesday Morning, 9:30 am.

Chief Ward and Detective Thompson were in uniform and out in the woods near Kotter's farm with a team of forensic specialists and two cadaver dogs from the state police. Forensic technicians Boyd Tremont and Cindy Sayer were also part of the team. After Chief Ward had shown the team where the first body had been found, a plan was developed on how the search was to be conducted. Meanwhile, Dylan Hudson and Jason Chapman were in a maple tree approximately forty yards from the scene. Dylan had brought along a pair of binoculars. The turning leaves provided excellent cover.

One of the dog handlers, dressed in a dark blue jumpsuit, explained to everyone present how the dogs worked. Everyone except the handlers had to remain twenty feet behind the dogs. Too many scents could distract the dogs. If the scent of a body was detected, the dogs would paw at the ground and begin barking. A forensic team would then carefully excavate the area looking for signs of a buried body. Once the instructions were understood, the search began.

Dylan and Jason watched intently from their perch in the maple tree. They passed the binoculars back and forth so each of them could see what was happening.

"You were right," whispered Jason. "This is pretty cool."

The dogs carefully walked side to side with their noses to the ground and tails wagging. Finding a body meant they would receive some type of treat as a reward. The dogs continued to walk side to side in a fifty-foot-wide pattern. At times, the handlers would have to help the dogs navigate around the trees and bushes.

As they watched the drama unfold, Jason's leg began to fall asleep. He attempted to adjust his position by moving his left leg to a smaller branch. As he pushed against the branch, it snapped, making a loud crack sound. The loss of balance caused Jason to lose his grip. The inside of his right arm scraped against the rough bark as he fell. It felt like a kick to the chest as he thudded against the branch below. Jason let out a yelp as he wrapped his arms around the branch, preventing him from falling further to the ground. Everyone looked in the direction of the tree. Both dogs turned and began barking.

"What's going on?" asked Thompson.

"Someone is out there," said one of the handlers.

The handler allowed his dog to lead him toward the source of the sound. Once they approached the tree where the boys were hiding, the dog saw them and began to bark incessantly.

"What are you boys doing up there?" the handler asked.

"Nothing. We were just climbing this tree," said Dylan.

"You boys need to come down right now."

Dylan and Jason both made their way down the tree. By the time they reached the ground, Chief Ward and Detective Thompson were there to greet them.

Ward shook her head from side to side. "Just what are you two doing out here? Shouldn't you be in school?"

"Yes, ma'am," said Dylan. "We just wanted to see what was happening."

"Do your parents know you're out here?" asked Ward.

"No," muttered Dylan.

"Didn't your mom tell me you were grounded from the woods?"

"Yeah."

Ward noticed Jason was rubbing his chest.

"Are you okay, Jason?"

"I'm fine," said Jason.

Ward turned to Thompson. "Have an officer take these two boys back to school. I'll call their parents once we are done here."

"Will do. Come along, boys. We'll get you a ride back to school where you belong."

Dylan and Jason knew it wouldn't be a pleasant evening once Chief Ward called their parents. Thompson walked the boys back to the road adjacent to the Chippewa Indian Burial Grounds. When they reached the road, a patrol officer was waiting for them. Dylan and Jason were placed in the back seat. An acrylic shield separated the front seats from the back. Once they were seat belted in, Thompson nodded to the patrol officer.

"Take these boys back to the high school."

"Will do."

Once they were on their way, Jason said, "This was a stupid idea, Dylan. Now we're really in trouble."

"You wanted to go too," replied Dylan.

"You talked me into it."

Dylan didn't respond. He knew Jason was right.

Back at the search site, the dogs continued to hunt for the telltale odors of death. Cindy Sayer continued walking with the ground-penetrating radar device. The dogs and Sayer walked in a side-to-side pattern within fifty feet of the Kotter property line. It was a slow process.

After an hour, Thompson looked at Chief Ward. "I was hoping any other bodies would have been close to the first one."

"You never know," replied Ward. "Remember, we don't know whether our body is that of one of the boys. However, assuming it is, the others could be buried in a completely different location."

"If so, I doubt we ever find them."

"They may be out here all day," said Ward. "We're just in the way. Let's head back to the office where we can get some work done, and I'll order lunch delivery for the crew out here."

Once at the office, Ward arranged to have sub sandwiches and drinks delivered to the work site at 12:30 pm. It was 1:25 pm when Ward received a phone call. It was from Boyd Tremont.

"I think we found something," announced Tremont.

"What do you have?" asked Ward.

"The dogs have hit on something, and the ground radar feedback is promising. We're going to start excavating if that's okay."

"Yes, please start. Greg and I will be there soon."

Once she got off the phone, Ward yelled, "Greg, grab your jacket. They believe they found more remains."

Back at the dig site, forensic specialists were carefully probing and digging into the ground. Three feet down, they found evidence of a decomposed body. Even after all these years, Boyd Tremont and Cindy Sayer could detect a slight odor of decay.

Chief Ward and Detective Thompson arrived just as they were uncovering the remains. While the flesh and organs had decomposed, the skeleton and items of clothing were still recoverable. The process would take the rest of the afternoon. Tremont stayed with the forensic experts working on recovering the remains and preserving evidence while Sayer and the search team continued looking for other remains.

"We may be luckier on this one," said Tremont. "Most of the clothing is still intact."

"How can that be after sixteen, seventeen years underground?" asked Thompson.

"It depends on the conditions and type of clothing. I've read about cases where clothing has been recovered after hundreds of years, even thousands."

"Are you thinking you might get foreign DNA from the clothing?"

"It's possible. If this is the result of a homicide and the killer had personal contact with the victim, then foreign DNA may still be present. If sexual assault were involved, the odds would even be better."

Thompson nodded. "I learn something every day. Did you know that Chief?"

"I did. We encountered stuff like this a few times in Lansing."

"Nothing's a sure thing," Tremont reminded them. "But I like our odds on this one."

"Thank you, Boyd," said Ward. "Do you mind if we stay to watch how your team recovers the body?"

"Not at all. It takes time to ensure we gather everything without compromising existing evidence."

"We understand."

Thompson was fascinated by the thoroughness and care the team took in recovering the remains. As he stood watching, Thompson noticed a barbed wire fence through the trees. It appeared to be about twenty yards away.

"Is that still Kotter's fence?"

"It is," replied Ward.

Neither said anything else until the radio cracked again. "We got another one," Cindy Sayer announced.

"Where are you at?" asked Ward.

"Keep walking north. We're approximately fifty yards from your location."

"Greg, you stay here. I'll go see what they have," instructed Ward.

Ward worked her way through the trees and brush until she reached the third site. Sayer was still going over the site with the radar. She looked up at Ward.

"This is going to be the third body."

Ward shook her head. "Unbelievable. To think our three missing teens have been out here the whole time."

Once the radar mapped the site, Sayer and the only remaining forensic expert began excavating it.

"Would you like me to find someone else to help you?" asked Ward.

"I think we'll be all right," Sayer answered. "Once the other team finishes, they'll help us here. It's starting to get late. We may need some lights to get this done today."

"I'll arrange for some flood lights," said Ward. "Do you need anything else?"

"Not right now."

Ward walked back to the first dig site and approached Thompson. "I don't think there's much more we can do here. I need you to arrange for some floodlights while I speak with Dylan and Jason's parents."

"That should be interesting," Thompson said with a smile.

Back at the office, Ward called the medical clinic where Karen Hudson worked. "Hello, this is Police Chief Paula Ward. May I please speak with Karen Hudson?"

"Please hold, Chief. I'll go find her."

Thirty seconds later, Karen Hudson was on the phone. "This is Karen."

"Karen, this is Chief Paula Ward. Sorry to bother you at work."

"Is everything okay?"

"Yes, but I wanted you to know we've been doing some searching in the woods out by the Kotter farm today, and we found your son and Jason Chapman spying on us."

"What? Spying on you?"

"We have a search party out there attempting to recover remains. The boys must have heard we were going to be out there looking. They were hiding in a tree trying to see what we were doing."

There were a couple of seconds of silence before Karen asked, "They weren't in school?"

"No. They were in the woods. I had an officer take both of them back to school."

"Those damn boys. I'm going to beat the crap out of Dylan."

"I wouldn't recommend that, Karen."

"I'm not going to actually beat him, but he's in big trouble now."

"Well, I knew you had grounded him from that area, so I wanted to let you know."

"Thank you for calling me, Chief."

After the call, Thompson walked into the Chief's office. "The lights will be out there by five o'clock."

"Thanks, Greg."

Thirty minutes later, Ward received a call from Cindy Sayer. "It's confirmed, Chief. We have a third body."

"Thank you, Cindy."

Ward sat at her desk, her head in her hands, rubbing her temples and forehead. She knew the case was about to explode in a media frenzy. It's not often three bodies are found in a matter of days in any jurisdiction, let alone in a small town like Swartz Creek. Ward called Thompson into her office.

"What do you need, Chief?"

"Greg, what do you think about confronting Kotter again before this hits all the news networks?"

"If we don't, we may not be able to talk to him again. I doubt he'll want to talk once the hysteria starts."

"Let's go then," said Ward. "Do you have a recorder?"

"I use my phone to record."

"Good. Turn it on when we get there, but don't let Kotter know we're recording the conversation."

"Got it. I'll go get the car and meet you outside."

Chapter 14

Ward and Thompson arrived at Kotter's farm before the evening news hit the airwaves. They found Kotter in his barn working on a motorcycle.

"Chuck, we'd like a few minutes to talk with you," said Thompson.

"I'm kind of busy at the moment," snapped Kotter.

"We understand, but it's important."

"I've seen lots of activity in those woods. What's this all about?"

"The three missing boys."

"You've already discussed that with me. I prefer you leave me alone."

Thompson looked at the Chief.

"Chuck, we found three bodies in the woods just outside your property line," barked Ward in a stern voice. "I think that makes this a priority, don't you?"

"Three bodies?" asked Kotter.

"Yes. We are excavating them as we speak."

Kotter stared at Ward. She couldn't tell if it was a look of surprise or concern.

"Let's go inside where we can ask you a few questions."

Kotter nodded and motioned to the house. The three of them walked to the porch and entered his home. They sat at the kitchen table.

"What is it you want to ask me this time?"

"Well, we just found three bodies buried near your property line," explained Ward. "I'd like to know if you knew anything about it?"

"The only thing I know of buried bodies is Indians. There are multiple Indians buried out there."

"These aren't Indians, Chuck. We believe they are the three boys who went missing sixteen to eighteen years ago."

Kotter looked down at the table. "I suppose you believe I'm the one who did it."

"You know a lot about it, Chuck. And now we find the three bodies just outside your property line. How did they get there?"

"I wish I knew," said Kotter in a soft voice.

"We think you do know," said Thompson.

Thompson looked closely at Kotter. It appeared as though Kotter's eyes were tearing up. He believed Kotter was on the verge of confessing.

"Chuck, if you tell us what happened, you can bring closure to the families," said Ward.

Thompson could see Kotter swallow. Another indicator of his stress level. Ward also picked up on it.

"Chuck, for the sake of the souls of these boys and the families, now is the time," said Ward. "What happened to these boys?"

"Where exactly did you find them?" Kotter asked.

Ward pointed in the direction of the fence line. "They were just outside the fence running along that property line, about fifty or so yards apart."

Kotter nodded, then rubbed his wet eyes. He then looked directly at Ward.

"How did they die?"

Ward squinted. "That's what we want to know, Chuck. What happened to those boys? I know they were special to you."

"I didn't kill those boys," Kotter softly replied.

Thompson spoke up. "Chuck, we will get DNA that will tell us who killed them. It's going to be your DNA. The charade has gone on long enough. Tell us what happened and why."

Kotter's demeanor suddenly changed. He looked at Thompson with an icy stare. "I don't really care for you too much, Detective. If I were to confess something to anyone, it would be to Chief Ward."

Thompson nodded. "Then tell her now."

"Why were they killed?" asked Ward.

"You're wasting your time, Chief," replied Kotter.

"Why won't you talk to us? These families need closure. It would be more noble to tell us what happened rather than wait for the DNA samples to reveal the truth. That won't look good for you. We saw the look in your eyes, Chuck. We know you cared about them. Show them you cared by coming forward with the truth."

"I've already told you and everyone who has asked me. I didn't kill those kids."

"Then give us the DNA sample we asked for."

"No!" snapped Kotter. "That's a violation of my privacy. Simply because you can't solve a case doesn't mean everybody should succumb to DNA testing. The government already knows too much about all of us."

"With everything we have now, I'll be able to get the search warrant that allows us to take your DNA. Giving us one now would save time."

"Then go get your warrant," growled Kotter.

Thompson interrupted. "Why were you crying?"

Kotter glared at Thompson. "Because I cared about those kids. I have always enjoyed teenagers. That doesn't make me a serial killer!"

"All right, we'll get our search warrant," said Ward. "But you're making this more difficult for yourself and the families."

"I'm not sure how since I'm not involved in any way. You would have solved this long ago if your department had any semblance of competency. The suspect has been right under your nose, and you don't even know it."

"What are you talking about, Chuck?"

"I'm not saying anything else. But you need to take a hard look at everything. I'd tell you if I were sure, but you need to investigate the right person. That's all I'll say."

Ward and Thompson looked at each other.

"Chuck, if you know something, tell us," Ward pleaded.

"I'm done talking. Please leave now."

Ward and Thompson left without saying anything else. Once in the car, Thompson turned to Ward. "What was that about?"

"I don't know," answered Ward. "The man talks in riddles sometimes. I'm very bothered by what he said. Is there someone else out there we should be investigating?"

"It seems like we've looked at everyone under suspicion."

"He said the suspect has been right under our noses."

"Yes, but he could still be talking about himself. The man is a master at manipulation. He's always telling tales. Remember what he told those kids about Indian spirits coming after them? He's full of crap."

"Hmmm. Maybe," agreed Ward.

On their way back to the station, Ward and Thompson stopped at the burial grounds and hiked back to the dig sites. It was now seven o'clock. As they approached the scene, they could see the floodlights. They found Boyd Tremont for an update.

"We should only be another hour or so," advised Tremont. "We won't have any results for several days."

"I understand," said Ward. "What about the first body recovered?"

"I think we'll have an identification by tomorrow. That's when the final DNA result should be in."

"Thank you," said Ward. "Let's go, Greg. I've got a flood of messages on my phone. Word on the bodies has gotten out."

****

"What the hell were you doing in those woods again!" screamed Karen Hudson.

"Mom, we heard about the investigation and just wanted to watch. We didn't do anything," Dylan replied.

"You disobeyed us again!" shouted Karen.

"I'm sorry, Mom. It won't happen again."

"I'm disappointed in you, Dylan. Hanging out near the Kotter farm is dangerous. What if he catches you snooping around?"

"We weren't snooping. The police were there."

"What about Jason? He could have been seriously injured."

"Mom, we climb trees all the time."

Jack Hudson interrupted. "Dylan, do you understand why we are upset?"

"Yes."

"You were grounded from going into those woods. You didn't even make it a few days."

"Yeah, I know. I'm sorry."

"Give me your phone," said Karen.

"I need my phone," protested Dylan.

"I know, but you don't need full functionality. I'm putting a lock on everything but the phone."

"No, mom. I need to use it for researching things and communicating with my friends."

"Too late for that, Dylan. You'll still be able to make phone calls."

"Dad, can you help?"

"No, Dylan. You violated the terms of your punishment. This is the result."

Dylan slumped in defeat.

"I'm also going to be tracking your phone, Dylan," said Karen.

Disappointed and angry, Dylan left the living room and went to his bedroom. Roxy, knowing Mom was angry, followed Dylan up the stairs with her tail hanging.

****

When Ward and Thompson returned to the police station, they found four news trucks parked outside the police department. Four reporters and camera operators approached Ward as she exited from her car. Bright lights shone in her eyes, temporarily blinding her. She held up her left hand until the lights were adjusted. Reporters started peppering Ward with questions about the remains found.

"Chief, we heard you've uncovered three bodies. Can you confirm this?"

"Have you identified the bodies yet?"

"Are the bodies those of the missing teenagers?"

"Who is the prime suspect?"

"I can't answer questions with everyone talking," shouted the Chief. "One at a time, please."

"Is it true you found three bodies?"

"Yes, we've found the remains of three bodies. None of them have been identified," said Ward.

"Do you believe they are the three missing teenagers?"

"It's too early to know. We need to wait for the DNA test results."

"Are you close to making an arrest?"

"No."

"Do you have any suspects?"

"We have several people of interest. There are no clear suspects at this time."

"How did you find the bodies?"

"We used cadaver dogs and ground-penetrating radar. That's all I'm going to say for now. We'll know more after testing is completed."

The Chief and Thompson then walked away and entered the police department.

"You handled that well," said Thompson.

"Thanks."

"It's been a week since we recovered the first body," said Thompson. "Why is it taking so long to get DNA?"

"It's a process, Greg. They first need to separate and process the DNA from the skeletal remains. Then, they need to test the DNA and compare it against samples obtained from the homes of each missing teenager. I was told we should know something tomorrow."

"It just seems like it should have been a priority," groused Thompson.

"Greg, while this is a significant case for us, you must remember it is a sixteen-year-old case. The state lab receives new evidence from recent crimes coming in every day. Our case is considered a cold case. I will feel fortunate to get some results tomorrow."

"Yeah, I suppose you're right," agreed Thompson. "After sixteen years, I doubt another day or week will make any difference."

"Greg, why don't you go home now."

"What about you?"

"I'm going to stay until they've cleared the crime scene."

"All right, I'll see you in the morning, Chief."

"Good night, Greg."

Chapter 15

On the following morning, Thursday, Chief Ward and Detective Thompson had already been in the office for several hours when the Chief received a call from the Michigan State Forensic Lab. It was Boyd Tremont calling.

"Chief, we have our first result. The DNA developed from the remains of the first excavation matched the DNA of Mike Taggert."

Chief Ward sat back in her chair and sighed. "We've finally found one of our victims. After all these years. Did you find any foreign DNA?"

"Not yet, but we still need to do some more work on the remains. Our director has made this case a priority now, so we should see results on the other two remains rather soon."

"Thank you, Boyd."

After taking a few moments to fully absorb the news, Ward stood and walked out of her office to Detective Thompson's desk. Thompson could see from Ward's expression that she had some positive news.

"What is it?" asked Thompson.

"The lab has confirmed the first remains are those of Mike Taggert."

Thompson sat back in his chair. "It took us eighteen long years, but we've finally found our victims."

"We only have one identification," Ward reminded him.

"Come on, Chief. We both know the other remains will be of our missing victims."

"You're most likely right, but I never rule anything out until it's proven otherwise."

Thompson nodded. "Understood. I submitted the affidavit for a court-ordered DNA collection from Chuck Kotter. We should have the warrant before noon."

"Good," replied Ward. "Were you ever able to find Mike Taggert's mother?"

"Yes. I forgot to tell you. I talked to Arleen Taggert earlier this week. She's in a senior living complex in Ohio. She didn't have any helpful information. Would you like me to make the notification?"

"No. I believe I should do that. Do you have her number?"

Thompson wrote the number down on a post-it note and handed it to Ward.

"Is there a father?"

"No. His father died when Mike was twelve years old."

Once she was back in her office, she called Arleen Taggert. Upon hearing the news, Arleen began to cry.

"Oh, you've finally found my boy," Arleen cried.

"I'm very sorry, Arleen."

Ward could hear Arleen crying over the phone. After several seconds, Arleen asked, "Where did you find him?"

"His remains were recovered from a shallow grave in the woods not far from the Indian Burial Site."

"How did he die?"

"We don't know that yet, Arleen. If we can determine that, we'll let you know."

"Who killed my boy?"

"We're still working on that as well. Detective Thompson will keep you updated."

"Okay. Thank you for calling," said Arleen, crying.

After the call, Ward felt a tremendous sense of sorrow for the victims and their families. The investigation had always seemed an arm's length away. Any thoughts of what happened to the missing boys had always been speculation. Now, with the finding of the corpses, it had all become more real for Chief Ward. Talking to Arleen Taggert only made it feel more personal. A stronger determination to find the killer grew inside of her.

"Greg!" shouted Ward. "Have you talked to the parents of Stanley Pollock yet?"

Thompson walked into Ward's office. "I've only talked to Peaky Cranski's father and Arleen Taggert. I just located the Pollock's late Wednesday. We were too busy digging up bodies for me to call them. They are now living in North Carolina."

"Give me the number. I'll call them."

"I can do it, Chief."

"No, I should do it. You have already talked with Dan Cranski. Why don't you call him."

"Okay."

Thompson took out his cell phone and texted Dave Pollock's phone number to Chief Ward.

"Thank you, Greg."

Once Thompson left her office, Ward called the number. Dave Pollock answered.

"Mr. Pollock, this is Chief Paula Ward with the Swartz Creek Police Department. I'm calling with some news about your missing son."

"Have you arrested someone?" asked Pollock.

"No, but we've recovered the remains of three bodies from a wooded area near the Indian Burial Grounds. One set of remains has already been identified as that of Mike Taggert. The other remains will likely be of your son and Peaky Cranski."

After a moment of silence, Pollock spoke. "When will you know for sure?"

"Probably within a day or so. They are comparing DNA from the remains with that collected from your home."

"That was seventeen years ago. The police took our DNA as well."

"Yes, that's for comparison purposes. We still have all that saved."

"We assumed our son was dead, so this is not a shock. But if this is our son, we will be so grateful for finally getting information on what happened."

"We will do our best, and I will keep you informed."

"Do you have any suspects?"

"Yes, we have a couple. Once we have positive identifications and additional DNA evidence, we hope to solve this horrific crime."

"That would be a blessing. Please let me know as soon as you get more information. It would be nice to finally have closure and a proper memorial service."

"I understand, Mr. Pollock. Is your wife still around?"

"Yes. She's not here right now, but we're still together."

"That's good to hear. Did you or your wife have any suspicions about anyone Stanley hung out with?"

"The only one we ever suspected was Chuck Kotter, the farmer. Our son had visited his place a few times. He seemed to always have teenage kids hanging out at his place. He didn't have kids and wasn't married, making it seem even stranger."

"Why did you allow Stanley to go there?"

"At the time, it didn't seem strange. All the kids liked Chuck. And Stanley never expressed any concerns. Stanley didn't have many friends, you know, so when Kotter befriended him, it initially seemed to be a good thing. But after boys started going missing, people focused more on why Kotter was so interested in teenagers. I fault myself for not being aware of what was going on."

"We don't know yet who abducted these kids," replied Ward. "We're exploring a few possibilities."

"You never forget, but this opens up old wounds."

"I'm sorry for that, Mr. Pollock."

"I appreciate you keeping us informed. You will call as soon as you know the DNA results, right?"

"Yes, of course."

"Thank you, Chief."

Once Ward was off the phone, Thompson walked in. "I've got it," he said while holding a sheet of paper in his hand. "The court just sent over the warrant. We can now go get Kotter's DNA."

"Good. Were you able to update Mr. Cranski on the investigation?"

"Yes."

"Okay, let's go."

As Ward and Thompson left the police department, they faced eight reporters in the parking lot shouting questions at them.

"Please, not now," Ward pleaded. "I will update you when we have information that can be released."

"Is it true the found remains are those of the three missing teenagers?" shouted a reporter.

Ward and Thompson ignored the question, got into Thompson's car, and drove off toward Kotter's farm. As they got closer to the farm, Thompson looked in the rearview mirror and saw someone following them.

"I think we have a reporter on our tail," said Thompson.

"It's hard to avoid the press once a case like this hits the news," replied Ward.

"What are we going to do?"

"We do our best to ignore them and do our job."

When they arrived at the driveway to Kotter's farm, two other news vans were parked on the shoulder of the road. One cameraman was filming as Thompson turned into the long dirt driveway. As they approached the barn, they saw Kotter's airplane parked just outside the barn doors.

"I wonder where he's going?" asked Thompson.

Thompson parked the car, and he and Ward approached the front door. The door opened before they knocked.

"You're here to take my DNA, aren't you?"

"We are," responded Thompson. "We have a court order granting us the authority to collect a DNA sample from you. Here's a copy for you."

Kotter shook his head as he opened the screen door and stepped onto the porch. He grabbed the order from Thompson's hand and read it without any expression.

Thompson took out two plastic tubes containing long-stemmed swabs from the large envelope in his hand. "I need you to open your mouth wide."

Kotter did as he was instructed. Thompson then swabbed the inside of Kotter's mouth. He then carefully placed the swab inside one tube and sealed the tube.

"I'll need to do this one more time," Thompson advised. "Open your mouth again."

Kotter complied. After getting the second swab, Thompson sealed it in the second tube and placed both tubes back into the envelope. He then sealed the envelope.

"Are we done now?" grumbled Kotter.

Ward pointed to his airplane. "Where are you planning to go?"

"I'm flying over the border into Canada," smirked Kotter.

"We can't allow you to do that," replied Ward.

"Am I under arrest?"

"Not yet," quipped Ward.

"Then you can't stop me. I'm free to go wherever I want."

"That won't be a good look for you, Chuck. Especially if this DNA matches that recovered from the bodies. And I don't think Canada will appreciate you flying over the border without proper clearance."

Kotter laughed. "You two are a couple of dumbasses."

"Excuse me!" shouted Ward.

"I'm not going anywhere. I had to change the oil and wash the plane. Look at the ground around it. Do you see how wet the soil is?"

"Regardless, I don't appreciate you calling us dumbasses," replied Ward.

"And I don't appreciate you accusing me of murder and taking my DNA. So, I guess that makes us even."

Thompson found the exchange somewhat humorous, but he dared not show it.

"Let's go, Greg," said Ward as she turned to walk away. Thompson followed her to the car.

As they drove away, they were again greeted by reporters at the end of the driveway. Ward drove slowly onto the roadway as reporters shouted questions. Once they were clear, Thompson broke his silence.

"I hadn't seen you get angry like that before."

"No, and I shouldn't have," said Ward. "He just frustrates me sometimes. Having those conversations with the parents got to me. I just wasn't ready to hear any more of his sarcasm or name-calling."

"I understand," replied Thompson.

Once back at the police department, Thompson asked whether he should put the DNA samples into their small evidence room.

"No. I want you to take them immediately to the state lab in Lansing. We need those results as quickly as possible. After that, you can go home for the night."

"Okay, Chief. I'll see you sometime tomorrow."

That evening, Chief Ward made herself a margarita and then sat to watch the local news. News about the Swartz Creek investigation was third in line. Ward was shocked when, after a brief update on the case, an interview with Chuck Kotter flashed onto the screen. She turned up the volume.

A blonde female reporter conducted the interview.

"Mr. Kotter, we understand the police were here earlier today and took a DNA sample from you. Is that correct?"

"Yes, it is."

"Did you have any involvement in the death of the three teenage boys found in the woods?"

"No, I did not."

"Why do you think the police suspect you?"

"Our Chief and her tiny police department is incompetent. They don't have the experience for a case like this. I think they should bring in the FBI."

"But why do they suspect your involvement?"

"You'll have to ask the Chief."

"Did you know the three boys?"

"I remember Peaky and Stanley. I don't remember the other one, but I may have met him."

"You say you're not involved. Do you have any idea who may have murdered these children?"

"I do, but I can't say. I don't need any more attention or someone suing me."

"Have you reported it to the police?"

"I told them they needed to look elsewhere, but they don't believe me."

"Okay, thank you, Mr. Kotter."

Ward could not believe what she was hearing. "That jackass!" shouted Ward to no one. She then called Thompson.

"Greg, did you see the news!?"

"I sure did."

"I can't believe he called us incompetent. We have multiple agencies helping us in this investigation."

"This is not the first time a small department has been scrutinized in a major investigation. You get used to it after a while."

"Well, I'm not used to it. If they find Kotter's DNA on any of those bodies, I'm slapping the cuffs on him myself."

Chapter 16

It was just after the lunch hour on Friday when Chief Ward received a call from Boyd Tremont.

"I have some updates for you," announced Tremont.

"Good ones, I hope," replied Ward.

"Yes, indeed. All three of your missing teens have now been positively identified through DNA. Peaky Cranski's remains were in the second burial site, and Stanley Pollock's were in the third burial site."

"Not a big surprise, but I'm relieved we've finally found the missing boys. It will bring some closure to the families and the community."

"I'm not done. Here's the kicker. We found unidentified DNA on the pants of Peaky Cranski. We also recovered some rope from around the neck of Stanley Pollock. We were able to recover foreign DNA from the rope."

"That is fantastic news, Boyd."

"It gets even better," said Tremont. "The foreign DNA samples from the second set of remains and the third set match each other. This indicates that the same person had contact with both victims."

"Oh, my god!" exclaimed Ward. "That's very positive news. Please thank your lab techs for us."

"There's more," said Tremont. "It's been confirmed that the hyoid bone in each victim had been broken. Our medical examiner is convinced all three died from strangulation."

"Next, you're going to tell me you've identified the killer, right?"

"We tried. The foreign DNA was run through both the Michigan and National databases. Nothing matched. Our suspect remains unknown."

"Damn," exclaimed Ward. "Does that include the exclusion of Chuck Kotter?"

"No. We haven't been able to process his DNA yet. That should be done no later than Monday. We can tell you the DNA recovered from the remains is that of a white male."

"But it eliminates Franklin and Morales as suspects, correct? Their DNA was already in the database."

"Assuming the foreign DNA belongs to the killer, then yes, your other two suspects are eliminated. The DNA also eliminates all family members."

"Did you ever find foreign DNA on Mike Taggert's remains?"

"No. His remains were too decayed. The digging done by the dog and two boys didn't help."

"I understand. Thank you, Boyd."

"I have another question," said Boyd. "If my information is correct, the order of the victims going missing was Taggert, Cranski, and Pollock. Do I have that correct?"

"Yes, that's correct."

"I thought so. We found it interesting that the victims were buried in a line by the order in which they went missing."

"You're right, Boyd. I hadn't even thought of that. What do you take from that?"

"It may mean nothing," said Tremont. "However, it may indicate someone who likes patterns. All three died in the same manner and then were buried in an orderly line."

I hadn't even thought of that. Thanks for pointing that out. When will you be releasing the remains to the families?"

"We're conducting further testing. Once that's done, we'll contact the families."

"Okay. Thanks for the great news. Please let me know when you've made the notifications. I'll then issue a press release."

"My pleasure. I'll call you as soon as the comparison with Chuck Kotter is completed."

"Thank you, Boyd."

Chief Ward immediately called Detective Thompson. "Greg! Where are you?"

"I'm at the intersection of Morris and Miller Road, helping with an accident."

"You've been in an accident?"

"No, I'm helping Officer Brock with an accident."

"Oh. As soon as you are able, come on in. I have some important news to share with you."

"Okay."

Thirty minutes later, Thompson walked into Ward's office. "What's up?"

"Boyd Tremont called with an update. They found matching foreign DNA on the remains of Cranski and Pollock. Both are from the same unknown white male."

"Hot damn!" shouted Thompson. "Did it match Kotter?"

"They won't know until early next week."

"Well, I bet it will match. He's just too obstinate not to be involved."

"He's obstinate and hard to deal with, but don't be too confident," cautioned Ward. "He's also intelligent, and the only thing on his record is a traffic ticket from thirteen years ago."

"Well, the BTK killer in Kansas had no prior record either," responded Thompson.

Ward leaned back in her chair. "I once read that statistically, we walk past thirty-six killers in our lifetime."

"What?"

"It was a statistical study that concluded we come across approximately thirty-six killers in a lifetime. It can be fewer if you live in a rural area. But in a major city, it could be significantly higher."

"That's a bit unnerving," said Thompson.

"I don't like the man, but two things give me pause about Kotter," said Ward. "The killings started and then suddenly stopped, yet Kotter has lived here the whole time. Second, his comment about a suspect being under our noses."

Thompson nodded. "Yeah, that comment made me pause as well. Although I think he likes to play mind games, which some killers like to do. He very well could have been referring to himself."

"Agreed. Therefore, we await the DNA comparison."

"And what if it's not him?" asked Thompson.

"Then we are left with having no suspects. The DNA of Franklin and Morales is already in the state database."

"That's right," agreed Thompson.

"Go home, Greg. Try to relax over the weekend. There's nothing else we can do today."

"What about you?"

"I have a few things to finish, and I'm waiting for Boyd to let me know when all the parents have been notified. I'll then issue a press release before leaving."

"All right, Chief. I'll see you on Monday."

Chief Ward spent the next hour going over reports from the week she hadn't had time to review. Most of them were minor accidents, illegal parking complaints, a few thefts, and a criminal mischief. She then prepared a press release announcing the identifications of all three missing teenagers from sixteen to eighteen years ago. It was 5:15 pm when she finally received the call from Boyd Tremont.

"Hello, Boyd."

"Hello, Chief. I'm just calling to let you know that all family members have been notified."

"Thank you for letting me know, Boyd."

Ward then sent her prepared press release via email to all the local Flint, Lansing and Detroit news stations. She then put on her blue blazer and walked out the door. On the way home, Ward stopped to pick up a tuna sandwich from Roland's Cafe. As she drove home, her cell phone kept ringing. Ward wasn't in the mood to talk to the press, so she ignored the calls. When she arrived at her condo, Ward checked her phone. She had twelve messages from various news organizations. While tempted to turn off the phone, Ward had to leave it on in the event of a police emergency. As the Police Chief of a small town, Ward was always on call.

Ward quickly changed into a robe, made herself a rum and coke, then sat in her recliner with her sandwich and drink in hand. She flicked on the TV, being sure to avoid the news. Ward found a lighthearted movie on Netflix to get her mind off the investigation, at least for a few hours.

The TV was on, and Ward was fast asleep in her recliner when a knocking on the front door awakened her. It took her a couple of seconds to realize someone was knocking. Ward rose from the chair while adjusting her robe to avoid being exposed. She walked to the door and peeked through the peephole. It was seventy-six-year-old Carol Newman from two doors down. Carol was wearing a pink sweatshirt and sweatpants. Her snow-white hair was uncombed. Ward opened the door.

"Is everything okay, Carol?"

"Oh, yes. I was watching the news and heard you recovered our missing boys. I can't believe it."

"Yes, we have."

"It's been so long. I feel awful about this. You know, I knew Stanley."

"How did you know him?"

"I worked in the office at the high school. It was a terrible time. This whole community was frightened."

"I understand," replied Ward.

"Do you know who did this terrible thing?"

"Not yet, but we're working on it."

"Yes, of course. I just can't believe that after all these years…. Those poor boys, buried like that. How were they killed?"

"We don't have all the information yet, Carol."

"Was it the gay guy from the library? That's who I've always believed was involved. Once he moved out of Swartz Creek, no one else went missing."

"We're still investigating, Carol. I'd like to talk more, but I've had a long week, and I'm tired."

"Oh, yes. Of course. I'm sorry. It's just so disturbing. Stanley was such a nice kid."

"I'm sure he was. I need to go now, Carol."

"Yes, I'm sorry. Good night, Chief."

"Good night, Carol."

After her neighbor left, Ward brushed her teeth and slipped into bed. As she lay in bed, a sense of loneliness came over her. As a divorced woman running a police department, she found little time for dating or other simple pleasures. The stress of the case had consumed her, and the thought of having someone to share it with would be a welcome relief. Ward and her ex-husband, John Logan, had been married for nine years. Logan was also a police officer in Lansing. They met while on the job, and after a year of dating, they tied the knot. Their marriage was great for about four years. However, Ward began to climb the police ladder while John remained at the officer level. Ward believed this created some jealousy on John's part. John eventually talked of having children, but with their different schedules, they could not agree on who would be the primary caregiver. They both tried to make the marriage work for another five years until John decided to move on. The divorce was amicable, and they remained friends after the divorce. John eventually remarried and had two children. Several years ago, he was promoted and is currently a Sergeant with the Lansing Police Department.

Ward wanted to call John but thought it might be inappropriate at such a late hour. She then considered calling Greg Thompson but realized that might also be uncomfortable. She was his supervisor and needed to maintain a proper balance between friendship and work. Ward lay awake in bed while her thoughts of the investigation kept her from falling asleep. After forty-five minutes of tossing about, Ward went to the bathroom, opened the medicine cabinet, and took two sleeping pills. She returned to bed and fell asleep soon after.

At 7:20 am, Ward's cell phone rang, waking her from a deep sleep. She could see it was dispatch calling her.

"Hello," said Ward. "Is something up?"

"Sorry to bother you, Chief, but we just got a report that Chuck Kotter has left the area."

"What do you mean?"

"He flew off in his plane. I thought you might want to know this."

"Who told us this?" asked Ward.

"A few reporters are staked out at the Kotter farm. They saw him fly off this morning at about ten minutes after seven. One of them called to let us know."

"Okay, thank you," said Ward as she disconnected.

Ward sat on the edge of the bed, thinking what, if anything, the police should do. She finally called Detective Thompson.

"Did I wake you up?"

"No. I've been up for a while. What's going on?"

"Dispatch just called. Some reporters observed Kotter fly out this morning in his plane."

There was a pause, and then Thompson spoke. "I'm not sure what we can do about it. One thing we might do is call the FAA to see if they can track the plane. He won't be able to fly over the border without special clearance."

"That's a good idea, Greg. I'll give them a call."

"Okay, let me know if you need me to do anything," responded Thompson.

After getting off the phone, Ward called the FAA to alert them to the situation. The supervisor advised her they would do everything possible to locate the plane.

Hoping it would be an easy task to locate Kotter's plane, Ward patiently waited for a return call. After three hours, Ward decided to go shopping. She had to do something to get her mind off the case.

Later that afternoon, Ward was having lunch at Chili's when Thompson called. "Have you heard anything?"

"No. Maybe he just disappeared," sighed Ward.

"They'll find him, or he'll return, in which case the press will let us know."

Ward chuckled. "Yeah, they seem to know things before we do. Maybe I should ask them to call me when they get the DNA results."

Thompson laughed. "It might be faster."

"Are you doing okay?" asked Ward.

"Yeah, sure. Why?"

"Well, this case is getting to me a bit. I thought maybe you were experiencing the same thing."

"Sure, I think about it all the time. But I'm not going to let it ruin my life."

"That's a great attitude, Greg."

Ward returned home at 3:15 pm. She was only home for twenty minutes when her cell phone rang. It was from the FAA.

"Hello?"

"Is this Chief Paula Ward?"

"Yes, it is."

"Chief, this is Randy Stewart from the FAA. I was told to call you if we found the plane belonging to Chuck Kotter. A small airport outside Columbus, Indiana, reported that his plane landed there this morning. The name of the airport is Munroe County Airport."

"Where is Columbus, Indiana?" asked Ward.

"It's a small town in southern Indiana."

"Is the plane still there?"

"Yes."

"Okay, thank you very much, Randy."

After the call, Ward called Thompson. "The FAA found his plane. It's located at a small airport near Columbus, Indiana.

"Okay," said Thompson. "I now recall that Chuck has an uncle and cousin living either in or near Columbus, Indiana."

"What do you think he's doing there?"

"I don't know. Maybe he needs to be around family right now. He's under a lot of pressure. The good thing is that he hasn't fled the country."

"I suppose," said Ward. "I'm going to call the Sheriff down there and ask him to keep an eye on Kotter."

Chapter 17

On Monday morning, Chief Ward drove past Kotter's farm on her way to work. To her surprise, there were no reporters at the entrance to the property. Ward drove down the driveway and parked her white Explorer between the house and the barn. She walked onto the covered porch and peered into the window. She could not see any lights on. Ward then knocked on the front door. Getting no response, she knocked again. Still no response. Ward then walked to the barn and tried to look between the crack in the barn door. It was too dark for her to see anything.

Ward arrived at the police station at 8:20 am. Thompson was already at work. Ward told him she had stopped by Kotter's home and could not see any sign of him being there.

"Did you hear anything from Columbus?" asked Thompson.

"Not yet."

"That's probably a good sign he's still there," said Thompson.

"I've got forty-two messages on my phone," Ward grumbled. "I'm sure most of them are from the media."

"Have fun listening to those," smiled Thompson. "On another topic, I received a tip on who the culprits are in the beer theft from last week. Unless you have something else for me to do, I'm going to go pull a couple of students from class for a conversation."

"Yeah, that's fine, Greg. I'll be here if the state lab calls. I hope to get an answer on Kotter's DNA sometime today."

Once Thompson left, Chief Ward began listening to each message. Most were from the media, with typical questions about the case. A few were from people providing names of individuals they believed could be involved, although none could provide good reasons why. One message was from Sheriff Joe Eagleman of Newaygo County. It was the county just south of Lake County in northern Michigan. Sheriff Eagleman asked Ward to call him when she had the chance.

Chief Ward called Marilyn Branch into her office.

"Marilyn, I have several messages from people providing names of potential suspects. I don't have the time to go through them. Could you run these names through state and national databases to see if any of them have a criminal background?"

"Do you have their date of births?"

"Unfortunately, no. However, all of them are supposedly located in Swartz Creek or somewhere in Michigan."

"I'll do what I can," said Branch.

"Thank you, Marilyn."

Chief Ward then turned her attention to calling Sheriff Eagleman. Newaygo County bordered Lake County to the north. The Newaygo County Sheriff's Office was located in White Cloud, a town situated on the banks of the White River. It was known as a "trail town" for its proximity to the North Country Trail.

"Sheriff Joe here," answered Eagleman.

"Sheriff, this is Chief Paula Ward from Swartz Creek. I received your message to call you."

"Yes, thank you for calling, Chief. I saw the media coverage this weekend on the cold case you're working on. I may or may not have information that could be connected to your case."

"Really? What is it?

"Again, it could be unrelated, but we've had two cases similar to yours."

"Tell me about it," said Ward.

"About six years ago, the body of a sixteen-year-old male was found in the forest not far from the North Country Trail. It was about thirteen miles north of White Cloud."

"Was he a local kid?" asked Ward.

"Yes. He was a student at White Cloud High School. His name was Max Caldwell, a shy, introverted kid. He'd been missing for over a year."

"How did you find him?"

"Two hunters found him."

"Had the body been buried?" asked Ward.

"Not really buried, but it looked like the body had been covered with dirt and concealed with tree branches. Animals had gotten to the body, so the remains had been disturbed."

"Were you able to get any DNA?"

"We identified the victim through DNA, but the remains were too disturbed and decayed to get anything but the victim's DNA."

"I take it you haven't solved the case?"

"No, we haven't. But there's more. Two years after that, another male teenager went missing from the same high school. A fifteen-year-old named Raymond Bearhart."

"It sounds like a Chippewa name."

"It is. In fact, I'm part Chippewa myself."

"I thought Eagleman might be a Chippewa name. Where did you find the second victim?"

"We haven't. He simply vanished."

"I seem to remember having a faint memory of that."

"Anyway, the reason I called is that perhaps our cases are connected. It sounds like you have a good suspect. If you make an arrest, I'd like to have one of my detectives interview him."

"Our suspect hasn't been very cooperative, but if we make an arrest, we'll help in any way we can."

"Thank you, Chief."

Two hours later, Detective Thompson returned to the office. "Have you heard anything from the lab yet?"

"No," said Ward.

"Damn, this waiting is killing me," replied Thompson. "What is taking so long?"

"It's a process, Greg. They need to do it right. Did you solve the beer caper?"

"Yeah. Two stupid kids. They agreed to pay for the damage to the lock, so I ended up issuing them a misdemeanor theft summons."

Ward then told Thompson about the call she received from Sheriff Joe Eagleman.

"That's interesting," agreed Thompson. "Hard to think they are connected given the significant time between our cases and theirs."

"I thought that too," Ward agreed.

Just then, Chief Ward's phone rang. "It's the FAA call-ing," said Ward.

"Hello?"

"Is this Chief Paula Ward?"

"Yes, it is."

"It's Randy from the FAA. I'm just calling to let you know the plane you're interested in took off from the Munroe County Airport twenty minutes ago. No flight plan was filed, so we don't know the destination."

"Thank you, Randy. We appreciate the notice."

Ward then gave Thompson the news.

"If he's flying back home, it should take him about two hours to get here," said Thompson.

"Yeah, and if the DNA comes back positive on Kotter, we need to be prepared. I'm going to call Mundy Township and ask if they can assist us on an arrest if needed."

Thompson nodded. "Before that happens, I'm going to go grab some lunch. Do you want anything?"

"No thanks. I'm not hungry."

"You look tired. Can I bring you a Starbucks or some-thing?"

"I'll be fine, Greg."

After Thompson had left, Ward began sifting through some of the old reports. She believed there had to be some-thing the police had missed. She paid particular attention to the old interviews with Chuck Kotter.

After an hour had passed, Thompson returned and handed Ward an iced tea.

"What's this?"

"I know you said you didn't want anything, but I got you an iced tea."

"Thank you, Greg. It does sound good. I'm reviewing some of these old reports. Interestingly, Mayor Strawski was in on some of the interviews. Was that normal?"

"I wouldn't say it was normal, but he was a hands-on Mayor."

"I'm glad our current mayor stays out of our way. I don't think I'd like a politician involved in one of our investigations."

"Strawski and Chief Braxton were good friends. The Chief didn't seem to mind it. Honestly, I think Chief Braxton was overwhelmed. He hadn't come from a large police department like you did."

"What time is it?" asked Ward.

"It's one-thirty."

"Let's go. Kotter could be back in the next fifteen minutes."

"What are you going to do?"

"I'm not quite sure, but I want to be there when he returns to see his reaction."

"You can't arrest him unless you get a warrant."

"If we receive word the DNA matches his, then we have probable cause to arrest him. We won't need a warrant if he's outside his home."

"That's why you want to be there. You're hoping to have probable cause before he enters the house."

"It would be nice," agreed Bones.

Thompson drove. They arrived at Kotter's driveway ten minutes later. Thompson pulled over onto the shoulder of the road.

"Do you see an airplane?" asked Ward.

"No. How do you know he's flying home?"

"I don't. But I'm betting he is."

Thompson nodded.

Twenty minutes later, Thompson looked at his phone. "It's been over two and a half hours. If he were flying here, he'd already be here."

"He'll be here. I can feel it," Ward said.

"You can feel it?"

Ward looked at Thompson and smiled. "Play a game on your phone or something."

Thompson rolled his eyes.

Ten minutes later, Ward heard the sound of an engine overhead. "I can hear an airplane."

Thompson listened. "Yep, I hear it too."

Thompson exited the car and looked toward the sky. Ward did the same.

"There it is," Thompson said, pointing toward the southern sky.

"Yep, I see it."

They both watched as Kotter flew the red and white Cessna above the farm. The roar of the engine grew louder as the plane got closer. Kotter circled over the farm, then lined up the nose of the plane with the east/west runway. The plane gently touched down on the blacktop and rolled to a stop at the end furthest from the barn. Kotter turned the plane and began to taxi back toward the barn and house.

"Let's go," said Ward as she jumped in the car.

"Where are we going?"

"I want to stall him before he gets into the house."

"We haven't gotten the DNA results yet."

"I know, but I have a sense the call will be coming soon. If he's a match, we can arrest him on the spot."

Thompson sighed as he got back in the car. He put it in drive and drove onto the Kotter driveway. Kotter was parking the plane in front of his barn just as Thompson and Ward pulled up behind him. Kotter looked surprised to see them as he stepped down from the plane.

"What do you want now?" grumbled Kotter in his gravelly voice.

"We just have a few more questions," said Ward.

"I'm done answering questions. Are you here to arrest me?"

"Where did you go, Chuck?" asked Ward.

"I don't believe it's any of your business."

"You went to Columbus, Indiana," replied Ward.

"How did you know that?"

"We have our ways."

"Yeah, well I don't have time for this. Unless you're arresting me, I want you to leave my property now."

Thompson looked at Ward.

"Can we just sit down and talk?" asked Ward.

"No. Now leave my property!"

Thompson motioned to Ward. "Come on, let's go."

"Stick around, Chuck," said Ward. "We'll have the DNA results soon."

Kotter grumbled something and walked toward the house.

Ward turned to Thompson. "Okay, we can go now."

As he drove out the driveway, Thompson asked, "Why did you want to confront him again?"

"Well, I was hoping we'd get the DNA results before he got home. Since that wasn't the case, I just wanted to keep his stress level high. You've got to keep the pressure on a suspect. You never know when they will do something or say something incriminating."

"I thought you had your doubts about him?"

"Oh, I do. But you can't stop pushing. At the moment, he's the only suspect we have."

"Okay, I get it. Keep the stress level high."

Once they returned to the police department, Marilyn walked into Chief Ward's office. "Boyd Tremont wants you to call him."

"Hmm. He has my cell number. I wonder why he didn't call that number? Does he have the DNA results?"

"I don't know. He wouldn't tell me."

"Thank you, Marilyn."

Ward called Tremont. "Hi, Boyd. Do you have some results?"

"We do. I'm sorry to tell you this, but the foreign DNA does not match Chuck Kotter."

Ward sighed. "Damn, I was afraid of that. We're back to zero in terms of suspects. Thank you, Boyd."

With arms crossed on her desk, Ward bent over and rested her forehead on her arms. Thompson walked in.

"The DNA doesn't match, does it?"

Ward looked up. "Nope."

"Now what?" asked Thompson.

"First thing tomorrow, we go apologize to Chuck Kotter and try to get more information about what he said earlier. He knows something he doesn't want to share."

Chapter 18

It was Tuesday morning, and it had been a week since all three bodies were discovered. Ward and Thompson were at Kotter's residence at 9:40 am. They found Kotter in his barn working on an old tractor.

"Okay, this is now harassment," growled Kotter.

"We understand, Mr. Kotter," Chief Ward said. "We are here to apologize."

Kotter rubbed his unshaven chin. "Apologize? Have you found the real killer?"

"Sadly, we have not," said Ward. "However, your DNA did not match the foreign DNA found on the remains. This pretty much clears you from suspicion."

"I tried to tell you," Kotter responded.

Thompson interrupted. "Yes, but you've been under suspicion for a long time, Chuck. Finding the remains just off your property line heightened the suspicions surrounding you. We had no choice but to thoroughly investigate you."

"He's right, Chuck," agreed Ward. "The DNA has also cleared Kent Franklin and Miguel Morales. Right now, we don't know where to turn. You commented earlier that the suspect was right under our noses. We are now asking for your help."

Kotter stared for several seconds before saying, "Follow me inside."

Ward and Thompson followed Kotter into his house. He took them into the kitchen. "Have a seat, officers."

Kotter sat across the table from Ward and Thompson.

"What do you know about this case, Chuck?" asked Ward.

"Detective Thompson, you were on the department back then, right?" asked Kotter.

"Yes, but I wasn't a detective then."

"But you remember how big the investigation was, right?"

"Of course."

"And you had help from other agencies."

"Yes. A task force was put together."

"Who managed the task force?"

"That would have been Chief Ron Braxton."

"But was he actually in charge? Did he have the final say on how the investigation proceeded and on who to target?"

Thompson frowned.

Chief Ward spoke up. "What are you getting at, Chuck?"

"You weren't here," quipped Kotter. "I want to know what Detective Thompson remembers. Who was pulling the strings? I know Chief Braxton was formally in charge. But who was running the show? Who was the face of the department?"

Thompson thought for a moment. "Are you talking about Mayor Strawski?"

"Just tell me what you remember."

"Well, the Mayor was involved, I know that. And he was the one who managed the press conferences."

"Was Chief Braxton ever frustrated by this?"

"Now that you mention it, yes. He thought the mayor was too much into police business. But that was with everything, not just this investigation."

"What was the mayor's attitude toward gays?"

Thompson looked down at the table, then back up at Kotter. "Now that you ask that, he was not very tolerant of gays. It was not unusual to hear him make anti-gay jokes around the office."

"And who was one of your suspects?"

"The guy from the library, Miguel Morales."

"Yes!" shouted Kotter. "Don't you find that interesting? There was nothing tying Miguel to the missing teens."

Thompson nodded.

"And I can tell you the mayor and I did not get along. And low and behold, I end up as a prime suspect. I was a patsy simply for getting along with kids and letting them use my property. And then eighteen years later, the bodies are found near my property line. I would call that one hell of a coincidence."

Ward and Thompson sat in silence for several seconds.

"You've raised some interesting thoughts," admitted Ward. "We probably need to rethink the entire investigation."

"What about the seventeen-year-old suspect, Kent Franklin?" asked Thompson.

"He was identified as a suspect only because he was the last person to see Taggert alive. Kent wouldn't hurt anyone."

"Why did you not share any of this before now?" asked Ward.

"Ever since this happened, I haven't been treated fairly by the police. And without any bodies, no one knew what had happened. Once those bodies were found, I suspected I would be targeted again. I knew the DNA would clear me, but I was in no mood to help. Your apology meant a lot to me. And I'm sorry I called you dumb asses, but it was difficult for me to believe no one would question the mayor's involvement and manipulation in the investigation."

"So, you believe Mayor Strawski was involved in the murder of these teenagers?" asked Thompson.

"I don't know. However, his behind-the-scenes manipulations should at least be examined. I understand why a lone, unmarried man like me who gets along with teenagers would be looked at. However, Strawski fits the same profile. Never married, lived alone, and was frequently involved in high school events. He also had a second home outside the city limits."

"That's right," Thompson interrupted. "He had a country home just outside the city limits. He sold it after he retired and moved away."

"That's right," agreed Kotter.

"We appreciate you telling us this," said Ward.

"I feel for those boys and their families," Kotter said softly. "I enjoyed having teenagers around because I didn't have kids of my own. Letting them use my property for fun events was a way for me to be involved and help them grow. The investigation ultimately brought an end to all that."

Ward felt empathy for Kotter. "Chuck, I'm sorry for the impact this investigation had on you personally."

"Thank you, Chief. That means a lot. And sorry I was such a jackass. It was born out of frustration."

Ward and Thompson both smiled.

"I understand," Ward said. "You have given us a fresh look at the investigation. We'll leave you alone now. But maybe one day you'll take me up in that airplane."

"Anytime, Chief."

On the way back to the police department, Ward checked her phone messages. There was a message for her to call Boyd Tremont. Ward hit the call button.

"Tremont here,"

"Boyd, it's Chief Ward calling you back. What's up?"

"I have some additional information regarding the foreign DNA we found on two of the remains. We continued to run the DNA through various databases and received a match from a case in Lake County."

"You have a suspect?"

"No, but we found another victim. Lake County found a seventeen-year-old male, Noah Simpson, in the national forest thirteen years ago. The victim had been strangled. Foreign DNA recovered from his body matched your suspect's DNA."

"Wow," said Ward. "Our killer didn't just kill in Swartz Creek."

"Nope. I'll email you all the information."

"Thank you, Boyd."

Ward turned to Thompson, "We have a much bigger issue on our hands. The lab found matching unknown DNA from a homicide victim in Lake County."

"The same suspect DNA as in our case?" asked Thompson.

"The same. Who knows how many victims may be out there buried or disposed in the woods of Michigan."

"Was the victim a high school student?"

"Yes. Seventeen-year-old Noah Simpson."

There was a pause in the conversation until Thompson spoke. "Maybe Kotter is right about Mayor Strawski. He now lives in Lake County."

"Unfortunately, I'm thinking the same thing," agreed Ward. "I'll call Sheriff Johnson back at the office."

Once in the office, Ward called Lake County Sheriff Mike Johnson.

"Hello, Sheriff. I'm calling to let you know the state lab just connected our case to one of yours from thirteen years ago. He was a seventeen-year-old named Noah Simpson."

"I wasn't the Sheriff then, but I know the case. How is he connected?"

"The suspect DNA in our case matches the suspect DNA recovered from Simpson."

"Have you identified the suspect?"

"Not yet, but we have some suspicions about our ex-mayor, Marty Strawski."

There was a pause. "Marty Strawski? The Marty that lives up here?"

"Yes. There are several behavioral issues that have recently come to our attention. Second, there have been no more cases in our area since Strawski moved from Swartz Creek. Finally, there are two similar cases from Newaygo County."

"This comes as a bit of a shock," said Johnson. "He seems very pro-police."

"He was very pro-police in Swartz Creek as well. In fact, we are learning that he may have manipulated the investigation here."

"I've only been Sheriff here for eight years, but now that you mention it, I recall Marty asking me once if we were still investigating our case. I never gave it a second thought."

"No reason you would, except now we have more information. Are you aware of the two teenagers from Newaygo County? One was found dead, and the other is still missing. The names are Max Caldwell and Raymond Bearheart."

"Yes, I do!" exclaimed Johnson. "We provided them some help on the investigations."

"Both of them sound like they could be related. I'm going to call Sheriff Eagleman next."

After the call with Sheriff Johnson, Ward called Newaygo County Sheriff Joe Eagleman. She updated him on the new DNA information and shared her suspicion of Marty Strawski. Sheriff Eagleman admitted he knew Marty Strawski and had discussed the cases with him.

"You know," said Eagleman, "after you telling me all this, I can see where you're coming from. Marty befriended himself to both me and Mike Johnson. I've just always thought he was a concerned citizen, and I knew he had been a mayor, so he had some credentials."

"To be honest," continued Ward, "I have a hard time believing it myself. However, the coincidences are just too much to overlook. We need to get his DNA."

"I agree. If you can be up here tomorrow, I'll have Marty come in for a DNA swab."

"That would be great, Sheriff. We can be there at ten tomorrow morning if that works."

"I'll call Marty to arrange it. If he can't make that time, I'll let you know. Otherwise, I'll see you then."

"Thank you, Sheriff."

After the call, Ward updated Thompson.

"We should leave by seven," said Thompson.

"Yeah, let's meet here tomorrow at 6:45. You can drive."

Wednesday morning started out cold. The first frost of the season covered the ground and car windshields. It was a damp, cold type of weather, with fog still lingering in the air. Thompson warmed up the white Explorer, allowing the windows to clear. By 7:05 am, Thompson and Ward were on their way to the Newaygo County Sheriff's Office. Ward had received a text from Sheriff Eagleman letting her know Strawski had agreed to meet at the Sheriff's Department in White Cloud. After about an hour of driving, the fog lifted. They arrived in White Cloud at 9:30 am.

Ward and Thompson checked in at the front desk and were escorted back to Sheriff Eagleman's conference room. Lake County Sheriff Mike Johnson was also present.

"I invited Mike here, given his connection to the other case," said Eagleman.

Everyone shook hands.

"Was your victim found buried?" asked Thompson.

"No," replied Johnson. "He was tied to a tree in the forest. The cause of death was strangulation."

"That's a different M.O. than our cases," Ward pointed out.

"Yes, but the same victim profile, and he was tied to a tree with a rope around the neck."

"Maybe the suspect is getting bolder," offered Ward. "We know it's the same suspect because of the DNA match."

"We all know the circumstances, but does anyone actually believe Marty Strawski's DNA will match?" asked Thompson. "Why would he voluntarily undergo a DNA test?"

"That thought crossed my mind as well," Sheriff Johnson admitted.

"I guess we'll soon find out," said Sheriff Eagleman.

A clerk walked in with coffees for everyone as the officers shared details on their cases. As they waited for Strawski, the conversation soon turned to the Detroit Lions, who had just won their third consecutive game to start the season, improving to 3-0.

"We might actually have a decent team this year," said Thompson.

"Let's hope our quarterback stays healthy," replied Johnson.

It was 10:10 am when Ward asked, "Marty was supposed to be here by now, correct?"

"Yes," said Eagleman. "I'll have my assistant call him."

Several more minutes passed before the assistant walked in. "I tried three times, Sheriff. There's no answer."

Ward looked at Sheriff Johnson.

"Oh, oh," said Johnson. "That's not a good sign. I'll call the office and have one of my deputies check his home."

Another twenty minutes passed before Johnson received a call. He listened briefly before saying, "Have you checked the garage? Okay, put out a bulletin to all officers with a description of him and his truck. If found, have him detained until I can speak with him."

"It sounds like he might be on the run," said Ward.

"Yes," agreed Johnson. "My deputies checked the house, and it's dark and locked up. His truck is gone as well."

"I'll have dispatch put out a BOLO," said Eagleman.

"Do you mind if Greg and I go up to his place to look around?" asked Ward.

"No, not at all," replied Johnson. "We can use the help."

Ward and Thompson left for the forty-minute drive to Strawski's cabin in the Manistee National Forest, north of Baldwin. When they arrived, no one was there. Both began to look into windows and walk around the property. A heavy chill filled the air.

"Let's walk the perimeter forest," suggested Ward.

"This forest is about as thick as a cornfield," noted Thompson.

"Yes, so let's stick together."

Ward took the lead as Thompson followed. "Do you think he's hiding out here?"

"Not likely," said Ward. "But maybe we can find something of evidentiary value, or maybe even more victims."

"That's a gruesome thought."

Back at the Newaygo Sheriff's Office, Sheriff Eagleman received a call from Marty Strawski.

"What the hell are the police doing at my property?"

"Marty, where are you?"

"Never mind that. Why are you looking for me?"

"You were supposed to be here at ten o'clock for a DNA swab so that the police could clear you of any suspicion."

"I spoke with my attorney, and he advised against it. He said it was too unpredictable without knowing more about the evidence and how DNA was found, collected, and tested."

"Marty, we just want to eliminate any suspicion about you. It's a common technique to clear people so that the investigation can move forward. Now come on in here and get this done."

"No way. It's absurd to think I had anything to do with what happened. I helped investigate the damn case!"

"Where are you, Marty?"

"None of your damn business!"

The phone then disconnected. Eagleman immediately called Sheriff Johnson to give him the news.

"That just further raises my suspicion about him," said Johnson. "Do you have any idea where he is?"

"He's an experienced outdoorsman. He could be anywhere."

"All right, I'll issue an all-points bulletin for Marty Strawski, notifying officers that he is wanted for questioning."

"He doesn't go anywhere without his guns," Eagleman reminded him. "Make sure to include that he is armed."

"I will," agreed Johnson.

Not finding any sign of Strawski around the perimeter of his property, Ward and Thompson returned to the front of the house.

"We need to search his house and garage," said Thompson.

"We don't have a warrant," Ward reminded him. "But maybe we can find something here that has his DNA on it. Let's look around."

Thompson looked at the covered front porch and noticed something on the small wooden table. Once he reached the porch, he observed a black coffee mug on the table next to a pair of gray leather work gloves. He looked into the mug and saw a small amount of coffee at the bottom.

"How about a coffee mug?" yelled Thompson.

Ward walked up onto the porch to observe the mug. "That would be perfect!" exclaimed Ward. "Let me grab a latex glove and paper bags from the car."

Ward returned to the porch with the latex glove on her left hand. She opened the paper bag, then carefully grabbed the mug from the bottom. She gingerly poured the remaining coffee onto the ground, then placed the cup into the paper bag, being careful not to touch the top half, handle, or lip of the cup. The bag was then sealed. She then picked up the leather gloves and sealed them in a bag.

"We need to get this stuff to the lab as soon as possible," said Ward.

"Where is the closest lab up here?" asked Thompson.

"Lansing and Detroit have the only DNA labs. We need to get this to Lansing right now. Let's go."

Once Thompson got into the driver's seat, he turned to Ward. "Check your text messages." He then fired up the Explorer, backed up, and spun the tires, spewing dust and rocks as he sped down the dirt driveway. Once he got to the roadway, Thompson flipped on the lights and siren, then headed toward Lansing.

Ward looked at her phone. She read the BOLO request issued by Sheriff Eagleman for Marty Strawski. "At least we have every cop in Michigan looking for him now."

While en route, Ward called Boyd Tremont to let him know they were coming from Lake County with items that needed to be tested for DNA as soon as possible.

Chapter 19

Thompson and Ward pulled into the parking lot of the Michigan State Forensic Laboratory at 2:05 pm. By 2:15 pm, they were meeting with Boyd Tremont. Ward handed him the paper bags containing the coffee cup and gloves.

"We believe these will have Marty Strawski's DNA on them. We found the items on his porch table, and the cup still contained a small amount of coffee," explained Ward.

"So, you don't know for sure if it was Marty who drank from this cup or wore the gloves?"

"No, but he lives alone. I doubt it belongs to anyone else."

"You'll need stronger evidence than that, Chief."

"Yes, Boyd, we know that. However, if it matches the DNA recovered from our victims, it will provide us with all the probable cause we need for an arrest warrant. We can later confirm the DNA with a controlled sample."

"Okay, that makes sense. When do you need it by?"

"Can you have it done in an hour?"

Boyd laughed. "You're joking, right?"

"Yes, but we need this as soon as possible. Strawski is on the run."

"We can run what we call rapid DNA processing. It is less precise, but if we get a preliminary match, it can be used to get a warrant. Follow-up testing would then need to be conducted."

"How long does this rapid testing take?" asked Ward.

"I can get a result to you by tomorrow morning sometime."

"Thank you, Boyd."

After speaking with Tremont, Ward called both Sheriff Eagleman and Johnson to let them know when the DNA results would be available.

"No luck in finding Marty?" asked Ward.

"I'm afraid not," Sheriff Johnson replied. "We have officers searching for him, but he's familiar with the terrain. He could be anywhere."

"We greatly appreciate your help in this," said Ward.

"We're all in this together, Chief."

After Ward's call, it was 2:50 pm.

Chief, sorry to bring this up, but I haven't eaten since we left Swartz Creek this morning," said Thompson. "I'm starving!"

Ward smiled. "I am too, Greg. Just pick a place. We've done all we can for now."

Just outside Lansing, Thompson found a Chili's restaurant. Thompson ordered the BBQ ribs while Ward ordered a Fiesta Chicken Salad. While eating, they engaged in small talk until Thompson turned the conversation back to Marty Strawski.

"There's something that's been bothering me," admitted Thompson.

"What is it, Greg?"

"With all this suspicion surrounding Marty, I've been doing a lot of thinking back to the days when he was the mayor of Swartz Creek. I now remember some things that, if I had been more aware, I might have seen Strawski as someone we needed to investigate."

"Like what?" asked Ward.

"He sometimes made comments about the investigation that I thought were inappropriate. I can't remember exactly what he said, but I remember feeling uncomfortable. But one stood out to me that I haven't forgotten. The Chief held numerous meetings during those days as part of the investigation, and Marty was almost always present. I recall a conversation involving Miguel Morales, the man who worked with children at the library. Marty was real firm in his belief that Miguel was involved. During the meeting, he called Miguel a gay bastard. I didn't remember this until my phone conversation with Miguel last week."

"I don't think anyone would suspect Marty based on that," said Ward. "He might have been a prejudiced jackass, but no one would connect that to being involved."

"It wasn't just that. Marty was also very involved with the students at the high school. Not much different from Kotter, although I'm not aware of any parties at Marty's country home."

Ward just continued to listen, knowing Thompson needed to vent his emotions.

"And I hadn't remembered this until our recent conversation with Kotter. There was a call to the police department one day, I think, sometime after the third disappearance. An anonymous caller suggested we investigate Marty Strawski. Everyone just kind of laughed it off, but maybe we missed a real opportunity. I remember Strawski being real pissed when the Chief told him about it. He wanted to trace the phone call, but it was too late, of course. And what a coincidence that no other teenagers went missing after that. If Marty's DNA matches, we really screwed up. We could have prevented these other victims. And who knows how many are out there?"

Thompson then fell silent.

After a few seconds, Ward spoke. "Greg, stop beating yourself up over this. There have been thousands of investigations where the police look back and think, if only we had done something differently. If anyone is to blame, it would be your chief. The mayor obviously had control over him."

Thompson sighed. "Yeah, I know that. But it still bugs the hell out of me."

"Here's a thought," said Ward. "Could Kotter have been the anonymous caller? That might help explain why he was so upset with the police."

Thompson's eyes widened. "Wow, I hadn't thought of that. I'll bet you're right."

Ward looked at her phone. "The word is out."

"What do you mean?"

"The news about the police wanting to interview ex-Swartz Creek Mayor Marty Strawski is now all over the internet. It even states that he is fleeing from the police, and there is a state-wide search."

"That was quick," said Thompson.

"Once that bulletin went out, I knew it would be in the news. But it's a good thing. Hopefully, someone will spot him or his truck."

Thompson nodded.

Ward then pointed toward Thompson's left shirt sleeve.

"I think you got some barbeque sauce on your sleeve."

Thompson looked at the sleeve. "Ahhh." He then dabbed his napkin in the melted remains of his iced tea and did his best to remove the stain.

"Did you just use your iced tea to clean your sleeve?"

"It's all water," replied Thompson.

Ward rolled her eyes. "Let's go. We need to get back to Swartz Creek."

After returning to Swartz Creek, Ward finished up some paperwork before heading home. On her way, she stopped by the home of Karen and Jack Hudson.

"Hello, Chief," said Karen after opening the door. "We've seen the news. What can we do for you?"

"May I come in for just a few minutes?"

"Sure."

Karen led the Chief into the living room. Jack was watching the news. When he saw the Chief, he turned down the volume. Roxy joyfully approached the Chief while wagging her tail. The Chief bent over to pet Roxy on her head.

"Hi, Roxy. You're such a sweet girl."

Roxy loved the attention as her tail wagged back and forth. The Chief then stood.

"I just wanted to stop by and see how you're doing."

"We're doing well, thank you," replied Jack.

"How are Dylan and Abby doing?"

"Abby is fine," said Karen. "Dylan's still upset about his restrictions, but otherwise fine."

"I wanted to talk to you about that if you don't mind."

"Sure, what is it?" asked Jack.

"It's been over a week since you grounded Dylan, correct?"

"Yes," responded Karen.

"I just wanted to let you know that if your children had not found those bones, we would not be where we are in this investigation. Those bodies may never have been found without Roxy and your children. Had they not brought that bone home, we still wouldn't know. We now have DNA that will help us solve this case. I wanted to thank your children."

Jack and Karen looked at each other.

"I hadn't thought of it that way," said Jack.

"Would you mind if I spoke to them?"

"Dylan! Abby!" shouted Jack. "Come on down for a minute."

Abby followed Dylan down the stairs into the living room. "Oh, what are we in trouble for now?" asked Dylan.

"You're not in trouble," replied Ward. "I just wanted to thank you for bringing the found bone to our attention. If not for that, we still wouldn't know what happened to those three boys. Thank you to both of you. Oh, and to Roxy as well."

"Thank you, Chief," said Dylan.

"Yes, thank you!" squealed Abby.

Roxy, with tail wagging, stood next to the Chief as she again reached down to scratch Roxy's head.

"This dog of yours acts like she knows what I'm saying."

"She's a smart dog," replied Abby.

"Now, I'd like to talk to your parents alone for a minute," Ward said.

"Go on back upstairs," ordered Jack.

After the children left, Jack asked the Chief what she wanted to talk about.

"I just want to say thank you to both of you as well. I understand the punishment for Dylan. However, given our current progress in the investigation, I feel maybe he could be released from his punishment. It's entirely up to you, but I wanted you to know how much their discovery has meant to this case. Every parent now has closure. That's because of your kids."

Jack and Karen were both silent for several seconds.

"Like Jack, I hadn't thought of that," said Karen. "I suppose Dylan has served enough time."

Jack nodded. "I agree. Thank you for sharing this with us, Chief. It means a lot."

Ward smiled. "Thank you for listening."

"Is Mayor Strawski responsible for these killings?" asked Jack.

"We don't know for sure, but it appears to be the case."

"Good luck, Chief."

"Do you get to go home now?" asked Karen.

"Just about. I have one more stop to make. I'm going to go thank Jason Chapman now."

Ward and Thompson waited most of Thursday morning for a call from the state lab on the DNA testing. While waiting, Ward talked with Sheriff Eagleman and Sheriff Johnson several times. No one had been able to locate Marty Strawski.

Thompson walked into the Chief's office. "Is there anything I can do? I hate the waiting."

"Yes. Why don't you go to Lake County and assist with the search? We need a Swartz Creek representative there should they find Marty."

"What are you going to do?"

"I need to wait on the DNA results. If they match, I'll obtain a warrant and then come up to assist with the search.

I'll put Officer Brock in charge here. Oh, and get two motel rooms. We may be up there a few days."

"Okay. I'll go home to pack my bag, then be on my way."

"Thanks, Greg. Be careful out there."

"I will, Chief."

After Thompson had left, Ward called Tremont to check on the DNA.

"No, we don't have it," Tremont told her. "I promise to call you as soon as the lab has the result. They need to follow protocol, even on a rapid test."

"Okay. Thank you, Boyd."

Ward completed an arrest and search affidavit in antici-pation of the DNA matching. She then went home to pack a bag for the trip north. Having nothing left to do but wait, Ward heated some leftover spaghetti and then settled into her reclining chair, turning on the TV to watch old episodes of Family Feud. Ward was asleep in the chair when her cell phone rang.

"Hello?"

"Chief Ward?"

"Yes."

"This is Boyd. We got your DNA result."

Ward sat up straight. "And?"

"The DNA recovered from the lip of the coffee cup matches the unknown DNA obtained from the remains of Richard Cranski and Stanley Pollock."

"I'll be damned. It's the mayor."

"You can't say that for sure, Chief. All we can say is that it most likely came from Strawski. Someone else may have drank from that coffee cup."

"It's good enough for a probable cause warrant. We can confirm it after we arrest him. Thank you, Boyd."

"You're welcome, Chief. Now go find him."

"We intend to."

Ward immediately called Thompson with the news. "Will you pass the information on to both Sheriffs?"

"Yes, I'm with Sheriff Eagleman right now. We'll get it out to all the officers in the area."

"Good. I'm heading to the office to add this to the affidavit. Then, I'll meet with a judge to obtain an arrest warrant and a search warrant for his house. As soon as I have them, I'll let you know."

It was after five o'clock when Ward finished the affidavits. She called the on-call county judge to arrange a meeting at his home to review and issue the warrants. The judge lived in Grand Blanc, about a twenty-minute drive away. Upon her arrival, the judge, a white male in his sixties, carefully read the affidavits.

"I remember when this was all happening," said the judge. "It's hard to believe it was your mayor."

"I agree, Judge. Who would have thought?"

Once the warrants were signed, Ward called Officer Glen Brock.

"Glen, we got the warrants for Marty. I've got to go up north to help with the search. I'm putting you in charge while I'm gone. Are you okay with that?"

"Yes, I'll take care of things here," agreed Brock.

Ward then called Thompson to advise him of the warrants. "Let the Sheriffs know," directed Ward. "Where are we staying?"

"There aren't many choices up here," replied Thompson. "I found a small motel between Baldwin and White Cloud. It's called The Pines Motel. It's not much, but each room has a bed and a small bathroom. We have rooms 105 and 106."

"Thanks, Greg. I should be there in about two hours. Still no sign of Strawski?"

"No, and with darkness setting in, we're done for the day. Every police agency in the state has been notified, so officers should be on the lookout for his black Ford pickup. But up here, there aren't many officers on duty."

"Okay, thanks. I'll see you in a couple of hours."

Ward arrived at The Pines Motel a little after 8:00 pm. The motel sat off the road, nestled among a cluster of pine trees. It consisted of a dimly lit office and twelve individual rooms. The motel was constructed of rustic faded logs with a covered wooden porch that ran the length of the motel. The vacancy sign above the office door was still lit a bright red. Ward noticed Thompson's white Explorer parked in front of the rooms, about halfway down from the office. Ward stopped in front of the office and went inside.

An older woman with white hair wearing a maroon Ferris State sweatshirt sat behind the desk, watching a small TV on a table to her right. She turned her head and looked at Ward as she approached the desk.

"You must be Chief Ward," barked the clerk.

"I am."

The clerk handed Ward a key with a tag bearing the number 105.

"You'll be in room 105, and your partner said you'd have a city credit card for the rooms."

"Yes, of course," replied Ward. "Here it is."

"I hear your mayor is a serial killer."

"Where did you hear that?" asked Ward.

"It's all over the news, and I've had two cops stop in today wanting to search the premises. Then your partner said they were looking for a suspect in a series of murders."

"Well, for clarification, the man we're looking for is not our mayor. He was at one time, but he's been gone for about fifteen years now."

"It's a shame. I hope you find him."

"Me too," agreed Ward. "Did you go to Ferris?"

"Nope. I just like the sweatshirt."

Ward just smiled. When she left, she re-parked her Explorer next to Thompson's in front of room 105. She grabbed her case portfolio and suitcase from the back seat, then walked to her motel room door. She found the room to be small. It had a queen bed with a table and lamp on either side. An older flat-screen TV was mounted to the wall opposite the bed and over a small dining table with two chairs. The bathroom was at the back of the room. The room was cold. Ward found the thermostat controlling the baseboard heater and adjusted it to a higher setting. Once settled in, she walked to room 106 and knocked on the door. Within seconds, Thompson opened the door.

"Ahhh, you made it! How was the drive?"

"Uneventful," replied Ward as she entered the room. "Do you have any updates?"

"Not really. There have been no sightings of Marty, and no one can reach him by phone."

"Where have we been looking?"

"They have search teams in both Newaygo and Lake County. The state police are also helping."

"The first thing we should do tomorrow is go search Marty's cabin," said Ward.

Thompson agreed, then said, "For now, I think we need to relax with one of my famous whiskey sours."

"Where did you get the makings for whiskey sours?"

"I may have stopped on my way to the motel," Thompson said with a smile. "Would you like one?"

"I believe I would."

After two whiskey sours, Ward was feeling very relaxed. "It's getting late, Greg. Your drinks were wonderful and relaxing. I'm going to get some sleep now. It could be a long day tomorrow."

"Good idea," agreed Thompson. "What time do you want to get started tomorrow?"

"Eight o'clock."

"I'll be ready."

"Good night, Greg."

"Good night, Chief."

Chapter 20

Friday morning was brisk, with a slight breeze creating a chill that Chief Ward could feel through her jacket. Ward knocked on Thompson's door at 7:56 am. Thompson opened the door, ready to go.

"Are we taking two cars?" asked Thompson.

"No. You can drive. I'll work the radio and phone. Sheriff Johnson and a couple of his detectives will meet us at Strawski's cabin at 8:30."

When Ward and Thompson arrived at the cabin, the Sheriff and two detectives were already on the scene. After introductions, one of the detectives used an electronic pick to open the front door. Once inside, a plan was devised to search the cabin. Ward and Thompson were asked to search the two bedrooms and a room used as an office.

Having observed the animal mounts on the wall and photos of Strawski hunting and fishing, one detective remarked that Strawski must really enjoy hunting and fishing.

"He did," agreed Thompson. "We now believe he also enjoyed hunting teenage boys."

"I'll search the office if you take the two bedrooms," said Ward.

"Got it."

Ward noticed the décor of the office was similar to that of the living room. Hanging on the wall behind a large walnut-colored wooden desk was a large map of the surrounding forest. Six red Xs were marked on the map. Ward took a photograph of the map. She then went through each drawer in the desk. Nothing of significance was found in the desk.

A closet with sliding doors was along the east wall. Ward opened the sliding door and found three hunting rifles stacked in one corner. A gray metal filing cabinet with three drawers stood in the opposite corner. Ward attempted to open the cabinet, but all the drawers were locked. Ward left the room to ask one of the detectives if they had something to pry open the cabinet. She was given a twelve-inch silver crowbar. Ward used the bar to pry open each drawer.

In the bottom drawer, Ward found twelve boxes of ammunition. Most of the boxes were rifle cartridges of various caliber sizes. She also found two boxes of forty-five caliber handgun bullets.

In the middle drawer, Ward found three rolls of silver duct tape, paper maps, a Taser, and a black metal box containing stacks of $100 bills totaling $12,000.

Ward then opened the top drawer and was shocked at what she found.

"Greg!" shouted Ward. "Come in here!"

Thompson entered the room. "What is it?"

Ward spread out some of the items on top of the desk. Thompson looked down and could see various driver's licenses and student IDs.

"Are these from our victims?" asked Thompson.

"They are. And look at these," said Ward as she placed photographs on the desk of three young males tied to a round wooden post.

"Oh, my god," muttered Thompson. "He took trophy photos of his victims. Those are the Swartz Creek boys. And as I recall, Strawski had a pole barn on his property in the county."

"Yeah, but look at these six," said Ward as she laid out six photos of boys standing in a darkened room with a rope around their necks at the end of a hanging rope."

"That's sick. It looks like they are in a garage."

"It looks like they are about to be hanged," Ward said.

Sheriff Johnson walked into the room. "What's all the commotion about?"

"Look at this," said Ward, waving her hand over the desk.

Johnson's eyes widened. "Are these photographs of our victims?"

"Yes, and he also kept ID cards. There are driver's licenses and student IDs here."

"Well, that monster," grumbled Johnson. "I had hoped Marty wasn't involved, but this proves otherwise."

Thompson examined the different photographs. "There are more photos here than we have victims."

"Yes," agreed Ward. "I count nine different victims."

"In total, we know of five with one still missing," said Thompson. "That means there must be four more bodies buried or hidden somewhere."

Ward sorted through the photographs and identifications. She found a photo each of Taggert, Cranski, and Pollock. She also found the driver's licenses for Taggert and Cranski. There was a student ID card for Pollock, who was only fifteen at the time of his disappearance.

"Look at this," Sheriff Johnson said. "Three of these photos show these kids tied to a post. The other six have a rope around their necks."

"Our three victims are tied to posts," observed Thompson. "I'll bet these were taken in Strawski's barn on his property outside Swartz Creek. I doubt he has a post like this in his garage here."

"No, he doesn't," said Johnson.

Johnson noticed Ward didn't look so well. "Are you okay, Chief?"

Ward wiped some tears from her eyes. "Yeah, I'll be fine. I just ache for these poor boys, having to endure such brutality. You can see the fear in their eyes."

Johnson nodded. "I understand. This is tough for all of us. I'll have one of my detectives collect and package each of these items."

"I'd like to take the items that pertain to our victims. We'll need them as evidence in our cases."

"Of course, Chief. I'll make sure our detectives keep our evidence organized by jurisdiction. We have all the necessary bags, boxes, and evidence tape. I'll have my guys process and label this evidence. Why don't you and Greg go search the garage?"

"We can do that," agreed Ward. "Thank you."

Ward and Thompson left the house and walked to the garage. The garage was built with the same log siding as the house. It had a double-car garage door in front and a walk-in door on the side facing the house. There were no windows. Checking both doors, Thompson found them to be locked.

"I'll get the crowbar from the car," said Thompson. Once he returned, he jammed the flat end of the crowbar between the door and door jamb just under the doorknob. He then applied pressure until the outside frame broke with a loud crack. Thompson continued to pry at the door, breaking out chunks of wood with each attempt. On his fifth pull, the entire frame pulled away from the deadbolt lock. Thompson stepped back, and with one hard kick with the heel of his shoe, the door flung open. Thompson reached inside until he found the light switch and flipped it on.

It was an oversized two-car garage. A red and white Polaris Razor ATV sat on the far side of the garage. A small trailer was attached to the ATV. There was also a small tractor sitting next to the ATV with a snowplow blade attached to the front. Various large gardening tools and shovels hung on the wall. A ten-foot aluminum ladder leaned against the far wall, and a wooden counter ran across the back of the garage with various power tools lying on top. Sturdy beams ran across the top of the garage. On the near side were three large white cabinets with double doors. Thompson and Ward stood for several seconds, taking in the scene.

"Well, let's have a look around," said Ward. "I'll take this side, and you start on the other side."

Thompson walked toward the ATV and tractor while Ward looked inside the cabinets. Most of the items in the cabinets were typical garage items such as cleaning supplies, oil, weed killer, and bug sprays. Additional power tools were also present. In the third cabinet, Ward found two unused rolls of half-inch rope and a half-roll of a third rope.

"Greg, come look at this rope."

Thompson walked over and examined the rope. "It appears to be the same type of rope we've seen in the pictures."

"I'm sure it is," replied Ward. "I'm taking it for comparison."

"You might want to take that rope as well," remarked Thompson as he pointed to the wooden beams above.

Ward looked up. She observed a rope tied and wrapped around one of the beams near the back wall. Approximately six feet of rope hung down.

Ward looked at Thompson. "You don't think…."

"Yeah, I do," said Thompson. "He couldn't tie them to a post, so he tied them around the neck like a dog on a leash. He probably hung them right there after he was done with them."

Both just stood silent for several seconds.

"Okay," said Ward, "you collect that rope, and I'll bag the rope from this cabinet. Take any towels, clothing, or gloves you see that could contain DNA."

As they were completing their search and collection of possible evidence, Sheriff Johnson walked in. "We're done in the house. Did you find anything in here?"

"Yes," answered Ward. "I believe we have the type of rope he used to tie up his victims, and we recovered rope hanging from one of the beams. We've also collected some rags that could contain DNA."

"Good. Let's pack up and get out of here," replied Johnson.

"Has anyone seen Strawski?" asked Ward.

"Not yet. But if he doesn't want to be found, it will be difficult to find him in these forests. We need help from the community."

"What would you like us to do?" asked Ward.

"You can stay in this area in case he returns. My guess is he will have to come back for the money at some point."

"Yeah, we can do that," agreed Ward.

"I have officers in four quadrants of the county, and Sheriff Eagleman is doing the same in Newaygo County."

"I'm not even sure he's still in the state," Ward sighed.

"I think he is," replied Johnson.

"What makes you think that?"

"Marty is arrogant enough to think he can outsmart us. He knows how to survive in the wild, and I'll bet he thinks he can evade us forever."

"I worked with Marty," said Thompson. "And I think you're right. He has that arrogance that he's smarter than everyone else."

"Sheriff, do you have any ideas where we might look for Marty?" asked Ward.

"He could be anywhere, but I do recall him telling me about a hunting blind he built in the forest somewhere near Twin Lakes. Twin Lakes is about a twelve-mile drive from here."

"Thank you, Sheriff.

"Well, we need to get this evidence back and have it processed," replied Johnson.

After the Sheriff's officers had left, Ward sighed. "Do you think we should try searching around Twin Lakes?"

"Might as well," said Thompson. "According to Google Maps, Twin Lakes is off North Hamilton Road northwest of here."

Twin Lakes consisted of two small lakes. The smaller lake was just to the west of the larger lake. The smaller lake had approximately twelve cottages along the western shore.

The larger lake, east of the smaller one, was undeveloped. A thick canopy of forest trees surrounded the lakes.

The road from the main highway to Twin Lakes consisted of dirt and gravel. Thompson bypassed the smaller lake with the cottages. He parked their Explorer along the dirt road near the larger lake. From there, they would hike to the lake.

Ward and Thompson both grabbed the AR-15 rifles from the back of the car. Both also put bulletproof vests under their jackets. Thompson began to walk toward the lake, navigating through thick brush and fall-colored maple trees, as well as lush green pines. Ward followed him. After about fifty yards, the woods opened to a beautiful deep blue lake. The lake was small enough to see from one shoreline to the other. Everything was quiet except for the periodic rustling of leaves and the calls of birds in the trees.

"This is beautiful," observed Ward.

"It would be relaxing if we weren't hunting a mass murderer," replied Thompson.

"True," Ward nodded. "How are we going to find anyone in this massive forest?"

"If anyone is here, they will likely be near the lake for water and fishing. Let's follow the lake line from about forty yards out," Thompson suggested.

"Okay, let's go."

Thompson led the way as they quietly worked their way through trees and brush. The crunching of fallen leaves hindered their ability to move silently. After twenty minutes, they had only traveled 200 yards. Thompson stopped.

"We need a tracking dog," said Thompson. "This forest is just too thick. He could be hiding anywhere."

"You're right. We need an entire search team up here."

"I doubt the county would agree to that unless we have some proof Strawski is here. Let's face it, he might not even be in Michigan anymore."

"He's out here somewhere," replied Ward. "I can feel it."

"You can feel it?"

"It's my cop radar. I don't know if he's in the Twin Lakes area, but Marty is somewhere in the Michigan forest. He hasn't left the state. He's too bold for that. He probably feels he can hide in the forest for as long as necessary."

"Yeah, that makes sense," agreed Thompson

Seconds later, a loud, explosive "CRACK" filled the air, and the pine tree trunk next to Thompson's head exploded into chunks of bark, wood, and pine dust, causing both Thompson and Ward to jump.

Before they knew what had happened, another loud explosion filled the air. This time, Thompson was lifted from his feet as he flew backward, hitting the ground hard on his back. Ward dove to the ground, lying as flat as she could. She waited for another shot as Thompson writhed in pain. After several seconds, Ward belly crawled to Thompson. She could tell he was still gasping for breath.

Ward put her hand on Thompson. "Greg, where are you hit?"

Thompson tried to respond but was still attempting to catch his breath. Ward ran her hand over Thompson's torso, trying to find an entry wound. "Where are you hit?"

After gasping for breath a few more times, Thompson struggled to say, "He got me right in the chest plate."

Ward felt some relief knowing he had been hit in his bulletproof vest. Hitting the chest plate meant the bullet had hit the metal plate in the middle of his vest.

"Just relax, Greg. I'll get you out of here."

Ward pulled out her cell phone to dial 911. To her dismay, she had no signal. "Damn it!"

Between heavy breaths, Thompson said, "What is it?"

"I have no phone signal. I need to get back to the car."

"Go, I'll be okay," moaned Thompson through pained breaths.

"No, I'm not leaving you out here alone. I'll wait until you can at least crawl out of here. How bad does it hurt?"

"It feels like a horse kicked me in the chest," moaned Thompson.

Ward opened his jacket and shirt. She could see the bullet embedded in the middle of Thompson's vest. The bullet had flattened against the steel plate. Ward used her pocket knife to pry the bullet off the metal plate. She then placed the bullet in her pocket.

"Had this missed the plate, it would have gone through your vest," advised Ward.

"Guess I'm lucky," grunted Thompson as he moaned in pain.

"You might have a broken rib or two."

Thompson didn't respond. Ward attended to Thompson while lying next to him.

"I'm starting to shiver," whispered Thompson.

"Yeah, that's the shock setting in. I need to get you in a warm car and to the hospital. Do you think you can crawl with me?"

"Yeah, I believe so," replied Thompson.

"Okay, roll over. We need to belly crawl out of here."

Thompson groaned as he rolled over.

"Now, crawl on your elbows and keep your butt down."

Thompson nodded.

"I'll be right behind you."

Thompson began to belly crawl through the fallen leaves, rocks, and sticks. Ward followed directly behind him while often looking back to see if Strawski was following them. After about fifty yards of crawling, Ward got up on her knees and looked back. She scanned the woods for any signs of Strawski or anyone else following them. She could not see anyone.

"Greg, I think we can get up and walk now. I can help you."

"Okay, I'll try," Thompson groaned.

Ward stood up and scanned the woods again. Seeing no one, she helped Thompson to his feet. Thompson moaned as he stood.

"Can you walk?"

Between heavy breaths, Thompson said, "My chest hurts like hell, but yeah, I can walk."

"Then let's get out of here," Ward said, putting Thompson's arm around her shoulders.

Once they returned to the car, Ward used the car radio to request assistance.

"Chief Paula Ward here. I've got an injured officer. I believe the wanted suspect, Marty Strawski, shot at us on the east side of Twin Lakes. Where is the nearest hospital?"

Another officer radioed back, "Reed City is the nearest hospital."

"Please advise them I'm en route with an injured officer."

Hearing the radio transmissions, Sheriff Johnson began to organize a search party for the Twin Lakes area. He contacted Newaygo County Sheriff Joe Eagleman for assistance.

With lights blazing and siren screaming, Ward drove as fast as she could to the hospital in Reed City. Thompson sat in the passenger seat with his hands clutched to his chest.

"It's painful to breathe," moaned Thompson.

"Hang in there, Greg. We're almost there."

Upon arrival, they were met at the emergency entrance by a female nurse and a male orderly. The nurse and orderly helped Thompson out of the car and into a wheelchair. He was then wheeled into the emergency entrance. Ward parked the car and then walked to the emergency room. She flashed her badge to the desk nurse and asked where Thompson was. Ward was directed to examination room number three. When she entered the room, a nurse was taking Thompson's pulse, and an I.V. was already dripping fluid into his left arm.

"How is he?" asked Ward.

"His heart rate is irregular, skin is clammy, and he has rapid, shallow breathing."

"What does that mean?"

"He's in shock. This IV will help calm him down and should bring his breathing closer to normal. He's in a lot of pain right now."

"I can imagine," said Ward. "He just took a high-powered rifle shot to the chest."

"We already have an x-ray scheduled for internal injuries. You look a bit rattled yourself."

"I suppose," agreed Ward. "I thought he was dying."

"Is this about the man the whole county is searching for?"

"Yes. Marty Strawski."

"If you'd like, there's a lounge down the hall. You can get a coffee or something," the nurse said.

"Thank you. I think I will."

Ward was sweaty, and her adrenaline rush was beginning to fade. Once she found the lounge, Ward removed her heavy jacket and bulletproof vest. She then poured herself a black coffee. Ward turned her portable radio back on and could hear officers coordinating a search for Strawski. A perimeter was being set up around the Twin Lakes area.

Ward had dealt with plenty of dangerous suspects during her time in Lansing, but she had never experienced being on a scene where an officer was shot. Once her adrenalin subsided, Ward felt nauseous, and her hands began to shake. Sipping the hot coffee helped.

Ward continued to listen to the radio. A perimeter had been established, but searching was difficult. It was clear the Sheriff was being cautious, not wanting another officer shot. As Ward listened to the radio chatter, a female county deputy walked into the room.

"Hi, Chief. I'm Deputy Howard. How are you doing?"

"I've been better."

"I'm sure. The Sheriff wanted to get some more information from you. They want to narrow down the search area. Where were you when Detective Thompson was shot?"

"We had parked on a dirt road south of the easternmost lake," explained Ward. "We then began hiking into the woods on the east side of the lake, probably forty yards from the shoreline. We only got about two hundred yards when Greg was shot. There were two shots. The first one hit a tree next to Greg's head. Before we could even react, a second shot hit him square in the chest."

"That must have been horrible. This will give the Sheriff a good idea of where to start the search. I will relay this information to the Sheriff, then I'll sit with you."

"That's not necessary," insisted Ward.

"It's by order of my Sheriff. He wants someone with you."

Ward smiled. "Thank you."

Ward spent some time telling Deputy Howard about the case of the three missing teenagers in Swartz Creek. She told Howard how three children and a dog named Roxy had helped in finding the buried body of Mike Taggert, which then led to the discovery of the other two victims.

After about forty minutes, a dark-skinned doctor with wavy black hair, dressed in a white jacket, walked into the room.

"Hello, I'm Doctor Hinduja. Detective Thompson is going to be just fine."

"Thank goodness," sighed Ward.

"He does have two broken ribs and a contusion to his heart. We will be keeping him for at least twenty-four hours for observation."

"Can I see him?" asked Ward.

"Yes. He is being assigned a room. Once he is in, a nurse will come get you."

"Thank you, Doctor."

Chapter 21

Sheriffs Johnson and Eagleman were coordinating the search of the Twin Lakes area. Specially trained SWAT officers were leading the search. Because the tree canopy created a dark environment, the SWAT team used infrared scopes to locate heat generated by mammals. This allowed them to see a human that may otherwise be hidden in the forest. The sky was overcast, making it even darker. The process was slow and dangerous.

It was late-afternoon, and there was no sign of Strawski or any other human in the area. Not wanting the search to extend into the night, the Sheriffs were discussing how much longer to continue. Moments later, an officer came on the radio announcing they had found the site where Strawski had been camping. Remnants of a campfire, flattened grass and leaves, and some trash were left behind. Further searching located an off-road trail with fresh tire tracks only forty yards from the abandoned campsite.

"The tracks look like truck tracks," one officer announced over the radio.

Sheriff Johnson radioed, "Collect the trash for possible DNA. Also, take close-up photos of the tire tracks for comparison."

"He's probably no longer in these woods," suggested Eagleman. "If he had his truck, he is far gone by now."

Johnson nodded. "Yep, it's time to call off this search."

Over the radio, Johnson announced the search was over.

Back at the hospital, Ward and Deputy Howard were in Thompson's room. It had been several hours, and the drugs given to Thompson had subdued his chest pain. Through her earpiece, Howard heard the command to end the search.

"The search is over for tonight," Howard announced. "They will re-group in the morning."

"They didn't find anything?" asked Ward.

"Yeah, they found his campsite, but he had already packed up and left."

"Damn," muttered Ward. "Will they go back out again tomorrow?"

"I'm sure they will, Chief. Sheriff Johnson is determined to catch this monster."

"As am I," Ward replied.

Thompson looked at Ward. "There's nothing more for you to do here. Go and help find Strawski."

"Are you sure?" asked Ward.

"Yes. I'm in good hands here."

Ward rose, grabbed Thompson's hand, then squeezed it. "We're going to find him."

It was after 5:00 pm when Ward arrived back at the motel. Her Ford Explorer was still parked in front of her room. She parked Thompson's Explorer next to hers. Once in the room, Ward threw her jacket onto one of the chairs and flopped back onto the bed. She let out a sigh and closed her eyes. It wasn't long before Ward was fast asleep.

At 5:50 pm, Ward was awakened by her cell phone buzzing. It was Sheriff Eagleman calling.

"Hello, Sheriff."

"Paula, we're organizing a large search party for tomorrow, following a media blitz asking for help from the public. I'm assuming you want to be part of that?"

"Yes, of course. Where and when?"

"We're all meeting at my office in White Cloud at nine in the morning."

"I'll be there."

"Are you still at the motel?"

"Yes."

"Well, get a good night's sleep."

"Thank you, Sheriff."

After the call, Ward realized she was very hungry. She hadn't eaten since breakfast. She walked down to the office and found the same older woman wearing the same Ferris State sweatshirt sitting behind the desk.

"What can I do for you?" asked the woman.

"Is there someplace close where I can get a decent meal?"

"Drive five miles south to Skillet Road. There's a blinking yellow light above the intersection. Turn right on Skillet and go about two miles. On the right-hand side will be Moon Dog's Diner. The food is good."

"Moon Dog's?"

"Yep. And be sure to dress up a bit. It's kind of high class."

"Huh?" Ward frowned.

The woman laughed. "I'm just pullin' your leg. But be sure to try a slice of the pecan pie for dessert."

"Thank you for the information," smiled Ward as she walked out. Following the woman's directions, Ward quickly found Moon Dog's Diner. The outside was painted a bright light blue with bright orange trim. *Quite noticeable,* thought Ward. A lighted sign on a single pole near the road had Moon Dog's Diner written in red neon lights. On the front of the diner was a screened-in porch with picnic tables. Inside, the restaurant had booths with light blue vinyl bench seats along the outside walls. Smaller silver-framed square tables with four matching chairs filled the center of the restaurant. Large ceiling fans hung from the ceiling.

Ward took a seat in one of the booths to afford her some privacy. A young, dark-haired waitress approached her.

"Are you here for our special?"

"What is the special?"

"Every Friday, we have all-you-can-eat fish and chips."

"What type of fish?"

"Lake perch."

"Yes, I'll take the fish and chips and a Diet Coke."

After ordering, Ward called Thompson's cell phone. To her mild surprise, he answered it.

"How are you doing?" asked Ward.

"They're keeping me full of pain pills, so I'm feeling quite well for being shot."

"Good to hear. Are you still getting out tomorrow?"

"As far as I know."

"We're going out on a county-wide search tomorrow. Johnson and Eagleman are putting it together."

"I wish I could be there."

"You just get well. You'll be out there soon enough. Let me know when they're releasing you, and I'll either come or have someone else pick you up."

"Sounds good."

"Sleep well, Greg."

As she finished her call, the food arrived. Three perch filets, fries, and coleslaw. The fish was crispy on the outside, tender on the inside, and perfectly seasoned. The fries were thin and crispy, just as Ward preferred. *That old woman was right. They do have good food here,* Ward thought.

After she had finished, Ward thought about ordering a slice of pecan pie but decided she was too full to eat it. After paying, Ward drove back to her motel for the night.

On Saturday morning, Ward showered and dressed before calling Thompson. "How are you feeling today?"

"The pain in my chest isn't so bad, but my upper body and arms are sore. The doctor said that was normal for the type of shock I took to the chest."

"When will you be released?"

"After the doctor checks me one more time. He said early afternoon."

"How long is the recovery time?"

"The doc said I can't work for six weeks. He wants the ribs well healed. He also referred me to a heart specialist in Flint."

"Are they worried about your heart?"

"No. He just wants a doctor to make sure there's no permanent damage."

"If I can't drive you back, I'll find someone who can."

"Thank you, Chief. Now go find Strawski."

"We intend to."

Ward arrived at the Sheriff's Office in White Cloud by 8:50 am. By nine, everyone had gathered in the conference room. Sheriff Johnson led the meeting.

"We're going to divide north Newaygo County and south Lake County into four quadrants," announced Johnson.

"We believe that at some point, he may try to return to his home. Should he return, I want a team of officers hidden near the house."

Sheriffs Johnson and Eagleman then assigned officers to the quadrants in their respective counties. Ward was not included.

"Chief Ward," said Johnson. "Where would you like to be today?"

"I think I'd like to be near his home. I also believe he'll return at some point."

"Okay," said Johnson. "Wherever we locate Strawski, we'll send additional officers to assist. Now, let's move out."

Ward followed the four vehicles carrying the team of eight SWAT officers assigned to Strawski's home. SWAT Commander Joe Wilson was in charge of the team. The team pulled onto a dirt road approximately a mile from Strawski's driveway. Once they were out of sight from the main road, everyone parked and gathered around the Commander.

"We're going to walk in from here. I want to clear these woods as best we can. Chief, why don't you go with Sgt. Connor and his team. Sergeant, I want you to approach from the southeast. Cover as much as you can. The rest of us will come in from the southwest. Stay out of sight, and no one will approach the house until I say so. Be careful. There could be booby traps the closer you get to the house."

Booby traps? Thought Ward. *I've never had to deal with that before!*

Each officer carried an AR-15 rifle. SWAT Sergeant Connor, assigned to Ward's team, took the lead. Ward followed behind Connor and the other three officers, one of whom was Officer Calkins, another female officer.

"We need to spread out to cover more area," said Connor. Sweep the woods as you go and watch for booby traps. Now spread out and cover as much as you can. When you see the house, stop and take cover."

Ward gingerly walked through the thick woods frightened by the thought there could be booby traps. Ward thought this was what it must be like when soldiers are in combat zones. The team was making good progress with no sign of Strawski.

Connor was in constant communication with the other team, which was led by Commander Joe Wilson. They had not yet seen any sign of Strawski.

After another twenty minutes, Wilson advised Connor that his team had a visual of the south side of the Strawski cabin. They would hold tight until Connor's team had visual as well. As they grew closer, Ward could feel her adrenaline level rising. She was thankful for the heavy-duty vest and helmet the SWAT team had loaned her.

"We found a camera," said Wilson over the radio. "He probably knows we're here."

"Copy," said Connor. He then motioned for his team to be on the lookout for cameras. Each member looked into the trees around them. Moments later, they heard a loud KA-BOOM!

"What was that?" shouted one of the other officers.

"That was a gunshot!" yelled Connor. "Everyone down!"

KABOOM! Three seconds passed. KABOOM! Another three seconds. KABOOM!

"It's coming from the front of the cabin!" shouted Wilson over the radio.

"Come on," waved Connor. "We need to reach the cabin."

Each officer rose and moved quickly in the direction of the gunshots. They ran hunched over at the waist to make themselves a smaller target. It was only another two minutes until Ward saw the front top half of the cabin through the trees.

Every three seconds, another ear-piercing shot rang out through the forest. Once the house was in view, each officer took cover behind a tree or a large rock.

"The shots are coming from the front picture window," announced Wilson. "It looks like he removed the glass."

KABOOM!.......KABOOM!.......KABOOM!

The shots kept ringing out every three seconds, spraying whizzing bullets through the forest.

Ward watched and listened as an occasional bullet whizzed above her head. It appeared and sounded like the bullets were being shot randomly in the direction of the officers. Ward waited for the next shot. Once she heard it, she got up and, in a hunched-over position, ran to a spot that gave her a better look at the window. She quickly flopped back down into a prone position. KABOOM! Another shot rang out just after she lay down. Ward wasn't sure, but it sounded like the bullets were flying closer to the ground than previously.

"We've got eyes on the window," announced Wilson. "It looks like an automatic rifle on a swivel stand. We do not have eyes on the suspect."

An automatic gun on a stand? Thought Ward.

Connor used his binoculars to look into the window. "The Commander is right. I can't see anyone operating the gun. It's sitting on a tripod and moving from side to side as it fires. It's either on a timer, or someone is operating it remotely."

A rifle operated remotely? Now that's different, Ward thought.

Ward could hear sirens in the distance. Having heard the radio traffic to dispatch, officers were on their way to help. Wilson heard them as well and got on the radio. "All officers need to stay back. We have an active shooting situation that is not contained. I repeat, all officers keep out of sight."

Ward agreed with the Commander's decision. She could imagine multiple officers being shot as they drove or ran into the scene.

KABOOM!...KABOOM!...KABOOM!

The shots were now more rapid, and bullets were barely above the officer's heads. Ward heard one bullet strike the base of a tree only ten feet away.

KABOOM!

"Officer shot!" screamed Calkins. Ward quickly raised her head to get a look. Only forty feet to her right was a SWAT officer screaming in pain. She could see Calkins run in a hunched-over position to his aid. Once she reached the officer, she slid onto the ground and lay beside him. Ward could see Calkins trying to stop the bleeding on the injured officer's right shoulder.

Once Commander Wilson heard an officer had already been shot, he decided to attack the cabin. His team would approach from the side of the house, out of sight from the front window. They would then crawl across the porch to the door and the open window. The plan was to blow open the front door while simultaneously throwing flash bangs into the front window. If someone were in the room operating the gun, the flash bangs would disorient him enough to allow the officers to take control.

It's a good plan if it works, thought Ward. Ward then belly crawled to the injured officer to see if she could help. An occasional bullet buzzed over her body as she crawled.

"How is he?" asked Ward.

"His shoulder is a mess," replied Officer Calkins while holding a blood-soaked washcloth-sized gauze pad on his shoulder.

The wounded officer had his eyes closed. Ward could hear his heavy breathing. She was amazed he wasn't crying out in pain.

"It's the adrenaline and shock helping him right now," Calkins said.

Ward flinched as another shot hit a nearby tree. "Anything I can do to help?"

"Yes. Keep an eye on the shooter while I keep him as comfortable as I can."

Ward nodded.

Wilson's team carefully approached the cabin from the south side. Each officer had his assignment. Two of them would breach the door, while Wilson and a second officer would belly crawl to the window, then throw four flash bangs into the home. One is usually enough to disorient someone. Four could knock a person unconscious.

Connor and his officers were pinned down. They could only watch and hope the plan worked. Connor watched through his field glasses. He announced the team's progress as they approached.

"They're at the side of the house," said Connor.

To Ward, it seemed like time was moving slowly. She waited for the next update.

"Okay, they're on the porch now," advised Connor. "They're belly crawling. At the front door. Looks like they are about ready."

Ward was not in a position to see the front of the cabin. She could only listen to Connor's narrative.

BAM!

BAM! BAM! BAM! BAM!

A succession of explosions rang through the forest. Then there was silence. Seconds passed.

"Officers are inside the home," announced Connor.

Again, silence. The shots whizzing above their heads and into the trees had stopped. Everyone waited. The seconds ticked away, and then the minutes.

Connor shouted to his team, "Don't worry. No sound is good."

Ward raised her head to get a better look. She couldn't see all of the window, but did see smoke emanating from it.

"All is clear," announced Wilson. "Suspect is not here."

"What?" shouted Ward. "How could he not be there?"

No one answered. Connor got on the radio, requesting immediate emergency assistance for the injured officer.

"They're going to come down the driveway," said Conner. "Can he walk?"

"I don't think so," replied Officer Calkins. "His shoulder is bad."

"Okay, you two stay with him. The two of us will meet the ambulance and bring the EMTs to you."

It took about twenty minutes before the ambulance and paramedics could reach the wounded officer. Once he was loaded on a tram, Ward walked to the cabin where numerous officers were now gathered. She walked up to Commander Wilson.

"What's the story?"

"He's not here. The gun was on a remotely controlled tripod and swivel. Go look at the setup. He even had a camera mounted on top of the gun. I don't know the range on his signal, but he could be anywhere."

"How did he know we were in the woods?"

"We found a camera mounted up high in a tree. I'm sure that's not the only one out here. Strawski was probably monitoring us and remotely operating the gun."

"But we were just here yesterday."

"He probably came back last night to set this all up. We should have had someone watching the house all night. I think everyone thought he was on the run."

Ward sighed. "I should have asked for surveillance. Now, another officer has been shot."

"No one thought anything like this would happen," Wilson assured her.

"Will you have officers assigned here now?"

"Yes. I'll make sure of it."

"Thank you, Commander."

After talking with the commander, Ward sought Sheriff Johnson. She found him in the driveway talking to several other officers. Johnson looked at Ward as she approached.

"How's the officer doing?" asked Ward.

"He'll live, but I'm not sure he'll be able to work as an officer again."

"I'm so sorry."

"This asshole mayor of yours is a raging maniac."

"He was never my mayor, Sheriff. He's a sick individual who needs to be stopped. What's the plan?"

"We're setting up a command post at the Lutheran church in Baldwin. Meet me and Sheriff Eagleman there at eleven-thirty."

"I'll be there," Ward assured him.

Chapter 22

After trudging back to her car through the woods, Ward removed her heavy outer vest and helmet. The cool air felt refreshing as Ward grabbed a bottled water from the car and chugged it down. She then called Detective Thompson.

"Are you still getting out today?" asked Ward.

"Yes, but after watching the news, I'm not sure I want to leave. Is it true Strawski had a remotely operated rifle?"

"Yes, Greg, it's true. I've never seen anything like it. It was an automatic rifle on a tripod being operated remotely."

"I heard another officer was shot. Is he okay?"

"He will live, but I wouldn't say he is okay. His shoulder was badly damaged."

"Oh, god," moaned Thompson. "Do we know where Strawski is?"

"Nope. There have been no credible sightings of him or his truck. People are calling in on every black Ford pickup truck they see. The Sheriffs have a meeting scheduled for eleven-thirty this morning in Baldwin. I'll head there soon to see what the plan is. When do you get released?"

"Sometime around noon."

"I'll come get you after our meeting."

"I can get a ride back to the motel."

"Don't be silly. Just text me once they're ready to discharge you."

Ward arrived at the Lutheran church fifteen minutes before eleven-thirty. Multiple police vehicles from the Lake and Newaygo County Sheriff's Departments were already in the parking lot. Several state police cars were also there. When she walked through the double doors to the church, Ward was directed to a large activities room. Sheriff Johnson was already there. Dozens of chairs and a podium had been arranged for a presentation. Several officers were already seated. Ward walked up to Johnson.

"Is there anything you want me to say or do?"

"Unless you have information to add, I don't think that will be necessary, but thanks."

Ward nodded, then found herself a seat in the first row. A poster containing recovered photographs of Strawski sat on an easel at the front of the room. Once everyone had arrived, Sheriff Eagleman joined Johnson at the front of the group. Johnson led the discussion by first giving a synopsis of what had occurred at the Strawski property. He then provided an update on Officer Howard, the SWAT officer shot in the shoulder. Howard had just been moved from surgery to the recovery room. No other information was available. He then began describing the next steps.

"We've gotten sightings from three separate civilians on Strawski's black Ford pickup."

Upon hearing this, Ward sat up straight with her full attention on what Johnson would say next.

"All three sightings came from Lake County. One from near his cabin early this morning, prior to the arrival of our SWAT team. A second report was received two hours later from Three Mile Road. Finally, he was spotted at a gas station in Wahalla, several miles west of Twin Lakes. That was about an hour ago. Officers were dispatched to each location, but obviously, he has not been found. Based on these reports, we have established a broad perimeter on the west side of Lake County. Officers have been stationed on major roadways. We have a combined SWAT team of sixteen officers who will be actively patrolling inside the perimeter. They will be doubled up in eight patrol cars. Sheriff Eagleman and I will also be out looking for Mr. Strawski. Chief, you can ride with me."

Ward nodded.

Sheriff Eagleman then spoke about the danger Strawski presented to officers.

"Be very cautious in how you approach him or his vehicle. He's already shot two officers. We don't need any more casualties. If you see him, keep him under surveillance until help arrives. He's a very dangerous individual."

Johnson then paired up the SWAT officers and dismissed the meeting.

Ward approached Johnson to remind him of Detective Greg Thompson's pending release from the hospital. "I was planning on picking him up and taking him back to the motel until I could arrange a ride back to his home."

"If you don't want to go out with me, that's fine."

"No, I do. I want to be there for Strawski's arrest. I was hoping you could arrange for someone to pick Greg up."

"Sure, that's no problem. I'll let dispatch know."

"Thank you, Sheriff. I'll call Greg to let him know. I'll meet you at your car in a few minutes."

Ten minutes later, Ward and Johnson were out on patrol. "Was Greg okay with you not meeting him?" asked Johnson.

"Oh, yeah. He wants us to catch Strawski as much as anyone," replied Ward. "I'll see him tonight at the motel."

"How's he feeling?"

"Much better. They have him on pain medication, so that helps. The ribs are very sore."

"I can imagine," agreed Johnson. "Have you eaten since breakfast?"

"No."

"There's a drive-thru just ahead. I'll stop there."

Johnson turned into an independent burger drive-thru on the right side of the road. The name was Louie's Burgers. Each of them ordered a hamburger and a soda. They continued down the road, with Johnson holding his burger in his left hand as he steered with his right.

Ward had just finished her burger when the radio came to life with a report of a Strawski sighting. A caller reported seeing an older white male driving a black Ford pickup matching the description of Strawski's truck in the parking lot of a plumbing supply store. Officers were headed that way.

"Hang on," said Johnson as he punched the accelerator, causing their cruiser to lurch forward. Johnson flipped on his lights and siren. Ward listened intently to the radio.

Officers arrived within minutes and surrounded the perimeter of the plumbing store. The license plate on the black pick-up matched that of Marty Strawski.

"I hope there isn't another shootout," said Ward, concerned over more people being injured. She continued to listen to the radio traffic.

Johnson and Ward arrived as officers were shouting instructions to the white-haired man who had just stepped out of the store carrying a plastic bag.

"Get on the ground! Get on the ground, now!"

Ward could see the man was dressed in a red plaid long-sleeved shirt, blue jeans and brown work boots. After some initial confusion, the man got onto his knees, then laid face down on the pavement as instructed. Officers quickly approached, then handcuffed his hands behind his back.

Ward and Johnson then walked into the perimeter. As they grew closer, Ward realized this man was not Marty Strawski.

Ward turned to the Sheriff. "That's not Marty."

"Huh? What do you mean?"

"I mean, that's not Marty Strawski. I don't know who that is, but it's not Marty."

"Isn't that his truck?" asked Johnson.

"Yes, but the man is not Strawski."

Johnson sighed. "You've got to be kidding me."

"I wish I were."

After frisking the man and finding no weapons, officers hoisted him to his feet and then obtained his identification from his wallet. His driver's license identified him as George Polanski.

Ward and Johnson walked up as a Sergeant was questioning the man.

"Where did you get this truck?"

"A guy traded it to me for my truck."

"What guy?"

"His name was Marty Straw or something like that. I have a bill of sale in my truck."

Officers quickly searched the truck and found a bill of sale from Marty Strawski.

The Sergeant continued. "You traded your truck for his truck?"

"Yes. This truck was much nicer than mine. He said he needed an older truck to haul something. He would rather trade his than ruin it. I thought he was crazy, but it was a great deal for me."

"What type of truck did you trade?"

"Mine was a brown Chevy pickup. It was much older than his and had a lot more miles. And the right back fender had some damage."

Chief Ward stepped forward. "Haven't you heard about the statewide search for Marty Strawski?"

"Huh?"

"Marty Strawski! He's wanted for murder and shooting two police officers. You didn't know that?"

Polansky shook his head. "I'm a farmer. I spend very little time watching TV. I'd never heard of Marty Strawski until we traded trucks."

"Didn't you think it was strange he wanted to trade a much newer truck for yours?"

"Of course. But he wanted to trade, so I did."

Ward shook her head and stepped back. "What the hell is going on here? I feel like I've stepped into the Twilight Zone or something."

"I know how you feel," replied Johnson.

"We probably have nine murdered young males, two officers shot, a surreal remote-controlled automatic rifle attack, and a sixty-one-year-old man who can't be found," grumbled Ward. "Then, he finds the only person in the state who hasn't heard of him and trades for his truck. Unbelievable."

A tow truck arrived to take Strawski's truck as evidence. Sheriff Johnson knew this would cause a scene. He moved over to be near Polanski, who was protesting the towing of his new truck.

"You can't take this! This is my truck now."

"Mr. Polansky," said Johnson. "I'm sorry, but we have to take the truck. It is evidence in a major crime investigation."

"How was I supposed to know that?" protested Polansky. "I need my truck to do my work!"

"Unfortunately, there's nothing I can do about that. This truck is evidence, and we must take it into our possession."

"Who's in charge here!" shouted Polansky.

"That would be me," responded Johnson. "I'm the Sheriff in this county."

"If you're the Sheriff, can't you help me?"

"We will do our best to find your truck and return it to you. Your truck was fraudulently taken from you. Contact your insurance company. In the meantime, I'll try to find a dealership that could loan you a used truck."

This appeared to calm Polansky down. "All right. Thank you, Sheriff. I really need a truck."

"I understand."

An officer then took Polansky to his patrol car to get more details about the trade for Strawski's truck.

As Johnson and Ward were preparing to leave, Sheriff Eagleman showed up.

"Did I hear correctly that Strawski traded out his truck?"

"You sure did," replied Johnson. "We're now looking for a twelve-year-old brown Chevy pick-up."

"Damn," muttered Eagleman.

"I'll say," agreed Ward. "We need to get this out to every officer and news organization."

"We're already on it," said Johnson. "Officers have been updated, and I have someone working on a new press release as we speak."

Ward nodded. "We need as many officers patrolling as available. Why don't you drop me off at my car, and I'll go out on patrol."

"Are you sure?" asked Johnson.

"Yes, we can cover more area that way."

Johnson dropped Ward off near her white Explorer. Ward then called Thompson's cell phone as she drove south toward Newaygo County.

"Hello?" answered Thompson.

"Greg, are you still at the hospital?"

"No. I was just dropped off at the motel ten minutes ago."

"Oh, good. I'm headed that way. I'll see you in about fifteen minutes."

Upon her arrival at the Pines Motel, Ward knocked on Thompson's door. "Come on in!" shouted Thompson.

When Ward opened the door, she found Thompson dressed and lying on top of his bed.

"How are you feeling?" asked Ward.

"Better than yesterday. But it still hurts to breathe heavily or bend over. The medication helps."

"I'm going to arrange a ride back to Swartz Creek for you."

"No, no. Let me stay here. I can rest here. I want to listen to the radio traffic. And who knows, you might not find Marty for days. I should be okay to drive in a day or two."

Ward chuckled. "I'm not giving you clearance to do any patrolling until you are fully recovered."

"I can at least make any phone calls you need. I'll go crazy not knowing what's going on up here."

"All right. So long as you stay here at the motel. I'd like you to monitor the news reports. It's always good to know what others are saying."

"Thank you, Chief."

"Can I get you anything to eat?"

"A sandwich and a large Coke would taste great."

"I'll go see what I can find and be right back."

Ward drove to Moon Dog's diner and ordered a pulled pork sandwich, some fries, and two large Cokes to go. When she returned to the motel, the time was 4:30 pm.

"Pulled pork? That's great. Thank you, Chief."

"Anything on the news?" asked Ward.

"Nah, just rehashing today's events. No reports of any sightings."

"Yeah, no news from the police chatter either. But the Sheriff's still have them out looking."

"Where's your sandwich?" asked Thompson.

"I ate not too long ago. A Coke is all I need right now."

"Are you going back out?"

"No. It's been one hell of a day, and I'm exhausted. I will relax while I monitor the radio, then try to get a good night's sleep."

"All right. Thanks for the sandwich, Chief."

Ward smiled and nodded as she left the room.

Chapter 23

It was early Sunday morning, and Chief Ward had just finished dressing for the day. Given that her uniform was dirty from the past two days of action, Ward dressed in civilian clothing. She wore a light blue blouse with a dark blue blazer to cover her firearm and handcuffs. Her first task was to check on Thompson. She hoped he was feeling well enough to go out for some breakfast. Otherwise, she would have to bring him something back to eat. After securing her weapon, Ward opened the door.

To her surprise and horror, the barrel end of a shotgun was shoved in her face. Ward froze.

"Get back inside," demanded Strawski.

"Take it easy, Marty," said Ward as she stepped backward into the motel room. Strawski followed her in and shut the door.

"Hold it right there," Strawski commanded.

Ward stopped with her arms in the air. "Take it easy, Marty. What are you planning to do?"

Strawski put the barrel end of the shotgun under Ward's chin. Ward swallowed hard.

"Don't move," said Strawski as he reached under Ward's jacket with his left hand and removed Ward's semi-automatic handgun from her waist. He tucked the gun behind him in his waistband. As he did, Ward could see he had a Smith and Wesson semi-auto handgun strapped to his right side.

"Now sit down on the bed," demanded Strawski.

Ward sat on the edge of the mattress. "What's your plan here, Marty?"

"You're getting me out of here."

"How am I going to do that?"

"By driving me to Chicago."

"Marty, there are officers everywhere looking for you and your brown truck."

"We're not taking my truck. You're going to drive me in your pretty white Explorer."

"You know I can't do that, Marty."

"You will or I'll fill your head with buckshot. And then I'll go get Thompson next door to do it."

Ward stared at Strawski for several seconds. "This is not going to work, Marty."

"Not for you if you don't do as I say," growled Strawski.

Ward could tell Strawski was serious. "Okay," agreed Ward. "I'll take you to Chicago."

Ward noticed Strawski was wearing a thick gray hoodie sweatshirt and jeans that looked soiled. He also wore brown hiking boots. The boots had dried mud around the edges of the soles.

"I need to tell Detective Thompson I'm leaving," Ward informed him.

Strawski huffed. "You ain't telling anyone. Just grab your keys and let's get going."

Ward's keys were on the round table in the kitchen area. She pointed toward them.

"Get the key!" Strawski huffed.

Ward slowly moved toward the table and, using her right hand, she picked up her car keys. Strawski then motioned for Ward to go outside. Ward slowly walked to the door, opened it, and walked outside with Strawski following. She got to the driver's side door of the Explorer and stopped.

"Get inside," demanded Strawski.

"Marty, don't do this. You're making a big mistake."

"I SAID get inside!"

Ward climbed into the driver's seat of the Explorer. Strawski then walked around the front bumper with his shotgun still pointed at Ward's head. He then opened the passenger door and got in. He set the shotgun on his right side against the door. Strawski then took Ward's handgun from the back of his waistband and placed it in his lap, his right hand holding it with the barrel pointed at Ward.

"Start the car," demanded Strawski.

"You don't have to keep that gun pointed at me," protested Ward.

"Yeah, I do. Now start the car and let's get going."

Ward started up the Explorer, then backed out.

"Go south," said Strawski.

Ward pulled out of the motel parking lot and headed south on Highway 37 toward Newaygo.

After several miles of silence, Ward spoke up. "What did you do with your new brown truck?"

"It's parked in the trees behind your little motel."

"Marty, just give it up. Otherwise, this is going to end in a bad way."

"Chief, just shut up and drive."

Back at the motel, Thompson was awake after his first good sleep since the shooting. He was still sore, but generally feeling much better. He looked at his cell phone and saw it was already eight-thirty. He was surprised that Ward hadn't yet checked on him. Thompson stepped outside and noticed Ward's white Explorer was gone. He figured she must have gone to get some breakfast. He then noticed the door to her room was slightly ajar. *That's strange,* thought Thompson. He placed his right hand on the door and slowly pushed it open.

"Chief, are you in here?"

Thompson got no response. He stepped into the room and looked around. He observed her uniform pants and shirt hanging over a chair, and her suitcase was on the small couch. Thompson pulled out his cell phone and punched in Ward's phone number. The phone rang until it went to voicemail.

"Chief, it's Greg. I'm just calling to be sure everything is okay. Give me a call back."

Meanwhile, Ward attempted to pull information out of Strawski as she continued south on Highway 37. "Where are we going?"

"I told you, Chicago. Just keep driving south to Grand Rapids."

The two then sat silently for the next ten minutes until Ward started to ask more questions.

"Marty, I have to know. Why did you kill those boys?"

Strawski turned and glared at Ward for a couple of seconds. Ward shuddered at the intensity of his stare.

"Why do you think I killed anyone?"

Ward was surprised at Strawski's response. "We know you did, Marty. We recovered your DNA from some of the victims, and we found your photographs."

After a moment of silence, Strawski spoke. "I liked those boys. In some ways, they reminded me of myself as an awkward teenager. I never intended to harm those boys."

"Marty, you did terrible things to them. You tied them up and strangled them!"

"Not all of them," replied Strawski.

"There were more?" asked Ward.

"I liked helping teenage boys. You know, Chief, I mentored many teenage boys over the years. Most of them moved on to have good lives."

"And the ones who didn't?"

"Yeah, sometimes it just didn't work out. I'd never survive in prison. I did what I had to do."

"You had to molest and murder teenage boys?"

"I never molested those boys," protested Strawski.

"The evidence and photographs tell a different story."

"Yeah, well, you can't believe everything, right Chief?"

Ward couldn't hold back the grimace on her face. She wanted to reach over and choke the life out of Strawski.

It was now 9:15 am, and Thompson still had not heard from Chief Ward. He decided to call Sheriff Eagleman.

"Hey, Sheriff. It's Detective Greg Thompson."

"Hello, Greg. Sounds like you're feeling better."

"I am, thank you. The reason I'm calling is that Chief Ward left without saying anything to me, which is unusual. I thought she might have gone for breakfast, but it's been almost an hour. Her car is gone, so I thought she might be with you at a meeting or something."

"No, we haven't had any meetings today. We're going to meet at noon."

"Have you heard from her?"

"No. Did you try calling her?" asked Eagleman.

"Yes, but I'm not getting an answer. I also found her motel door slightly ajar."

"I'm sure she's fine. But I'll put out a request to officers to look for her Explorer and have her give you a call."

"Great, thank you, Sheriff."

Ward and Strawski were about halfway to Grand Rapids. "When we get to Grand Rapids, I want you to take I-196 south. We'll follow it to I-94 south toward Chicago," Strawski instructed.

"What's in Chicago?" asked Ward.

"My escape."

"The whole country will be looking for you, Marty. What's your plan?"

"You must think I'm stupid. I'm not telling you my plan."

"No, I don't think you're stupid, Marty. That automated machine gun trap was something else."

"You know I could see you guys remotely, right?"

"Yes. How did you do that?"

"Not that hard. With the right equipment and cameras, you can do almost anything."

Ward hoped she could convince Strawski to stop for gas and a bathroom break while in Grand Rapids. It would be her best chance to escape.

"Hey, we're below a half tank of gas, and I'm going to need to use a bathroom soon. Can we stop in Grand Rapids?"

Strawski glared at Ward. "Nice try, Chief. You want to stop in a busy area with people and police nearby. You'll be fine until we get through Grand Rapids and into a more remote area."

Meanwhile, Thompson knew something was wrong. Ward would not have left without letting him know, and too much time had passed without her calling someone. Thompson decided to have a look around. He checked the parking lot for any evidence. There was nothing out of the ordinary. He then went to the motel office and found a twenty-something white male with blond hair working the desk. After introducing himself, Thompson asked, "Have you seen Chief Ward this morning?"

"Who is Chief Ward?" asked the clerk.

"She's the Chief of Police who has been staying at this motel for the last two days. We are looking for a serial killer in this area. Does that ring a bell?"

"Oh, yeah. Um, I haven't seen any police officers this morning."

"How about a woman in her forties, slim build, with dark red hair?"

"No, I've only checked out two people this morning, and neither fit that description."

"Okay, thank you."

Thompson left the office and began walking around the motel property. *Something is wrong,* thought Thompson. As he walked, he looked into every parked vehicle. He then walked around to the back of the motel. An open area of gravel, grasses, and weeds separated the motel from the thick woods. Thompson scanned the ground as he slowly walked around. He then looked up and was surprised to see an older brown Chevy pickup parked against the trees. Thompson moved as quickly as he could without causing too much pain toward the truck. *This matches the description of the truck Strawski traded for.*

Thompson couldn't believe it. His fears were accurate. Ward was in trouble. Thompson reached for his phone and called Sheriff Eagleman.

"Sheriff, this is Detective Thompson again. I believe Chief Ward has been taken hostage by our suspect."

"What? How do you know that?" asked Eagleman.

"She's gone, her car is gone, and there is an older brown Chevy pickup parked behind the motel."

"What's the license plate number?"

Thompson read it off to the Sheriff.

"Yep, that's it all right. I will get this information out statewide. Do you know the license number of Ward's car?"

"No, but I'll get it and text it to you."

"Great."

Thompson then called Swartz Creek's City Clerk, Marilyn Branch, to get the license plate number of Ward's vehicle.

"It's Sunday morning and I'm at home," said Branch.

"Marilyn, we believe Chief Ward has been kidnapped by Marty Strawski in her Explorer. We need the license plate number to put it out to all officers."

"Kidnapped!" screamed Branch. "How did that happen?"

"I believe Strawski came to the motel this morning and grabbed her as she left her room. But that doesn't matter right now. I need you to go get her license plate number."

"Right. I'll go into the office right now and find it. I'll text it to you."

"Good. Make it fast."

As Thompson disconnected, a Newaygo County Deputy drove up behind the motel. Thompson introduced himself.

"I'll watch the truck until we get a tow truck out here to haul it back to the department for processing," said the deputy.

"Thank you," replied Thompson. "I'm going to wait in my room if that's okay. The ribs are hurting me."

"No problem, I've got this," the deputy replied.

Thompson returned to his room and opened the app he had to locate cell phones. The app could not provide exact locations, but could tell what cell sites a phone was pinging. Thompson stared at his phone while waiting. It took over a minute for the app to find Ward's phone. His phone dinged.

The app provided a location north of Grand Rapids.

"Grand Rapids?" said Thompson to himself. Just then, his phone rang. It was Branch calling him back. She read off the license plate number to Ward's Ford Explorer.

"Thank you so much, Marilyn. I think they are heading toward Grand Rapids."

"Grand Rapids?"

"Yes, according to the location of her phone. I need to go."

As soon as Thompson disconnected, he called Sheriff Eagleman to give him the news.

"You've tracked Chief Ward's phone to Grand Rapids?" asked Sheriff Eagleman.

"Yes. I have an app that will do that. If this is accurate, they are driving toward Grand Rapids."

"Okay, I'll put out a new alert and contact both the Grand Rapids Police Department and the Kent County Sheriff's Office."

"Thank you, Sheriff."

With all his movement, Thompson's ribs were causing him some pain. He took a pain pill to ease the discomfort. He then quickly gathered up his stuff, strapped on his gun and handcuffs, and loaded up his Explorer. Thompson also carried a scoped rifle in the car. He then gingerly got into the car, backed out, and headed toward Grand Rapids.

"Can we stop?" pleaded Ward. "I've really got to use a bathroom."

Ward wanted to stop to attempt an escape, but she also really had to pee.

"Not yet. We'll stop somewhere between here and Holland."

"That's too far," complained Ward.

Strawski didn't respond and still held the handgun in his right hand resting in his lap.

"You like torturing people, don't you?" asked Ward.

This angered Strawski. "Just shut up! I already told you I don't torture people."

"Well, you won't let me pee!"

"If it's that bad, just pee in your pants. No one will see it. Now shut up."

Ward shook her head and continued to drive. As she drove, Ward looked for any state or local police officers on the highway. *Cops are never around when you need them,* thought Ward.

Ward continued driving south. Once they reached Grand Rapids, Strawski told Ward to get onto I-196 southbound. This would take them the rest of the way through Grand Rapids and the suburb of Wyoming. Meanwhile, Ward continued trying to pull information out of Strawski.

"I'm curious. Why did you bury the three Swartz Creek victims near Chuck Kotter's place? Were you trying to set him up to take the blame?"

Strawski continued to stare out the windshield for several seconds.

"Chuck is an interesting guy. He likes young teenagers, just like I do."

"Not in the same way," Ward responded. "He never abused or murdered anyone."

Ward glanced over and was disgusted to see a sly smile on Strawski's face.

"How did you hide your criminal activity from Chief Braxton?"

Strawski chuckled. "Braxton was like a lap dog. He would do whatever I told him to do."

"Did he know?"

"Know what?"

"Come on, Marty. You know what we're talking about. Did he suspect you in the disappearance of three teenage males?"

"No. He was clueless. You're the only one who figured it out. Congratulations."

"Actually, it was a dog named Roxy who found one of the bodies. Without her help, we still wouldn't know."

"Yeah, I saw that in the news. If it weren't for that damn dog, I wouldn't be in this situation."

Detective Greg Thompson was driving as fast as he could with his lights blazing and siren wailing. If possible, he wanted to catch up to Strawski and Ward. He was only fifteen minutes from Grand Rapids.

Ward continued driving through Grand Rapids and into the smaller city of Wyoming.

"We're through Grand Rapids," said Ward. "Let's stop at the next exit for a bathroom break. You must need one as well."

"No. It's too busy here. Wait until we are in a less congested area."

"I can't wait. I'm pulling off."

Strawski raised the gun in his right hand. "If you get off now, it will be the last thing you do."

Ward looked at Strawski. The look in his eyes gave her the chills. "Okay. Take it easy, Marty. But I can't wait much longer, and we're getting low on gas."

After several nervous seconds, Strawski said, "Once we get past Grandville, we'll get gas and take a bathroom break. But if you try anything, I will not hesitate to shoot you, Chief."

Ward believed him.

Chapter 24

Once they were through Grandville, Ward pointed out a Circle K coming up at the next exit.

"I'm stopping whether you shoot me or not. I have got to use the bathroom."

"Yes, this looks safe enough," agreed Strawski. "But I won't hesitate to shoot your ass if you try anything."

"I understand," said Ward.

Ward pulled off at the next exit and drove into the Circle K lot.

"Pull up next to those far pumps. We need to fill this baby up to get us to Chicago," directed Strawski.

Ward pulled up next to a gas pump and shut off the engine. She started to open her door.

"Whoa! Not so fast. You stay in the car while I gas up. After that, we'll both go inside to use the restroom."

Strawski looked around before exiting the Explorer with his shotgun behind his right leg. He then filled the car with gas while scanning the area. He hid his shotgun as best he could. Another car pulled in to gas up, but the occupants paid no attention to Strawski. After he was done, he returned to the passenger side and re-entered.

"Drive us closer to the store," commanded Strawski.

As Ward drove closer to the store, Strawski pointed out a space apart from other cars. "Park there."

Strawski carefully scanned the store. He could see two employees and three customers inside.

"Now, when we go inside, you walk with me directly to the bathrooms. You're going to use the men's bathroom, and I'm going in with you."

"No. I'm not going into the bathroom with you," Replied Ward.

"Then you might as well get us back on the road because I can pee on the side of the road if need be."

Ward's bladder felt as though it was about to burst. "Okay, but you're not coming in the stall with me."

"I'll have my hand on my gun. If you try anything, I'll have to shoot you and anyone else in the store. I can't leave any witnesses behind. Do you understand?"

"Yes, now can we go use the bathroom?"

"All right, let's go."

Ward exited the car, as did Strawski. As Ward approached the front door of the Circle K, Strawski was directly behind her. She walked to the back corner where the restrooms were located.

"Can't I just use the women's bathroom?"

"No. You come in with me or not at all."

Ward nodded and pushed the men's door open. Strawski followed her in. To Ward's relief, there were no other men in the room. Ward entered the only stall while Strawski used one of the urinals.

"You stay seated on that toilet until I'm done. If you come out before I tell you to, I'll shoot you. No one wants to die on a dirty restroom floor."

Ward didn't respond. When done, she did as Strawski demanded. After about fifteen seconds, Ward heard the sink water running.

"Okay, you can come out now. And don't forget to wash your hands. I hate germs."

Ward frowned but did not respond. She exited the stall and washed her hands. All the while, she was thinking of a way to disarm or disable Strawski. When they exited the bathroom, Ward saw several other customers in the store. She believed it was too risky to attack Strawski in the store. She didn't want any more innocent people to die.

When they got outside, Strawski kept his distance with his right hand holding his gun under his sweatshirt. Ward climbed back in the driver's seat. Strawski then got in on the passenger side.

"Where to now?"

"Get back on the highway and head south," replied Strawski.

Ward was disappointed she hadn't had the chance to disarm Strawski during their stop. He was cautious in how he maintained distance and control. She wondered if he would kill her once he no longer needed her.

Meanwhile, Thompson was still driving with his lights and siren on. His speed reached up to 95 miles per hour when traffic allowed. He sometimes had to slow to 45-50 miles per hour when traffic was heavy or slow to move to the right. Thompson was frustrated by the slow reaction time of some drivers.

The word had gotten out to all police agencies across Michigan to be on the lookout for Strawski and Ward. The

Grand Rapids Police and Kent County Deputies had officers searching for Ward's white Ford Explorer.

Thompson pulled over onto the shoulder of the road to check his phone app. According to the phone locator, Ward's phone was now in Grandville, Michigan, southwest of Grand Rapids.

Damn, I'm too far away, thought Thompson. He then called Sheriff Eagleman.

"Sheriff, we need to put out another bulletin. Our suspect is driving through Grandville right now."

"By the time I get this out, they will be past Grandville," said Eagleman. "Are they still on Highway 196?"

"I believe so."

"Then I'll notify the state patrol and Hudsonville to be alert to Ward's vehicle."

"Thank you, Sheriff."

Thompson continued to drive with a heavy foot while weaving in and out of traffic. He had to get to Ward before Strawski did any harm.

The State Police, Kent County Sheriff's Department, and officers from Grand Rapids were all sending officers onto the highway to locate the escaping fugitive and his captive.

While driving toward Hudsonville, Ward noticed a state trooper pass in the opposite direction. *I wonder if he saw us?* Strawski had shut off the police radio in Ward's car, so she was unable to listen to the police chatter.

"What's your plan in Chicago?" asked Ward.

"If I told you, it wouldn't be much of a secret now, would it?"

"Do you have family there?"

"Shut up, Chief."

"I'm just curious. A smart guy like you has a plan. I admire a man who knows how to get what he wants. So, what's in Chicago?"

"A chance to get lost from all you cops."

"Not much of a plan," replied Ward.

"You'll never find me, Chief."

"How can you be so sure?"

"I've avoided detection and capture for eighteen years. I know what I'm doing."

Ward frowned. "Do you understand how wrong it was to kidnap and kill innocent teenagers? The police will track you down no matter where you go."

"They were abnormal kids. One might say I saved them from a life of ridicule and isolation."

"Did you just say you saved them? You're a sick bastard, Marty."

Strawski raised his semi-automatic pistol toward Ward's right temple. "What did you just say?"

"What are you going to do? Shoot me while I'm driving at seventy-five miles an hour? That would be suicide."

There was silence for several seconds until Strawski lowered the gun. "I won't shoot you yet."

Ward read each road sign as they passed small towns and landmarks. They were coming up on Zeeland as Ward continued to look for patrol cars on the highway. The time was 10:20 am. Ward started to pull off at the next exit.

"What are you doing?" asked Strawski.

"I haven't had anything to drink since you abducted me, and you're threatening to kill me. My mouth is dry from nerves, and I've had nothing to drink for over two hours. I'm stopping to get a drink."

"No!" screamed an angry Strawski. "Stay on the high-way!"

"Nope. I'm stopping. There's a McDonald's at this exit. I'll use the drive-thru."

"I said, stay on the highway!"

"Or what? You'll shoot me? You've already said that."

Strawski glared at Ward. Ward could feel the anger in his stare, but she was reasonably sure he wouldn't shoot her, at least not yet.

"There's the McDonald's over there," said Ward. "It will only take a minute. Would you like something to drink?"

"No. Just get your drink and get out of here. If you try anything, I WILL shoot you."

Ward pulled into the drive-up lane behind a small red Toyota and a white Chevy Blazer. Ward hoped their orders were large and would take a few minutes to get served. The more time she could burn, the better.

Meanwhile, Detective Thompson continued to check his tracker app. Ward's phone was just outside of Zeeland.

Sheriff Eagleman called Thompson. "Thompson here."

"Detective, we now have a state police helicopter in the air. Do you have any idea where they might be?"

"I believe so. According to my app, they're near Zee-land."

"Great. I'll let the state police and Holland police know."

"Thank you, Sheriff."

Thompson had passed through Grand Rapids, but heavy traffic slowed him down. "Get out of the way!" screamed Thompson.

As they sat in the drive-up window lane, Ward looked around. To her surprise, she observed a Zeeland patrol car passing by on the street. *Please look over here.* The officer glanced toward McDonald's but then continued on.

"This is taking too long," complained Strawski. "Let's just go."

"No. I'm getting something to drink. Are you sure you don't want anything? I'm buying."

Strawski glared at Ward, then said, "Sure, get me a Coke."

Ward approached the speaker and ordered a regular-sized Diet Coke and a Coke. She then moved up to the service window. Ward reached into her jacket for her wallet and pulled out a debit card. She handed the card to the attendant.

The female attendant handed Ward a small clipboard with the pay slip to sign. Ward signed the paper, then handed it back. The attendant then handed Ward two Cokes.

"You didn't have cash to pay for that?" asked Strawski.

"No, I don't carry cash."

"Now, get back on the highway."

Ward pulled the Explorer out of the parking lot and back to the road taking them to the freeway.

The McDonald's attendant went to put the receipt into her drawer when she noticed the slip had been written on but not signed. She then looked at the writing. The note said, Kidnapped - Call Police. She immediately took it to her manager.

"What is this?" asked the manager.

"This is a note a lady passed to me at the window."

"Really? What kind of car was it?"

"A white SUV. I think an Explorer."

The manager's jaw dropped. "It's been on the news. There's a manhunt for a guy who kidnapped a Police Chief in her own Explorer! Was there a man in the car?"

"Yes, an older gentleman."

"That has to be the car. I'm calling the police."

As Thompson continued in his quest to catch up with Ward, he heard the latest police bulletin update come over the radio. A vehicle matching the description of the stolen police vehicle, with a white female with red hair and an older white male inside, had just been spotted at a McDonald's in Zeeland. The suspect was to be considered armed and dangerous.

Ward and Strawski were now between Zeeland and the outskirts of Holland, heading southwest on I-196. As she was driving, she kept looking in the rearview mirror. Finally, Ward saw a Michigan State Patrol car approaching them from behind. The officer had not yet turned on his overhead lights.

The patrol officer continued to follow Ward for several miles. Ward figured the officer was waiting for backup before initiating a stop. At least she hoped that was the case. Strawski noticed Ward was looking into the mirror more than usual.

"What are you looking at?" growled Strawski.

"Just checking traffic behind me, like I always do."

Strawski turned and looked over his left shoulder. He saw the state patrol car.

"Don't do anything stupid," Strawski advised. "Just keep driving."

After Strawski's warning, Ward only used the movement of her eyes to check the rearview mirror. She could sense Strawski becoming nervous. He would periodically look back at the officer.

Several more miles passed, and still no attempt was made to initiate a stop. *He doesn't want to stop me on the highway,* Ward thought. Ward glanced at the mirror again. This time, she observed a second patrol car. She couldn't tell what jurisdiction it was from. This gave Ward more confidence that the police knew who they were following. She felt an inner feeling of relief while still knowing she was in grave danger of being killed.

Another mile passed as Ward now heard a faint thumping sound. She listened for a few seconds before recognizing it as the sound of a helicopter. As it grew closer, the sound intensified, drawing Strawski's attention.

"Damn it!" said Strawski. "They're on to us."

"It's time to give it up, Marty. No one else needs to get hurt. Let me pull off at the next exit."

Thompson was listening to the radio traffic on the state police channel. He knew Ward and Strawski had been located and were being followed. Thompson figured he was only fifteen minutes behind. He pressed a little harder on the accelerator.

"I'm not giving up," replied Strawski. "Our only chance is to get off the freeway. They're probably setting up a roadblock ahead. Take the next exit."

"No," replied Ward. "I'm not taking us into a community. This is over."

Strawski raised his handgun in his right hand and pointed it at Ward.

"Are you crazy? We're going 65 miles per hour."

"I'd rather die in a flaming car crash than go to jail."

The helicopter now sounded like it was directly overhead.

"What's it going to be, Marty?"

BAM!! Strawski fired a round. The bullet traveled two inches in front of Ward's nose and smashed out her side window. Ward could feel the bullet pass in front of her, and the concussion of the blast inside the car was deafening. Her ears were ringing.

"The next one goes through your thick skull, you bitch!" yelled Strawski. "Don't test me."

"Okay, okay, I got it. Now put the gun down."

Ward could feel herself shaking.

The officers following Ward now turned on their overhead lights. There were now three patrol cars. They used a rolling roadblock tactic to keep civilian traffic back. The constant thumping of the helicopter blades could be heard above. And now Ward had wind blowing in her face.

Thompson continued to listen to the radio traffic. Once he heard a shot had been fired, he feared the worst.

"Here's an exit coming up," said Strawski. "Take it."

Ward didn't respond.

"I said take it!"

"I heard you!" Ward screamed back. "I'm focusing on driving."

Strawski held up his gun again. "Turn the lights and siren on."

Ward followed his instruction.

"Now, I want you to keep going without stopping, just like you're on an emergency run. Head toward the forest."

They were now between cities and in open farmland and woodlands. Ward signaled and pulled into the exit lane. She did as Strawski ordered. Ward slowed but drove through the stop sign and turned right onto a county road. All three patrol cars pulled off the highway and followed behind her.

"Faster!" yelled Strawski.

"I'm going fast enough. The officers will keep up no matter how fast I drive. What's the plan here, Marty?"

"I don't know yet. Just keep driving."

"They're probably setting up a roadblock," Ward advised.

"Then you'll run it."

Ward shook her head but didn't respond.

After another minute of driving Strawski saw an intersection ahead, and it looked like a dirt road that went into a wooded area.

"Take a right onto this road coming up."

At the same time, Thompson was taking the exit off the highway. He was now only five minutes behind the pursuit.

Chapter 25

As Ward drove down the dirt road, her car tossed up dirt and gravel, making it more difficult for the officers following them to see.

"Now, if you want to live, listen to me carefully," yelled Strawski above the noise of the wind and tires on gravel. "When I say pull over, I want you to pull to the far right off the road and into the weeds. Do you understand?"

Ward nodded, "Yes."

"Good. Now get ready. Unbuckle your seatbelt."

"Huh?"

"Unbuckle your seatbelt!"

Ward reached down and released her seat belt. A warning bell started beeping. Strawski then did the same.

"See that little grassy area coming up?"

"Yeah."

"When I yell now, I want you to immediately pull over into the grass."

Ward nodded, "Okay."

As they approached, Strawski hollered, "Now!"

Ward quickly pulled off the gravel and into the grass while braking. The Explorer skidded to a stop. Strawski grabbed Ward by the hair and yelled, "Let's go!"

Ward scooted across the bucket seats as fast as she could. Her right hip hit the shift lever as she was half-dragged out of the car. As she exited the passenger side, Ward saw multiple patrol cars coming to a skidding stop. Dust, dirt, and small rocks were flying everywhere.

Strawski put his left arm around Ward's neck, and with his right hand, he held the barrel of his gun against Ward's right temple. He then began to walk her backward toward the thick trees.

Shielding themselves behind their patrol cars, officers had their guns pointed at Strawski. One of the officers was shouting for Strawski to drop the gun. He ignored them as he continued to walk Ward into the trees.

Strawski had to leave his shotgun behind. He now only had his and Ward's handguns. He also had some extra ammunition in a pouch on his belt. Once he was deep enough in the woods to feel safer, Strawski released his chokehold on Ward and turned her in the direction he was walking. Ward was now in front of Strawski as they walked. They could both hear the sounds of officers approaching through the woods behind them. They could also hear the helicopter above.

Officers on the scene included Kent and Ottawa County deputies, State Police Officers, and Freeland Police Officers. Officially, they were now operating in Ottawa County.

When Thompson arrived at the exit, he wasn't sure where Strawski had gone after getting off the highway. Fortunately, other officers from the area were still arriving. He simply followed them to the spot where Strawski and Ward had gone into the woods. As Thompson exited his car, his ribs ached from all the sitting. He had driven the entire way without stopping. The first thing Thompson did was find a spot behind a tree to relieve his bladder. He then approached State

Police Sergeant Burns, who appeared to be in charge. Thompson introduced himself before asking about the situation.

"Your suspect just took off into the woods with your Chief," said the Sergeant. "We have six officers here now with a SWAT team on the way. Pursuing him through these trees is difficult because he could be hiding anywhere."

"I'd like to help search."

"You're not even in uniform," replied Sergeant Burns.

"No, but I do have a ballistic vest in my car."

"Hmmm. Well, it's up to you."

"Thank you, Sergeant."

Thompson returned to his car and painfully put his ballistic vest over his shirt. He then grabbed a police baseball-style cap from the backseat. It had POLICE printed across the front of the cap. He then approached Sergeant Burns again.

"I know the suspect from my time in Swartz Creek years ago. He was our mayor, and we got along well at the time. I might be able to talk Marty down."

"That might work. But right now, we're waiting on our SWAT team. I'll let them know you're available."

"Thank you, Sergeant."

Fifteen minutes later, a Kent County SWAT team arrived. As they were gearing up, Sergeant Burns and Thompson approached the SWAT Commander, Steve Corey.

"Yes, I think you might be of help to us," agreed Corey. "Once we get him pinned down, we'll bring you in to talk."

"Thank you, Commander," Thompson replied.

Strawski had bunkered down behind a stack of logs someone had cut years ago. He made Ward lie on the ground face down. Strawski then placed his right knee on her back.

"That hurts," protested Ward.

"Not as much as shooting you would."

Strawski scanned the woods for officers. He could periodically hear and see officers moving among the trees. He kept checking his rear flank to prevent someone from coming up behind him. Every once in a while, he would shoot off a round in the direction of officers. *If only I had my scoped rifle.*

The plan developed by the SWAT team involved stealthily moving officers to the right or east side of Strawski. The commander did not want Strawski to escape to the north. No officers would be posted to the west, as the commander wanted to avoid a crossfire situation should a gunfight ensue. Other SWAT officers would move to the front. Two officers, one in front and one on the right flank, would be armed with scoped rifles. Others carried their AK-47s.

Strawski carefully watched the maneuvers of the SWAT team officers. The officers were well trained in maintaining concealment, making it difficult for Strawski to see what was happening. This made him uncomfortable. He no longer felt in control of what was happening.

"Let me up, Marty," pleaded Ward. "It's hard to breathe with you on top of me."

Strawski ignored the plea. "Tell me what they are planning to do."

"How would I know? You're on top of me."

"You're an experienced officer, right? What would you do if you were running this operation?"

Ward didn't answer. Strawski raised one knee and slammed it into Ward's kidney area.

"Yeow!" screamed Ward. "What did you do that for?"

"I asked you a question," growled Strawski.

"Okay, I'd have my sniper shoot your brains out."

Strawski lowered his pistol to the side of Ward's head. "Do you want to say that again?"

"Well, what do you expect, Marty? Do you think they're going to throw you a party? Just give yourself up. This is not going to end well."

"Did you hear that?" asked Commander Corey. "It sounded like Chief Ward screamed."

"Yes," said Sgt. Burns and Thompson in unison.

Commander Corey turned to Sgt. Burns. "We're ready to go. Try to call him out."

Sgt. Burns turned on his bullhorn and began to speak. "This is Sgt. Burns with the Michigan State Police. There is no way out of this, Marty Strawski. Release Chief Ward, drop your guns, and walk out slowly. We will not shoot."

"If you want me, come and get me," shouted Strawski.

"There's no other way out. This is over. Come on out, and no one will get hurt."

"I'd never make it in prison. You know that."

As Marty talked, his weight made it difficult for Ward to breathe.

"Marty, please let me up. This hurts."

"Good idea," Strawski replied as he reached down, grabbed a handful of hair, and pulled Ward off the ground. He then lifted her head above the logs with his gun to the back of her head.

"You want to shoot someone? Here you go!" Shouted Strawski.

Both police snipers tried to get a good target on Strawski's head. The movement and proximity of Ward's head to Marty's made a shot too dangerous to take.

"Let me try," said Thompson.

Commander Corey agreed. "Just be careful."

Thompson took the bullhorn. "Marty, this is Greg Thompson. You knew me well during your time in Swartz Creek."

"Yes. I remember you. Not much of an officer if I recall correctly."

Thompson shook his head. "You were a good mayor, Marty. Don't go out this way."

"I'm not going to prison, Greg."

"Let Chief Ward go. Then you can do whatever you want."

"She's the only thing keeping me alive right now."

"The Commander has assured me you will not be shot unless you shoot at someone. Let Chief Ward go. She's never done anything to you."

"You and the Chief started this manhunt. You and that dog!"

"What dog is he talking about?" asked Commander Corey.

"A kid's dog dug up a bone of one of the buried bodies," explained Thompson. "It ultimately led to finding the other two bodies and Marty's DNA."

"Ahhh, I see," replied the Commander.

Thompson got back on the bullhorn. "Marty, you can't just sit in the woods forever. You have no other way out. Save yourself. Throw down your weapons and step out slowly. Show Swartz Creek and the world you're a man of integrity."

"Are you on crack?" yelled Marty.

"Marty, you have a story to tell. You'll be famous, and every news station will want to interview you. If you get yourself killed, no one will know the whole story."

This made Strawski think.

"He's right," said Ward. "You could even write a book."

The idea of being famous, even as a criminal, was enticing.

"Yes, he may be right," agreed Strawski. "I could write a book explaining my life and why I took the lives of those boys. I could explain they would not have been successful in life and would struggle, maybe even becoming criminals or just psychos."

"Yes, Marty. That's why you must end this before anyone, including you, gets hurt."

"What's it going to be, Marty?" asked Thompson over the bullhorn. "Let the Chief go first."

"Hang on," yelled Strawski. "I'm thinking."

"Sounds like you have him thinking of surrender," said Commander Corey.

"We'll see," Thompson replied.

"What's it going to be, Marty?" asked Ward.

"It's probably the only way I can tell my story."

"Yes, it is. People need to hear your story. Now, can you let go of my hair? It hurts."

"Chief, I like you, but I can't just let you go."

"What do you mean?"

"I need to tell the story my way. I can't have you telling people you're version."

"I'm not going to write a book!"

"I've said too much to you."

Chief Ward realized Strawski was mentally deranged and that she probably wasn't getting out of this alive unless she helped herself.

"I need a moment with your Chief," yelled Strawski. "Then I'll surrender."

"I don't like the sound of that," stated Commander Corey. "Put the snipers on high alert. If they can get a shot, take it."

"Will do," replied Sergeant Burns.

Strawski whispered in Ward's right ear, "I'm sorry it has to end this way, Chief."

Ward knew this was it. She had to make an attempt to save her life. She wasn't about to be executed without a fight. Strawski placed the barrel of his semi-automatic handgun to the back of Ward's head. Ward could feel the cold steel against her skull. The time was now.

With all her strength, Ward quickly raised her right arm at a 90-degree angle, then swung the arm while twisting her body to the right. As fast and as hard as she could, Ward swung her elbow into the right side of Strawski's head, striking his right cheekbone just below his right eye. As Ward stuck Strawski, the gun went off with a deafening sound. Ward felt the blast and heat from the barrel, but the bullet narrowly missed her head.

"Shot fired!" yelled the Commander.

As he was struck, Strawski fell backward, pulling Ward down on top of him. Ward quickly grabbed his gun hand, attempting to disarm him while keeping the gun pointed away from herself. Strawski managed to fire another round, again missing Ward.

"Another shot, and they're down!" Commander Corey yelled. "Move, Move, Move!"

Swat members immediately began approaching the stack of logs, serving as a bunker.

Ward and Strawski continued to struggle on the ground. Ward attempted to knee him in the groin, which only seemed to make him angrier. Strawski drew the gun down toward his waist with Ward still trying to control the weapon. As they struggled, another shot rang out. Ward let out a loud guttural scream as searing pain ripped through the flesh of her left thigh, shattering her femur bone. She could feel the immediate rush of warm blood gushing from the wound.

Upon hearing this, Thompson left his position and rushed toward the scene.

Ward still clung to Strawski's right arm, praying for help to arrive. Strawski then took his left fist and slammed it into the right side of Ward's head. The force of the strike caused her to lose grip of his gun hand and knocked her to the left. Strawski then propped himself up and aimed the gun toward the middle of Ward's chest. Ward was too dazed and injured to defend herself.

BAM! BAM! BAM! BAM! BAM! BAM! BAM!

The noise and smoke from the gunshots were deafening. Ward's ears were ringing, she was dizzy, and her leg felt like it had been cut off. The next thing she remembered was Detective Thompson propping her head up and a SWAT officer applying pressure to her shattered leg.

"You're going to be okay, Chief," was the first thing Ward could understand. Someone put a smelling salt under her nose, quickly awakening her from her half-passed-out state. When she looked around, Thompson was cradling her head, and at least a dozen SWAT officers were standing over her and Strawski.

"What just happened?" muttered Ward.

"These SWAT officers got here just in time, Chief. They plastered Marty full of holes. He'll no longer be anyone's problem."

Ward managed a weak smile. "How did you get here?" she softly asked.

"Once I knew you were taken, I followed you."

Ward smiled, then closed her eyes. Within minutes, paramedics were on the scene attending to Ward. Once they had her stabilized, she was moved to a gurney and then carried out of the woods to a waiting ambulance.

"Where are they taking her?" asked Thompson.

"She'll go to the Corewell Hospital in Zeeland," replied Commander Corey. "It's the closest one."

"Thank you, Commander."

Thompson trudged through the woods back to his car. Once the adrenaline faded, Thompson felt the pain in his ribs.

"You don't look so well," said Sergeant Burns.

"I'll be fine. I just need to take a pain pill."

"What did you do?"

"That asshole Strawski shot me in the chest two days ago. Without my vest, I'd be dead right now. As it is, I have two broken ribs."

Burns had a surprised look. "You came out here with broken ribs?"

"I did. I wasn't about to lose my Chief."

Burns smiled and patted Thompson on the shoulder. "Do you need a ride?"

"No, I'll be fine. Thank you."

Chapter 26

When Thompson arrived at Corewell Hospital, it was 2:30 in the afternoon. He went to the emergency room to check on Ward. He was told she had been rushed into surgery. Thompson found a restroom to clean himself up as best he could. He then found the waiting room for surgery patients and collapsed in a chair. He was hungry, exhausted, and feeling pain from all the moving around.

After about fifteen minutes, Sherriff's Johnson and Eagleman entered the room. Thompson opened his eyes.

"How are you doing?" asked Eagleman.

"Huh? Oh, I'm okay. Just waiting for Chief Ward to get out of surgery. I'm surprised to see you."

"This is just as much our case as yours. And we are here to support you and Chief Ward."

"We're sorry and praying for Chief Ward," said Johnson. "You don't look so well."

"I'm just tired. My ribs hurt, and I haven't had anything to eat today."

"That's not good," replied Eagleman. "Come on, let's get you to the cafeteria for something to eat."

Thompson nodded his head. "Okay, I do need to eat."

While eating cafeteria chicken fingers, Thompson described the entire ordeal in the woods.

"Your Chief is very lucky. I hope Strawski rots in hell," admitted Eagleman.

"I suppose the press is all over this?" asked Thompson.

"Are you kidding?" replied Johnson. "This is national news. We've got FOX News and CNN here."

Thompson shook his head. "Wow."

They then returned to the surgery waiting room for any news about Ward. The food and fluids helped improve Thompson's well-being. The pain pill he took lessened his chest pain and removed his headache. After another forty minutes of waiting, a doctor walked in.

"Are you all waiting on patient Paula Ward?"

"Yes!" exclaimed Thompson as he painfully stood up. "How is she?"

"She's in recovery now, but still in critical condition. Her left femur was shattered, and she lost a lot of blood. We also believe she suffered a concussion."

"But she's going to live, right?"

"Yes, I believe she will survive."

"Thank you, Doctor. When can we see her?"

"It won't be today. If all goes well, she will be moved to a room tomorrow."

While disappointed, Thompson understood.

"Well, I guess there is nothing more for us to do today," Johnson said.

Thompson nodded in agreement. "I need to return to retrieve the rest of Ward's stuff at the motel."

"Don't be crazy," said Eagleman. "I'll have someone gather everything and transport it to Swartz Creek. You go home and get some rest."

Thompson smiled. "Thank you, Sheriff."

Rather than making the two-hour drive back to Swartz Creek, Thompson checked into the Days Inn Hotel in Zeeland. He planned to visit Ward in the morning. He then called Officer Brock and Marilyn Branch to provide them with an update on Chief Ward. Both of them had already heard the news.

"How is she doing?" asked Branch.

"She's in recovery right now. I haven't been able to see her yet. I'll go back tomorrow."

"How are the ribs feeling?"

"After today, they're very sore. But I'll be all right."

"Thank you for the update, Greg. We'll see you when you get back. Give our best to the Chief."

"Thanks, Marilyn."

Thompson was exhausted from the day's events. He walked from his hotel to a small bar across the street named the Broken Arrow. After consuming a burger and two whiskey and cokes, Thompson was ready for bed. He returned to his hotel room, showered, and climbed into bed. It was only 7:15 pm, and Thompson was fast asleep.

Thompson awoke the next morning and looked at his iPhone. The time was 9:15 am. He couldn't believe he had slept for so long. He quickly dressed, brushed his teeth, and then checked out. He was at the hospital by 9:55 am.

Thompson checked at the front desk and was told Ward had not yet been moved to a room. Thompson sat in the waiting room killing time by playing word games on his iPhone. At 11:00 am, a nurse walked in and told Thompson he could now see Ward. She explained that Ward had extensive surgery on her leg, and several pins were used to secure the femur. She also suffered a concussion during the fight.

When Thompson walked into Ward's room, Ward was lying on her back with her left leg heavily wrapped and elevated. Her face was scratched, and her right cheek was swollen. Ward's eyes were closed.

Thompson placed his hand on Ward's left forearm. Ward opened her eyes, turned her head, and smiled slightly.

"How are you feeling?" asked Thompson.

"Very sore and tired," Ward whispered.

Thompson could tell she was drugged up.

"The nurse said you're doing well considering your injuries."

Ward nodded.

"Marty Strawski is dead. The SWAT team shot him just before he was going to kill you."

Ward nodded her head yes with a slight smile. She then said, "We got him, Greg. We got him."

"Yes, we got him, Chief. But it was mostly you."

Seven Weeks Later

On a Tuesday evening, a large gathering of people filled the Swartz Creek High School auditorium. Guests included all the officers and staff of the police department, other city officials, school employees, many students and their parents, interested residents, and members of the media. Chuck Kotter was also present, standing in the back corner. In the front row, special guests included Dylan Hudson, Abigail Hudson, Jason

Chapman, and their parents. Roxy, the dog, was sitting with the Hudsons. Many people stopped to pat her head as they walked by. Roxy enjoyed every bit of attention.

Once everyone was settled, the ceremony started with the City Mayor, Gary Engles, giving a speech about the great effort and sacrifice so many made in working on the case of the missing teenagers from many years ago. He praised the work of the police department, city employees, and the victims' families. He specifically mentioned the Hudson family, the Chapman family, and Chuck Kotter for their assistance in the investigation. Engles also spoke about healing and moving forward as a community. Once his speech concluded, Engles called Police Chief Paula Ward and Detective Greg Thompson to the front.

Chief Ward approached the podium with the assistance of two crutches. Detective Thompson walked beside her. Once they stood with the mayor, he presented them with an award for their bravery and sacrifice in apprehending the suspect, who was not mentioned by name. Included with a gold-plated plaque were blue ribbons with a gold medallion for courage and sacrifice. The ribbons were placed over their heads. Once he finished, he turned the podium over to Chief Paula Ward.

"First, I want to thank all of you for coming here tonight to support us," said Ward. "Both Greg and I very much appreciate it. Many people have asked if I will be able to return to work. The answer is yes. With time and physical therapy, the doctors say I will return to about eighty-five percent mobility. I may not be able to run as fast, but I will be able to proudly serve you as Police Chief. As for this case, we could not have solved it were it not for the work of many others, including community members and many agencies across our state. However, there are a few special people I'd like to recognize and honor tonight for their help in solving this case. Will Dylan Hudson, Abigail Hudson, and Jason Chapman please come forward."

Everyone in the auditorium stood and clapped as the three teenagers approached the podium. All three of them had big smiles on their faces.

"These three young people, while hesitant at first, eventually told us where their dog had found the bone that re-opened this investigation. For this, they will each receive a medallion and a one-hundred-dollar gift card."

Thompson handed each teenager their awards. As she did, the crowd stood in applause. After the applause, Ward said, "Dylan, will you please bring your dog up here?"

Dylan turned to Roxy and called her up to the podium. Mr. Chapman unhooked her leash, and Roxy gleefully romped up to Dylan, her tail wagging.

"This has to be one of the friendliest dogs," said Ward as she reached down to pet Roxy's head. "The reason we are honoring Roxy tonight is that had she not dug up that first bone, we would not be here right now. Her discovery ultimately led to the reopening and solving of this case. For that, she gets a crime dog pendant for her collar. Furthermore, the Blue Buffalo dog food company has agreed to provide Roxy with a lifetime of free dog food. Please give Roxy a hand."

Everyone in the auditorium stood and applauded. Roxy enjoyed every minute of it. She showed her pleasure by dancing in a circle, then stopping to bark twice as though she was saying thank you. In the back, Chuck Kotter smiled and nodded. He then turned and walked out.

Dylan knelt down and hugged Roxy. In return, Roxy gave Dylan a quick lick on his left cheek. "Roxy, you're the best crime dog ever! I love you, girl."

Thank You

I want to thank my readers for supporting me in my book-writing endeavors. I hope you enjoy my stories as much as I enjoy writing them. It would be greatly appreciated if you would leave an online review of my book. It really does help. Thank you.

And if you haven't yet read my first five books, please check them out. They are titled **Behind The Lies,** a book of three novellas full of action and drama; **Death From Desire,** two short novels of more crime action, mystery, and suspense; and **Naked Evidence,** two more crime thrillers with mystery and intrigue. My fourth book, **Silent Waters,** is a full-length mystery crime thriller that takes place in Boulder, Colorado. My fifth book is titled **Cactus View Book Club.** It takes place in Surprise, Arizona, and is about a women's book club that turns deadly. They are all available from various vendors, both online and through bookstores.

Please look for additional future releases of my crime thrillers. For further information and an inside look, please visit my webpage at:

beccknerbooks.com

Thanks again.

Mark R. Beckner